Cozy Author
2017

THE INHERITANCE

Center Point
Large Print

Also by Charles Finch and available from
Center Point Large Print

The Last Enchantments

The Charles Lenox Series
The Laws of Murder
Home by Nightfall

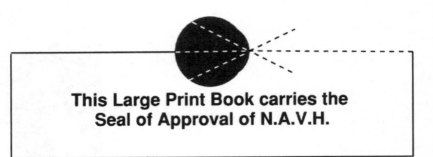

**This Large Print Book carries the
Seal of Approval of N.A.V.H.**

THE INHERITANCE

Charles Finch

CENTER POINT LARGE PRINT
THORNDIKE, MAINE

Library of Congress Cataloging-in-Publication Data

Names: Finch, Charles (Charles B.) author.
Title: The inheritance / Charles Finch.
Description: Center Point Large Print edition. | Thorndike, Maine :
Center Point Large Print, 2017.
Identifiers: LCCN 2016048759 | ISBN 9781683242802
   (hardcover : alk. paper)
Subjects: LCSH: Lenox, Charles (Fictitious character)—Fiction. |
Private investigators—England—London—Fiction. | Large type books. |
GSAFD: Mystery fiction.
Classification: LCC PS3606.I526 I54 2017 | DDC 813/.6—dc23
LC record available at https://lccn.loc.gov/2016048759

This book is dedicated to Rachel, Matt, John, and Ben. For why? For Bingham, for Broadway Pizza, for the CCDC, for Summer '05, for Praha mismatches, for Cashier #4, for Jane Street, for upstate, for AFV, for doing it right, for 1377, for walking the dog, for E3s, for fweakin', for public consumption, and for setbacks. Thank you for being my best friends! Without your splendid company this book would have been finished in half the time.

Acknowledgments

Every year at this time I thank my editor, Charlie Spicer, and my agent, Elisabeth Weed, and then somehow immediately fall deeper into their debt. I think this is the economic model Greece was working on. But it's mostly their fault: they're such thoughtful readers, such warm people, and such true friends that my deficit can only continue to grow.

There's a group of professionals at Minotaur who really understand and love Charles Lenox and who make publishing these stories about him a joy. Andy Martin, April Osborn, Paul Hochman, Martin Quinn, Sarah Melnyk, Hector DeJean—you're a dream team.

My family and my friends are the best part of my life, and whatever is good in this book I owe to them. It would be convenient to blame them correspondingly for whatever is bad in the book, but those parts, alas, are always the writer's own.

THE INHERITANCE

CHAPTER ONE

L ondon was silent with snow; soft flakes of it dropping evenly into the white streets; nobody outside who had somewhere inside to be. It was the third day of the year. Already the light was fading, though it was scarcely past two o'clock in the afternoon, and in his study in Mayfair, Charles Lenox allowed his watchful eyes to rest upon the large set of windows at the opposite end of the room, the long room, far from the dying fire by which he sat.

He was alone in the house but for servants. His wife, Jane, and their four-year-old daughter, Sophia, were still at her brother's house in the country, but business, on behalf of the detective agency of which he numbered one of the three partners, had drawn him back to London earlier than he had anticipated.

But not enough business, alas, to keep him occupied for more than a few hours the previous afternoon, so that on this lonely and endless Sunday he had already reorganized the long rows of books that lined the walls, had gone through several pots of tea—and above all had waited, waited, waited, all the infinite day through, for a certain visitor to come.

And still no sign of him.

Lenox hadn't looked at the letter heralding this visit since late that morning, but he was conscious at every moment of just where it sat on his desk in its long, crisp envelope, its cryptic contents never far from his thoughts. Out of sheer nervous energy he wanted to open it again. But if he closed his eyes he could probably recite it.

It was on the stationery of the hotel from which it was addressed.

> The Collingwood
> 3rd January 1877
>
> Lenox,
> I am writing in some haste—too much haste, certainly, to set down the reflections I wish I could of our distant friendship. As you can see, I am in London at the moment. Only briefly, however. Your address (I hope it may still be the correct one) was in the school directory.
> It comes to this: I am in trouble. And yet I am not even quite sure how I am in trouble. I think it may be connected to that business that you and I once

Here the letter broke off abruptly.

It began again after some space on the page, with the darkness at the outset of this new passage making it clear that its author had taken a fresh nibful of ink—had resumed his communication after being momentarily drawn away from it.

> I must go. No time to explain further. Send word by return post and I will call upon you there in Hampden Lane, most likely after three o'clock.
>
> Even in such circumstances I will be pleased to meet again. Until then believe me to be, in sincerest regards and fondest remembrances, your friend,
>
> Gerald R. Leigh

The carriage clock on Lenox's desk had just swung its small bells to tap each other together once, which meant it was two forty-five. Sitting motionless in his armchair, after his restless day, he felt an irrepressible urge to do something—to act. But there was nothing to do, and no act to perform. He had forbidden himself another examination of the letter.

Which of course meant that at 2:48 he found himself, not quite consciously, standing up out of his chair and striding across the room to examine it again.

The hotel's stationery revealed precious little. Lenox was forty-seven now—a tall and thin man, with a close brown beard and a thoughtful, kindly, but undeceived face—and had been a detective since roughly the age of twenty-two, first as a private investigator, now as a professional in the agency he had founded with two close friends. (For several years between these stages of his career, he had been in Parliament, the ancient family game, but that was in the past now.)

Across that long period, one of the few things he had very definitely learned was how to look at a letter. Some of the most innocuous among them had also been the most decisive—in an early case, he recalled, the Hoxley silver thief had been sent away for life on the strength of a note to his partner that said "A bit peckish"—but this one stubbornly refused to reveal anything to him.

The Collingwood was a first-rate hotel. That was just faintly surprising, perhaps, since Leigh was an unpretentious soul.

His handwriting here had a ghost of familiarity to it, long-ago familiarity, dormant now for nearly thirty years. (Gerald Leigh, no less! Well, he could marvel at this reappearance at his leisure. For now he must concentrate.) There was one obviously notable thing here, the letter's sudden interruption and its reference to Leigh's trouble. And one more subtly interesting clue: He had sealed the envelope with a signet ring, and Lenox could just make out that its looping intertwined initials were not Leigh's own.

RSR, he thought. Or perhaps, upon closer scrutiny, *BSB*. Maddening, the artistic freedom these jewelers felt it within their rights to take with the alphabet.

Lenox stood up from his bent position, tapping the envelope thoughtfully against the desk, a hand thrust in the pocket what his wife had named his study-jacket. Brushing its torn lining with his fingers he felt, just somewhere in the back of his consciousness, a pang of anxiety about Lady Jane, and a puzzlement, too.

Study-jacket, that was her all over—a denomina-tion designed to remind him, not especially gently, that it was a garment unwelcome in any other room of the house, the jacket being a deeply injured old quilted blue smoker, covered with burn marks and the stains of innumerable spills from coffee and teacups, its wrists singed and smudged.

But she also knew it was the jacket he thought best in—he didn't care if that was silly; a detective needed superstitions—and as a consequence made certain, in her loving way, that it was always on its hook, brushed as clean as it could get in these latter stages of its life, and with a charcoal pencil in the pocket in case Lenox needed to jot something down.

He hoped they were all right, he and Jane. They had to be, of course.

The hands of the little clock on the desk ached forward. Two fifty-four, two fifty-five. Outside, the snow fell. The little bookshop across the way had a drowsy low fire in its window, and Lenox knew that its proprietor, a friend of long standing, would be sound asleep in his armchair with a book open across his belly. The image made him consider what could have brought Leigh to London, and what problem (or what "trouble," to use his word) could have driven him out of doors on a day such as this one.

That business that you and I once.

This was the sentence that had kept its hooks in Lenox throughout the day. For he knew full well, or thought he did, to what it referred: his very first case as a detective, in a way.

The clock took Lenox past the hour and he went to sit in the cushioned window seat that looked across Hampden Lane. The panes were very cold to the touch; the snow was relentless, reckless with the plans that Londoners had made.

Three-fifteen and the bells touched once; three-thirty and they did it again, twice now.

At four, Lenox began to worry.

It was at five o'clock, having spent the hour in no more fruitful activity than willing it to pass, and, now that it had, having nothing to show for it, that he cried out "Kirk!" in a loud, irritated voice.

After a long beat the house's phlegmatic, pear-shaped butler appeared. "Sir?"

"You can tell Rackham to get the horses ready. Ten Arlington Street—the Collingwood."

Kirk raised his eyebrows very slightly, which

was the equivalent in him of asking outright whether Lenox had gone insane, and perhaps needed to check into a sanatorium known for its particular specialty in madness, and should he call a doctor.

"Yes, sir," he said.

"It's no use giving me that look. I don't want to go out any more than Rackham does, or in all likelihood the horses for that matter."

"Yes, sir. You would not care for the footman to call you a cabriolet, sir."

"No, I wouldn't care for the footman to call me a cabriolet, Kirk, because I might need to make several stops and you never know where the *next* blasted cabriolet will come from in weather like this, unless you want the footman to follow me around London stalking cabriolets for the next several hours."

"I see, sir."

"Cabs, you know, is what we started calling them at the advent of the modern period, oh, a thousand years ago."

Lenox was rarely in such an acid mood, and Kirk inclined his head deferentially to the celebrity of the moment. "Of course, sir. It will be heavy sledding, but I'm sure Mr. Rackham won't mind."

"Ha, ha," said Lenox bitterly.

"Will there be anything else, sir?"

Lenox said no, there wouldn't be, but then

remembered to ask Kirk to fetch him a proper jacket, too, after he had gone to alert the grooms-man that his services were required.

When Kirk had withdrawn, Lenox looked out the window at the weather. It was night out now. They said the year was lengthening, but on the present evidence he doubted it. Barely five and dark as pitch, except for the eerie black-violet light that a snowy street colored back up into the sky.

He sighed. But then, Gerald Leigh: a very old and deep call upon his loyalties, one that would have drawn him into taking far greater troubles than this one; and might yet, he thought. For he felt a real uneasiness about that letter.

CHAPTER TWO

What would he be like, Leigh, thirty years on?

Their friendship had begun when they were schoolboys at Harrow. In this age that valued education so highly, there were now a dozen or so great British public schools, among them famous ones such as Charterhouse, Westminster, Rugby (which had already lent its name to a sport), Shrewsbury, and Wellington—but two stood preeminent still, Harrow and its infamous rival, Eton, each ancient, each situated upon beautiful grounds, each a nursery for the aristocracy.

Eton was the more hallowed of the two, Harrow the more sophisticated and smarter. Each was snobbish about the other. The nation and the empire bent the knee to both—one needed only look at their cricket match, the oldest in the world, played each year since 1805 upon the hushed springy turf of Lord's Cricket Ground, with the batting and bowling skills of carbuncular little boys drawing, for a day, the attention of an entire globe and its news services.

Harrow lay ten miles of rural road north of London, a miniature Oxford. Lenox's family had always gone to Harrow, and despised Eton, and his older brother, Edmund—now Sir Edmund, having ascended to a baronetcy upon their father's death—had cut the trail there ahead of him, smoothing Charles's way into a group of amiable fellow students, most neither too brilliant nor too athletic nor too brutally arrogant. It had been a soft transition from home.

Not quite so for Leigh. He had been one of the school's strangest fellows, and by some stretch Lenox's most unusual friend. Also one of his dearest, however, even if the two had barely spoken in the decades since their long afternoon rambles across the countryside.

Leigh had been famous within the houses for the most part as a singularly awful student. Indeed, it was commonly accepted that he was one of the worst students in the history of Harrow School. That was never thought to be an exaggeration: The beaks said it themselves.

A dimwit, though, was one thing—plenty of space remained for them at the school, if they had other qualities. Half of the education was Latin or Greek, and the boys understood intuitively that Latin and Greek did not form half of the sum total of life's potential achievements. There were young ladies, for one thing; the school nurse, Miss Farquhar; and cricket, for another.

But an awkward boy was another kettle of fish. Leigh had been shy, undersized, hopeless at sport, and had had an unfortunate, fatal tendency to color brightly the instant anyone mocked him.

On top of that he had arrived late. The four forms at Harrow, from youngest to oldest, were numbered Third to Sixth, though by common parlance they were called Shells, Removes, Fifth, and Sixth. Leigh hadn't come in until Removes, the second year, after all the friendships of Shells had already been consecrated by the things that tie boys at boarding school together so tightly: rising on miserable winter mornings to trudge to chapel, unfair canings, shared sweets from home, minor triumphs on the game fields, late-night chatter between beds.

If Leigh had been either a sportsman or a swot, he would have found his group, no doubt. But neither had been the case.

And so he had been utterly alone for the entirety of his first year at Harrow; alone in a way it is possible to be only among four hundred other fellows of your age when you are fourteen, and even the teachers despair of you. So alone that he hadn't even been among the regular targets of the older, bullying chaps, because he was such a diffident specimen. They gave him the occasional jibe—his background was undistinguished for their taste—but for the most part he was simply undetectable, isolated. Nobody.

How, then, had Lenox found himself friends with Leigh, for the five months the latter had ultimately survived into Fifth Form?

Thereby hung an hour's tale.

As Lenox sat huddled upon the bench of his carriage all these years later, wind slicing remorselessly through its smallest points of contact with the outdoors, like sad memories late at night, and Rackham up on the box guiding the horses toward the Collingwood, he brought Leigh into his mind.

Trouble.

They approached the hotel swiftly, the horses moving well over the untrammeled snow. Two men in greatcoats stood outside of the Collingwood's brightly twinkling glass doors. Both stepped forward to the carriage as it pulled to a stop.

Lenox, after he had climbed down the two weak steps, called up, "Give me five minutes, Rackham,

21

don't stable them if you can help it. I'll send someone out if I mean to stay longer."

The driver touched his cap. "Aye, sir."

As he entered the hotel, Lenox felt an immediate and welcome warmth, originating from the enormous fireplace, taller than the average man, which stood next to the stairwell. Everything was clean and comfortable at the Collingwood, shined wood and shined brass, a fine series of portraits of racehorses along one wall. None of the dust of an old coaching inn. There was a splendid oceanic crimson rug across the whole stone floor. A few discreet groupings of armchairs and sofas were ranged upon it.

Hard to picture Leigh here, Lenox thought again. He had never been overly solicitous of his own personal comforts. Nor had he been rich.

Lenox approached the hotel's counter, which was spaced evenly with small brass bells. There was no occasion to use them, however, since a nattily dressed young man, one hand resting on an open ledger, had been observing him since he entered.

"Good evening, sir," he said as Lenox approached. "May I help you?"

"I hope so. My friend Gerald Leigh is staying here. I wondered if you might ring up to him for me."

Looking as if he wished for no more from life than that he might, the clerk shook his head, rueful. "Mr. Leigh is out, sir."

Lenox frowned, wondering if they had crossed

each other's paths, and Leigh was at Hampden Lane after all. "Did he leave just now?"

"This morning, sir. I would be happy to take a message for him on your behalf."

Behind the young man there was a large wall hived with pigeonholes, some full, most empty, each with a number upon it and about half with keys hanging from hooks above them. "I would appreciate it. You may tell him that Charles Lenox called. Here is my card."

The clerk accepted it. "Of course, sir."

He transcribed the name, tore a page theatrically from a small notepad, folded it, and placed it along with the card in the pigeonhole belonging to room 29.

Where faithfully sat, Lenox saw with a sinking in his heart, his own letter from earlier that day. He could have recognized the dark blue trim of his envelopes from a hundred paces.

"Can I ask what time Mr. Leigh left this morning, if you were here?" he said to the clerk.

"I was, sir. It was just after eleven o'clock."

"Alone, was he?"

"Yes, sir."

"And you are absolutely certain he hasn't returned? I only ask because I was meant to dine with him."

"All but certain, sir. His room key is still behind the desk. I could check his room, however, if you liked?"

Lenox nodded. "I would be extremely grateful."

The clerk gave a signal to the bellman by the door that he would be gone a moment, took the key to 29, then left. He returned very quickly, without ever giving the slightest impression of haste—very good at his job, indeed. "He is out, sir."

"But his things are still there."

"Oh, yes, sir. He is booked with us for several more nights."

Lenox thanked his stars that this clerk's professionalism didn't make him closemouthed—but then, he didn't know he was speaking to a detective, and Lenox was a gentleman and had given his name. "Thank you very much. Please do tell him I'm sorry to have missed him."

"Certainly, sir."

Lenox went back out to his waiting carriage in an unsettled state of mind. As Rackham led them slowly away from the hotel, Lenox thought that he wished he knew more of Leigh's habits, his circle of acquaintance.

He was briefly distracted from these contemplations, as the carriage turned onto Hampden Lane, by an unfortunate list in its posture. Lenox tapped hard on the roof of his small chamber to wake Rackham up—the driver being an unrepentant dipsomaniac, who had concealed within his cloak and breeches at all times, like a pirate with never fewer than thirteen knives stowed away upon his person, various bottles of alcohol. He was completely safe from the sack, too, because he had once, his most glorious moment, flown into action when some scoundrel tried to rob Lady Jane as she stepped from the carriage, thrashing the fellow and then standing on his supine form until a constable arrived.

"Thank you, Rackham," said Lenox dryly when they were in front of the house again.

"Not at all, sir."

Having survived this ride and come into his front hallway again, Lenox took off his cloak and hat in a brooding mood. Kirk greeted him; Lenox returned his word with a clipped hello, then went off to his study. He sat there late into the night, nursing a glass of ruby port, without hearing anything from Leigh.

The next morning he awoke early, dressed quickly, and set out into the streets on his own, stalking heavily through the drifts of snow upon the pavement. It would be quicker to walk back to the Collingwood himself than to wait for the horses.

On the corner of Hampden Lane was Pargiter, the newsman. "Out again after the blizzard?" Lenox asked.

"I was out yesterday, wasn't I?"

"Were you, though? I'm amazed."

"Sold seven bleeding papers in two hours and called it quits." Pargiter shook his head moodily. "Even the regulars not about."

Lenox smiled. "I'll take the four usual, at least. Anything worth reading?"

"No," said Pargiter firmly, pulling copies of each of the morning newspapers from his small wooden stand, which had two wheels. He couldn't read and was deeply biased against the practice. Somehow he always knew the contents of the papers, however. "A little pother at the Parliament, that's your lead in three of'm. Broken window. Vandals suspected, 'n'all."

Lenox frowned. That was a matter of some professional interest to him, as it happened. "I didn't see it in the *Times*."

That was the paper he subscribed to, and Pargiter shook his head. "I always tell you if you want the *final* edition you have to come here, Mr. Lenox. I've told you that up and down, you know."

Lenox handed over a few small coins. "So you have, yes. I have myself alone to blame."

He scanned the headlines as he walked toward the Collingwood, then, realizing that he was cold, folded the papers over and began to walk more briskly. It took him fifteen minutes to reach the hotel. Despite being heavily enfolded, gloved, booted, scarved, he was freezing. It gave him a new feeling of tolerance for Pargiter's habitual gloominess.

He entered the hotel. There was a small group of gentlemen in the armchairs this time, each with a pipe and a cup of tea, each positioned comfortably behind a newspaper.

None of them Leigh, as Lenox took in at a glance. He approached the desk—a different clerk this morning—only to perceive, with an unnerving jolt of recognition, that his letter was still waiting in the pigeonhole of room number 29. The key was there, too. Apparently Leigh hadn't returned to his hotel since writing to his old friend for help.

CHAPTER THREE

L enox's concerns, which had been pressing insistently but lightly upon his conscience, suddenly felt more serious.

The new clerk confirmed that Leigh hadn't returned while he was on duty. It had been no night to remain out abroad, either. Lenox was nearly tempted to ask if he could see the room Leigh had been staying in, but he knew that the answer would be no, and that he would only alarm the clerk with the request.

And yet what was his next step to be?

By the time he had returned home he had at least one or two ideas. He'd eat breakfast; wire to let Polly and Dallington, his partners at the detective agency, know that he wouldn't be by until the afternoon; then head outdoors once more, though it was already beginning to snow again.

As he approached the house, however, he saw that he would be spared at least the sending of the wire. A figure stood in front of his door, a young woman in a slim gray coat, her hansom still waiting at the curb.

This was Polly Buchanan, one of the agency's two other partners.

"There you are," she said. "I've just been speaking to Mr. Kirk, who told me that you were away. I asked him what could have taken you out on a morning like this before breakfast, but he didn't know."

"I don't tell him all my secrets, believe it or not, schoolgirls though you think us. Please, though, come inside, you must be a block of ice. Is Anixter in the cab?"

This was Polly's enormous and taciturn dogsbody, implacably loyal and also implacably silent, a hulking fellow who in all weathers wore the same peacoat. "He is—but he doesn't mind. He fell into the waters of Newfoundland once when he was in the navy and he says that he's never been cold since, though when I asked him to explain how freezing half to death keeps you warm he couldn't explain it. In fairness, he isn't a biologist."

"Dead nerve endings, perhaps."

"I say, there's a jolly thought."

They had come into the front hallway. There was a small brazier burning its hot coals on the floor next to the coatrack, and Polly warmed her hands and face over it, the flakes of snow in her light brown hair melting quickly into wetness, invisibility.

"What brings you?" Lenox asked.

"I wasn't sure if you intended to come to Chancery Lane later today. I'm on my way there myself. Did you see the papers?"

"Yes, I did," said Lenox, hanging his coat.

The headline Pargiter had dismissed—the broken window at Parliament, and the possible break-in it meant, though nothing had been reported missing—might in fact prove extremely meaningful to the agency, as Lenox had known right away.

The reason for this was that the agency was on retainer there. It was the crown jewel of the many businesses and organizations that paid them an annual sum in order to remain on call should any trouble arise.

So far it had involved tasks both great and small. There were minor, niggling problems, problems that were either of too little consequence or too much confidentiality to involve Scotland Yard. Small missing amounts of money, misplaced documents, even disputes over bar bills. The agency had handled all of these on behalf of Parliament.

"I was calling to see if you wanted to go and see Mr. Cheesewright with me."

Jacob Cheesewright was their point of contact, an officious, pedantic fellow with proudly fat muttonchop whiskers. "Let's discuss it—I can give you a decent breakfast, I'm sure, even without Jane here, though it will have to be a quick one for me before I go back out."

Polly looked at him curiously. "Out again already? Is it a case?"

"I'm not sure, to be honest. Come have a bite and I can explain."

He led her to the small paneled breakfast room at the back of the house. It was filled with bright snowy daylight, the sun gleaming more fiercely against the windows than it did in the streets. On the sideboard there was a large pot of coffee with steam rising from it. Lenox poured a cup and would have offered it to Polly, if he hadn't known she took tea.

As he sat, gesturing for her to join him at the round table, he took a grateful sip. Kirk must have heard him enter, for at that very moment he came in carrying a tray laden with plates of eggs and kippers and buttered toast, as well as a porringer full of hot oats under a small mountain of dark sugar. Without betraying any surprise, he inclined his head toward Polly, set down the food, and laid a second place on the table from the drawers of the sideboard.

"I'll bring more eggs shortly, sir," he said, "and strong tea, ma'am."

"Oh, thank you, Mr. Kirk," she said. "I found him after all."

"Very good, ma'am."

"Yes, I thought so. I am a detective."

That Kirk knew what she drank showed the intimacy of Polly's connection to Lenox's home, despite the fact that two years before he wouldn't have known her from a stranger in the street.

She was a young widow, with a pink coloring that seemed to reflect some certain recklessness of spirit, the same quality that led her more quickly than other people into impatience, even combativeness—perhaps because she was so often smarter than those other people. It was a trait that had gotten her into trouble after her husband's death, when she spoke pertly in one too many drawing rooms, and gained a slightly gossiped infamy, without any real cause.

She had ignored it, and, needing money and spying what she thought was an unfilled space in the marketplace, had opened a detective agency that catered to women. She had called it Miss Strickland's. It was a success from the first—she had proven herself a pragmatic, sharp-eyed detective, with a gift for finding lost jewelry, missing beaux, all the small cases that came her way.

She had taken the great gamble, then, of joining her career to Lenox's and to that of Lenox's protégé, John Dallington—and it had paid off.

Indeed, she had become their leader, they would both likely have admitted, first among equals. She had the greatest gift of the three of them for organization, for seeing the longer arc of the agency, sensing when they ought to increase their staff, when to cut it back, which cases to take, which rooms. Her own small custom hummed along, and the few larger cases she had taken on she had handled well.

Already, Lenox considered her family. Certainly there were not many young women of less than thirty with whom he would speak so freely as he already had that morning, or dine alone—and he respected, too, her character, which was open and yet reserved, passionate but with some suffering behind it, originating, he would have guessed, though he rarely mentioned the subject, with the loss of her husband.

After inviting him to start his food, an offer he happily accepted, she asked what he had meant about the case. "I had a letter from a friend, and he promised a visit to follow it up—except that now he seems to have disappeared."

"Disappeared!"

"Perhaps that's too dramatic a word." He recounted his two trips to the Collingwood. "I would like to chase him down."

"Is it anyone I know?"

"No, I've barely seen him myself in the last thirty years. He's lived abroad nearly the whole of that time. A fine fellow, though. Gerald Leigh."

She frowned. "And where do you suppose he's gone?"

His morning walk had made Lenox ravenous, and having dispatched an egg in five bites he pulled the oats toward him, lifting a spoon, his cheeks still tingling from the bracing air outside. "I wish I knew." Kirk, his stately bulk somehow always graceful in its motion, reappeared with more eggs and with tea. Lenox thanked him, and added, "Please have them get the horses ready, too, would you? Quickly, if possible."

"Of course, sir. A telegram for you, as well, sir."

Lenox accepted the paper with a thanks and tore it open. He scanned its brief contents, while Polly, raised by a scholarly country clergyman and his aristocratic wife, attended with scrupulous politeness to a piece of toast.

"There, what do you think of that for an inventive daughter," Lenox said, passing over the telegram. He realized that there was relief flooding through him—the tone of the note so friendly, once more so intimate, as Jane's usually were, after the unwonted coolness of their last day together in the country.

Polly read it out loud.

Weather heavy here STOP imagine we shall be another day while they clear the tracks STOP Sophie three uninterrupted hours of snow angels STOP much love to you don't wither in absence STOP Jane

She smiled—but Lenox thought he caught, fleetingly, a look of sadness in her face, and realized that perhaps he had been selfish to show her the message. Her family was mostly gone; she had no person with whom to share her life, or from whom she might receive a telegram like this one. She lived alone in her small, elegant house. Anixter happily roomed, like a sailor in quarters, in the smoky fug of the cellar.

As they were bundling themselves back into winter clothes in the entrance hall, Polly, having received a full summary on Gerald Leigh, returned to the subject of the smashed window at the Parliament. "You do not wish to go to the House with me, then?" she asked.

"In the normal course of things I would."

"No, I can handle it. The police must already be in," said Polly. "From the accounts in the papers, it sounded serious enough that I think Cheesewright would have called them."

Lenox nodded. "Yes."

"And so of course we ought to be there. It's one of our most lucrative contracts. As you know."

"Of course." He hesitated. "Cheesewright hasn't called us then?"

"No. I had Anixter run over to the office earlier and check. No wires, no letters."

34

"I would go, but really I am worried for my friend Leigh, you see."

The understood subtext of this conversation was that Cheesewright, an old country Tory, loathed dealing with Polly; indeed, would have released the agency from their obligations without the intervention of Graham, Lenox's friend, who was a sitting Member of the Commons.

He loved a lord, on the other hand, Cheesewright. "Let's have Dallington go and speak to him. And then you can help me find Leigh. I could use a hand."

She looked doubtful. "Dallington seemed slightly—"

He interrupted. "He'll be fine now."

Their third and final partner, Lord John Dallington, was a wry, handsome young fellow of thirty, youngest son of a duke and duchess, who in his earlier years of adulthood had earned a terrible reputation as a rake—but had mostly reformed of drinking and late nights now, and possessed a tremendous innate gift for detection, even if he was prone, still, to the occasional lost night. At their meeting two mornings before—the morning following New Year's Eve—he had seemed barely aware of their conversation. But deeply aware of even the softest ray of sunlight that happened to pierce the cover of clouds, wincing sharply at each.

They fetched Anixter, however, and went to find

Dallington. It was four days past the celebrations, and their partner could summon up his strength and go to the House of Commons on their behalf, Lenox thought, and if he felt ill afterward he could full well have barley water to drink until he improved.

CHAPTER FOUR

As it happened, Dallington was in excellent fettle. When Lenox's carriage slowed before the building in Half Moon Street in which he had his rooms, the young lord leaned from his window and called out a hello. He was dressed, his jet black hair smoothed down, and a small white flower in his buttonhole to match the city's glistening shell of snow.

"What do you two scoundrels need now? Bail money again?" he called.

"LORD JOHN!" cried an anguished voice from within—his landlady, an extremely proper widow.

"Apologies, Mrs. Lucas! Apologies! Come up, Lenox and Polly, come up."

He met them at the top of the stairs and ushered them into his rooms with a smile. There was breakfast on his table, the newspapers spread out among the plates. Polly accepted a second cup of tea. "You're reading the papers," she said.

"Well spotted."

She rolled her eyes. "I only meant—you saw the story."

"Yes. 'Vandals.' Not so dramatic a culprit, but it's a slow day for news, I suppose."

"There were one or two intriguing details, were there not?" asked Lenox, who had looked at the papers on the way over. "That it was so close to the main chamber of the Commons, for instance. We came to see if you would talk to Jacob Cheesewright for us."

Dallington nodded. "I thought you might have. But wouldn't he prefer to see you?"

Because Lenox had been a Member, Cheesewright was extremely deferential toward him, even more so than toward Dallington. If the Yard was being difficult—territorial—it was Lenox who stood the better chance of putting the agency on the inside of the investigation.

He explained, briefly, about Leigh, Dallington's face becoming more solemn as he attended to the details. When Lenox had finished, the young lord stood up and said he was ready to go to the Commons immediately.

"Thank you," said Polly. "I would do it myself, but—"

"Oh, I understand, of course," said Dallington, and in his polite reply there was almost even a bow, a ghost of a bow in the angle of his head.

This was their usual interaction: teasing, until there was any point of consideration that they might pay to each other, at which time it became entirely respectful.

Their relationship was all that Lenox could wish for either of them—except that they had no relationship, properly speaking, beyond work and an amiable, easy camaraderie, a complete comfort with each other, which nevertheless never strayed from within certain rigid bounds.

Yet he knew that Dallington felt very, very strongly for Polly! And had since they first encountered her as Miss Strickland, the anonymous detective who had been a step ahead of them all the time in the case of Godwin, and his attempt upon the life of Queen Victoria. The plain truth was that he loved her. Every gesture betrayed it, every look, as vigilant as he was not to let them.

Why then did he not ask for her hand?

Lady Jane, who was close friends with Dallington's mother, had strong opinions on this question: She felt that the young lord, for all his blitheness of demeanor, had perhaps been wounded by the animus that London society had developed toward him during his years of debauchery, and feared either Polly's rejection, because of it, or else feared burdening her with his reputation.

And while there was no doubt that she, too, had a deep affinity with Dallington, Polly was in no wise short of admirers—and a girl could not wait forever, as every aged aunt from Oxford Street to the Strand would have been pleased to inform her.

A very small part of Lenox was relieved that their romance had progressed no further, because the agency had never run more smoothly than it did in its current iteration, the three of them equal friends.

And yet.

When Polly had finished her tea and Dallington had donned his greatcoat, the three of them descended the stairs ("If I have any visitors tell them I'm in Peru, Mrs. Lucas," their host called out cheerfully, not bothering to listen for the reply) and stepped into the carriage, Polly and Anixter on one of the benches, the two gentlemen facing them from the other.

"We'll drop you at the Commons, Dallington," said Polly, "but then, Lenox, where shall you and I begin?"

"The Collingwood again, I think."

She nodded. "Very well. And we'll all meet in Chancery Lane at two o'clock this afternoon—or at least, I shall be there, Dallington, if Lenox is still out upon the trail. We must show our faces, I think. And assign work."

There were several detectives, all formerly of the Yard, who worked for the agency. The bulk of their business was commercial: acting more swiftly and with greater energy than the police could on behalf of various businesses when they had internal troubles, just as they did for Parliament.

Dallington debarked with a wave at the Commons, and then they turned back toward the Collingwood, Rackham driving them in as straight a line as he could manage, through the snow—the now dirtied snow, life, as was its habit, having resumed.

"Off to the Collingwood, then," said Polly. "Before we get there, can you remind me again how you know Mr. Leigh?"

"I—"

There was a pause as he considered how to answer that question.

In the very brief duration of that pause, Lenox felt himself transported into the past. It felt almost physical, as if he had been thrust backward in time, to the first real conversation he had ever had with his friend.

"It's a very involved story," he said, finally.

That conversation had taken place thirty years before, along the country road that separated Harrow School from the high street of the village of Harrow.

Lenox, sixteen then, had been strolling along that road alone in the mid-afternoon; a hot mid-afternoon, because it was only just September, and the weather still more August-like, the trees so heavy with their late-summer leaves that the wind could barely shift them.

There had been in those days a rough-hewn wooden fence running along this empty road.

40

Lenox had spotted a figure sitting upon it, hunched and wretched-looking.

As he drew closer, he had seen it was Gerald Leigh.

"Ahoy," he said, which for some lost reason had become the customary greeting of all the boys in school.

Leigh looked up. "Oh."

Not a customary greeting, by contrast. There was a very awkward silence, as it became perfectly clear that Leigh had been crying, and then it became clear that Lenox knew, and then it became clear that Leigh knew that Lenox knew. "Good summer?" Lenox asked.

"Yes. Fine."

"Mine, too."

"How rippingly splendid," said Leigh.

Lenox's spirits, that day, had in fact been very high. Not many boys were back at Harrow from his year. (He had come up early with Edmund, who was head of his house.) There was no prospect of work for a week or so still, only games, riding, and perhaps a bit of fishing.

Lenox had almost walked on. But something in Leigh's posture—his hands stuffed into his pockets, his face grim with the determination not to cry any further in front of a schoolmate— held him back. "Would you like to go into town?"

"Not at all."

"Look here, there's no point being proud. We've all been snotty once, or crying."

"Thanks, no."

The truth was there really was no excuse to be crying. They were fifth formers now. But Lenox, young and carefree, had been in such a decent mood that he had tried again. "I think I've a parcel in the mails from my aunt. There's bound to be some gingerbread in it."

Chocolate, too; but that he was not going to share with a person he barely knew. "I'm fine," said Leigh.

"Be stubborn, then, go on."

Leigh had colored—his unhappy tendency—and said, "Don't think I'm not appreciative that you're being friendly. It's just that you'd rather feel rotten alone, wouldn't you?"

"But why feel rotten? Come along to town and forget about it."

Leigh looked conflicted, but after a beat, said, "Well—all right. I've nothing else to do."

"Good chap."

Leigh hopped down from the fence and ambled alongside Lenox. "Cheers."

"Although you do have something to do, if it's anything like last year. You ought to be studying."

"I'm never going to study any of that rot again if I can help it."

They walked along in silence for a few moments, Leigh occasionally grabbing moodily

42

at the high grasses at the side of the road. He really did ought to have been studying, Lenox had reflected. At Harrow a bad paper received a "skew," which was a black mark, and a truly terrible paper a "rip," which involved the beak literally ripping the paper in half and returning it to the pupil. A skew was shameful enough— Lenox had gotten two in his first year—but a rip was an event of such embarrassment that his own father still winced at the word, when Edmund spoke it. Leigh was nearly always skewed; and had been ripped at least weekly the year before.

This was none of Lenox's business, however, and soon enough they came to the post office.

If it had been any other time of year, Lenox probably would have shared his gingerbread at this point and bade Leigh good-bye. But none of his own friends would return for another day or two, he knew from their letters, and Edmund, though he would have helped him if anything was wrong, in the normal course of a day at school wouldn't even deign to look at his younger brother.

And so Lenox suggested that they take the long way back around, by way of passing the day.

Leigh had agreed. This roundabout route took them across some pretty countryside, past a dairy farm and then a lord's meadow with a small, idyllic pond in it.

To Lenox's surprise he found that Leigh was not

such an appalling companion for a walk. Once he started talking his temper improved, and he surprised Lenox by mentioning with great care the names and properties of one or two plants they passed. In fact he seemed to know quite a lot in that field, for all that he was a dunce—he told Lenox the name of a bird, and then, when they came near a huge oak tree, stooped to feel its roots, saying that he thought it was sick.

"You're talking rubbish," Lenox said, bending down.

"I'm not," said Leigh hotly.

"How do you know, then?"

"You can see whiteness under the bark of the roots." He pointed. "It'll be a while, but that's the end of that."

Lenox looked up at the massive tree. "Hm."

"Nothing to be done."

They stopped when they reached the edge of the pond. They had been discussing some of the boys in the upper forms, the bullies, with satisfying mutual expressions of loathing. Lenox, hot, had taken off his jacket and tossed it to the ground. Leigh picked up a flat stone and hurled it sullenly toward the water.

"No, no," said Lenox, who found a similar stone and threw it at a low parallel to the pond's surface, then watched with gratification as it skipped seven, eight, nine times, before jagging the water and disappearing.

They skipped stones for ten minutes before Leigh got the hang of it. "Ah!" he called triumphantly after a decent shot.

No older brother, Lenox reckoned. "What were you so weepy about back there?" he ventured to ask.

"Oh, mind your own business," said Leigh.

"Fine."

They started slowly around the pond, still some ways off from school. Only after they had been strolling in silence for a few minutes did Leigh say, in a burst of confidence, "I hate being here again."

"I'm happy to be back. The summer was a million years long, I thought."

"You *would* be happy," said Leigh, bitterly.

"You'll never make a friend if you're so down at the mouth all the time."

Leigh shook his head furiously, as if he knew it just as well as Lenox did. There was another long period of silence.

And then, suddenly, as if he couldn't help himself, he began to pour out the whole story in a great torrent.

They walked slowly. He told Lenox about his father, about his mother's insistence that he come to Harrow, about his odd anonymous patron (whom they would come to call in their investigations that fall the *MB,* short for "Mysterious Benefactor"), his misery at being forced to sit in the Harrow classrooms, surrounded by boys who hated him and teachers who were indifferent.

Lenox was as selfish as most sixteen-year-olds, but he had mostly been a good sort even then, and after a while the boys had taken up places opposite each other, sitting against two trees at the edge of the school meadow, and sat there for a long time, discussing Leigh's misfortunes.

It helped that they were interesting—and Leigh, silent amid his schoolmates for a whole year, was furiously talkative, in a way that he had never been and Lenox would never know him to be again. Indeed, they sat for so long that they only realized they had to be back at school when the first bell for supper rang. "Damn it," said Leigh.

Lenox leaped up, tugging his jacket on. "We can make it."

"No chance."

"You have to get your chin up. Come on. It'll mean sprinting it, but I certainly don't intend to be caned on my second day back."

CHAPTER FIVE

Lenox recounted none of this history in response to Polly's question. All he said was that he and Leigh had been friends at school together—but that Leigh had spent the ensuing years abroad.

Polly tilted her head thoughtfully, as the carriage juddered along. "I don't wish to be indelicate," she said, "but your friend wouldn't be the first gentleman in London to be enticed into spending the night away from his hotel room."

Anixter frowned pointedly, which Lenox thought was a little bit rich given that he had called at every port from here to Bombay with Her Majesty's Navy, an association not remarkable for its high morals ashore.

"Yes, but I think he would have written that he couldn't come, after the alarmed tone of his first letter," Lenox said. "That's what worries me. He is not an inconsiderate person."

Polly nodded. "A fair point." She thought for a moment, then added, "My own father was at Eton."

"I'm amazed he stayed out of prison long enough to have a daughter."

"Ha, ha." She drew her arms around herself. "I don't envy your poor Mr. Leigh a night out, either. It's colder than a witch's heart."

"They say it warms up during a snow and gets colder afterward."

"That sounds like balderdash."

Whether it was true or not, the cold told in the streets of the capital: As Lenox stepped down from the carriage he had a long view of the street, tapering into the distance, and saw that the chimneypots were smoking furiously from each house along the way. He hoped Jane and Sophia weren't so very cold. He knew from his childhood that certain rooms in a country house could never be coaxed into real warmth, no matter the number of fires lit in their hearths.

"Why are we here, then?" Polly murmured to Lenox as they entered the hushed entryway of the lobby.

"I want to find out who paid for Leigh's room."

"Paid for it?"

"He wouldn't have stayed here of his own choice. At least I don't think he would. He would have found someplace simple, and preferably closer to a park."

"Perhaps he's changed."

Lenox smiled. "No. He hasn't changed."

There was a short line at the clerk's desk, and as they took their place in it, Polly said, "He's a natural philosopher, you said?"

Lenox shrugged. "Yes. Or a 'scientist,' as McConnell keeps insisting the more up-to-date term is. A generalist of some sort anyhow. We had lunch together—oh, ten years ago, I suppose, and my impression then was that he was some sort of a jobbing scientist, taking whatever work he could find, acting as shipboard apothecary. He had gone on a great many sea voyages, jumping aboard ships wherever they happened to be going. Rather romantic."

"Not successful, then. In spite of being at Harrow."

"He was expelled from Harrow and never went up to university at all—no, not traditionally successful. But happy, I hope. His coat was in tatters when we dined, as if mice had been at its edges. He was very sunburned, too. If I recall he had just been in Brazil."

"And you've no idea what's drawn him back to London now?"

The answer to that was complicated, given Leigh's note. Lenox was spared from offering it when the clerk greeted them, inviting them forward.

Lenox was about to speak when he realized something: His letter was gone. Leigh had apparently claimed it within the last hour. And yet the key was still there, on its hook.

"Is Mr. Leigh in?" he asked.

"No, sir."

"He was just by?"

"Sir?"

"I see the card I left for him earlier is gone."

"Ah! No, sir, his secretary was here."

"His secretary."

"Yes, a red-haired young man. He took Mr. Leigh's letters."

"Did this person say where Mr. Leigh was waiting for his letters?"

The clerk looked blank. "No, sir."

"I see."

"Can I take another message for you?"

Lenox glanced at Polly. She shook her head. The same thought had occurred to them both: that this secretary, this supposed secretary, might be the very person Leigh feared. For his part Lenox felt that his friend was unlikely in the extreme to employ a secretary.

And so Lenox declined the clerk's offer. He then asked under whose auspices Leigh was staying at the Collingwood—who was paying for the room—and the clerk immediately grew suspicious and then silent, which would have been Lenox's reaction, too.

He looked happy when Lenox and Polly turned and left.

"Where now?" asked Polly.

"I'm going to find him," said Lenox grimly. "But first I suppose we had better go back to my house to be sure he hasn't popped up there, or had my letter from this 'secretary' and replied to it. Unless you would prefer me to drop you in Chancery Lane."

"No. I'm curious now."

In fact there *was* a guest waiting at Hampden Lane, but it wasn't Gerald Leigh. It was Thomas McConnell, one of Lenox's closest friends.

He had a telegram himself. "Jane and Toto are still in the country," he said, holding it up. "I stopped by to see if you thought we ought to go down and retrieve them. Hello, Polly."

50

"Hello, McConnell. We were hoping that Lenox here had received a letter. Kirk?"

The butler, hovering nearby, stepped forward and said that no letter had arrived.

"Were you working overnight, Thomas?" Lenox asked.

McConnell looked at him inquiringly. "How did you know?"

"Iodine on your right cuff. A tired face. Your collar crimped in a neat line, where your stethoscope loops it."

"Ah! Yes, so. As it happens I was there overnight. It was a hard one as well with this weather," said McConnell. "New patients."

McConnell was a physician. A Scotsman, he had come to London riding a crest of academic success—papers published, a brilliant future foretold—and immediately become one of the most respected practitioners in Harley Street. Then he had made an extremely illustrious marriage, which nearly ruined him.

His wife was one of Lady Jane's cousins and also one of her closest friends, a sprightly and feckless young person named Victoria Phillips, though everyone, from dukes down to the gossip columnists of the penny papers, called her Toto. When she had defied her family and married McConnell—who was well but not nobly born—they had insisted that he sell his practice before the marriage take place. The idleness that this

51

decision let him in for, combined with the tempestuousness of both his own character and his new wife's, had made for several dark years, full of long periods of estrangement and, in his case, drink.

Two things had pulled him back from the edge: the daughter he and Toto had had, and, more recently, his return to work, at the Great Ormond Street Hospital, where indigent children received treatment without any charge. It was here that he had evidently been working through the previous night.

The three of them had moved into Lenox's nearby study, where McConnell perched on the arm of a chair, and Polly took a seat behind the detective's desk and studied the small swinging silver clock there, its gears visible through glass.

"I would go down to the country if it weren't for the case Polly and I are working upon," Lenox said.

Over the years McConnell had assisted upon innumerable matters for his friend, as a medical man. "Is it a serious one?"

"A friend of mine, recently returned to London."

"Anyone I know?"

"No—as I told Polly, he's been away from England these thirty years. A very fine chap, though. Gerald Leigh."

McConnell, who had just been flipping idly through a copy of *Punch*, looked up suddenly. "Not *the* Gerald Leigh," he said.

"What do you mean, *the* Gerald Leigh?"

"Not the scientist? The colleague of La Rhome?"

"I don't know. I don't think so. He would be about our age. He's been aboard ships most of the last decade, I believe."

McConnell's eyes were wide. "That's him. Gerald Leigh. He's traveled extensively in South America, I know. Several of his most profound discoveries occurred there."

Lenox frowned. "Profound?"

McConnell wasn't listening, however. "You're telling me that Gerald Leigh is in London!"

"I earnestly hope he is, anyhow."

"Yes—missing! My God! We must find him!"

"I concur."

Polly, drawn in by McConnell's reaction, said, "What makes this fellow so noteworthy?"

McConnell looked as if he didn't know where to begin. He shook his head. "I think him probably the finest living British scientist. There are those who would cite—oh, Meriweather, Ashgate. But I would argue with them all down to the end of the matter, I assure you."

McConnell began to describe some of the works Leigh had published in recent years, and soon Lenox felt an odd displacement, the kind that happens when it turns out we have misestimated someone. Or perhaps only misunderstood: the description McConnell was giving didn't fit Gerald Leigh, perhaps, and yet in a strange way it did, too.

Lenox interrupted to say, "Do you have any idea why he would have been in London? A conference, a meeting?"

McConnell frowned. "There are no great conferences impending. Where was he staying?"

"The Collingwood."

At this the doctor brightened. *Punch* was curled in his hand, forgotten. "Why, that's where all of the guests of the Royal Society stay, of course, per immemorial custom. But Gerald Leigh is not on the Society's schedule. I would have noticed immediately."

"The Royal Society!" said Lenox. "Can he really have been their guest?"

It was the most august of institutions, located in a beautiful alabaster building on Carlton Terrace.

McConnell looked at him with chastising solemnity. "It is Leigh who would bring honor to the Society, Charles, and not the Society who would bring it to Leigh. I know for a fact that he has been invited to speak there dozens of times— so often that he ceased replying to the invitations some time ago, according to a friend of mine who is a fellow."

There was a wistful inflection to that word, for to be a fellow of the Society was perhaps McConnell's truest ideal of happiness.

"We could ask after him there," said Polly.

"May I come?" McConnell asked.

"Aren't you tired from working overnight?" she said.

"I'll pull the carriage if it means shaking hands with Gerald Leigh."

Lenox shook his head. "You may come," he said. "But not to the Royal Society. I suddenly have an idea where he might be."

It took just over an hour to find him.

Three stops in that time; two angry encounters; and a few pieces of tidy detective work.

And there, at the end of it, sitting at a small table, dressed more shabbily than ever, a copy of the newspaper and a huge bowl of coffee in front of him, sat Lenox's old friend, looking very much changed and also utterly the same.

"My God, Charles!" he said, rising, as the detective, in his breast, felt a huge surge of relief to find his friend among the quick. The mystery was solved; the mystery could begin. "How did you find me? Never mind that—thank goodness you did, thank goodness you did!"

CHAPTER SIX

Leigh pulled an extra chair to the table, adding it to his own and the two empty ones nearby, beckoning his three seekers to be seated.

They were in a comfortable and low-lit coffee-house that had no name, only a sign advertising coffee and newspapers. It was known far and wide as Mr. Covington's—the name of its proprietor once, no doubt, now as impersonal an appellation as "The Queen's Arms" would be for a pub.

It was a cheerful, warm place, particularly with the wind howling in the streets. On the scarred bar was a line of glass jars filled with pickled onions, hard-boiled eggs, and squares of chocolate. Two huge copper urns steamed at the very end, leaving the whole room fragrant with the scent of coffee. At their side was a small glowing orange rack with pieces of toasted cheese beneath it, the house specialty.

Lenox was shaking his head. "For heaven's sake, Gerald," he said, "where did you go? Why did you not keep the appointment you set to come to Hampden Lane? I've been worried."

Leigh's face clouded. "Yes. I must offer you my apologies."

Middle age suited his friend better than adolescence had, Lenox thought. His small, trim figure had never run to fat, and the gray at his temples and the scored lines around his eyes bespoke seriousness, enterprise, intelligence, qualities valued more highly in men than in boys. "Well?"

"The trouble is that I know that you have a family now," said Leigh, "and I didn't wish to risk bringing whoever is chasing me to your doorstep. I mean to leave London as soon as humanly possible. I've been skulking here until I could do so. I intended to write you from Paris."

"Chasing you!" said Lenox. "Who was chasing you?"

"I don't know." Leigh looked from McConnell to Polly. "This is a question I would never normally ask, but might I inquire as to your—your identities, sir, madam?"

"Oh, in my haste—these are my very good friends," said Lenox, "Dr. Thomas McConnell, a well-known physician, and Mrs. Polly Buchanan, my partner in our detective agency. You may trust them as you trust me."

"Gerald Leigh. A pleasure," said Leigh, bowing his head to each of them. Lenox had rather forgotten his old-fashioned, rural manners, which had been teased at Harrow but evidently remained intact withal. "If you are friends of Charles's, you may as well know what I had hoped to tell him—that for the second time in two days, yesterday, somebody tried to kill me."

"Twice!" cried Polly.

Gerald Leigh nodded. "Yes."

In nearly any other man, Lenox would have suspected either grandiosity or error in such a declaration. But Leigh had always been precise, and had never been one to affect any posture to his own benefit, nor to become dramatic over a small incident. It was partly what had made him unsuited to life at school: a completely pragmatic approach toward life, verging on blindness to the basic things expected of him. He had once written "I don't care" at the top of a history paper he handed in about Herodotus, for instance, for which he had been skewed, ripped, caned by old Fairfield, caned again by the headmaster, and nearly expelled.

Lenox grimaced. "Do you know who tried to kill you?"

"No. I wish I did. By appearance I might know him again."

"Have you a secretary, Gerald?"

Leigh raised his eyebrows. "A secretary! No, I do not. Nor an equerry, nor a butler, nor a pack of hunting dogs."

McConnell, who was agog with admiration (and had a butler himself, the hypocrite), laughed with merry delight at this sarcasm. Lenox said, "I ask because someone answering to the description of your secretary picked up your correspondence at the hotel this morning. A redheaded fellow. Among it my own card."

"Ah! So I have led them onto your heels even as I meant to protect you." Leigh looked distressed. "I'm very sorry for that."

"No, it's in our jobs. We have strong bars on the lower windows of the house—and the address on the card is my office's."

Polly looked around. "I wonder whether perhaps we ought to go there now," she said. "The office.

This is a very fine coffeehouse, but not the last word in sanctuary."

Leigh looked at her and then to Lenox. "But wait, that reminds me—how did you find me?"

How indeed?

Lenox and Dallington had been arguing the week before about whether London was large or small. Large, indisputably; and just as indisputably small. For one thing it was made up of uncountable small overlapping communities, as little as a kitchen, as large as a neighborhood. For another, everyone had their own London—a huge London, in the case of, for instance, an omnibus driver, a far smaller city for most others.

Leigh had spent so little time in the city that Lenox had almost immediately felt he could isolate the few places where his friend might go. Covington's was one of them—the third they tried, as it happened.

The heyday of the London coffeehouse was now a century in the past. In 1750 there had been thousands of them, including many hundreds jammed close to each other around Exchange Alley, and the most famous of these, for instance Garroway's, might plausibly have been called the very epicenter of the British Empire, which controlled a quarter of the entire world, from the Leeward Islands to the Windward Islands, from Manchester to Bombay. For men of every conceivable commercial and artistic interest, the coffeehouse had been where the day began and ended, lords sitting cheek by jowl with poets and merchants. It was the place from which news spread and toward which it was directed. Lenox's own grandfather had often recalled going into a coffeeshop and sitting down next to any perfect stranger to discuss the news.

In the century since that peculiarly fluid and democratic moment of British history, when fortunes had been made and lost upon the nearby 'change with breathtaking rapidity, class, England's old bugbear, had reasserted itself: now there were gentlemen's clubs for the gentlemen, taverns for the workers, and often something in between for the professional classes: supper clubs, members' lounges, public houses with particular affiliations to, say, journalism, or politics.

But the one profession that had never abandoned the coffeehouse was science. This might have been because its most natural home was either in the field or at Cambridge, which meant that its practitioners were often slightly lost in London; or it might have been that it was a naturally collegial field, in which the mingling of its knowledge was pleasant to both amateur and professor; or it might have been that its customs changed more slowly, since its debates often took place across continents and decades, at their own leisurely pace.

Whatever the reason, it was to the coffeehouses

that Lenox suspected that his friend, unpretentious, afraid, and mostly unfamiliar with London, must have betaken himself.

That still left dozens of choices, and they had guessed and missed a few times before Lenox and Polly had grown frustrated and begun to consider practically where they ought to try. Which coffeehouses were open through the night? Which offered drink but also food? Which had been here at least ten years, since Leigh had last passed a significant amount of time in London?

And most importantly, which had a naval association, since Leigh had spent most of his previous sojourns in search of a ship to sail away on?

They had posed these questions to a few unhelpful people, before a boy of fourteen, who was out buying coffee grounds for half a farthing the pound, stopped and answered them thoughtfully and good-naturedly.

Either Lugaretzia's or Covington's, he had said, finally, and happily taken the coin Lenox passed him, flipping it in the air and catching it overhand.

They had tried Covington's first and found success.

Lenox described this trek briefly, Leigh smiling at the tale. "I ought to have been more intelligent about where I hid, if it was as easy as all that."

"We are dogged, and know your habits," Lenox pointed out.

"I fear that they are dogged, and know me, too," Leigh replied. "But I had nowhere else to turn."

"Any member of the Society would have been more than pleased to offer you a welcome," said McConnell. "And I still would."

"Are you a fellow, sir?" asked Leigh, with interest. "My contacts there are few."

McConnell looked sick at the question. "I! No. No. But I attend all of the lectures—and let me say how wholeheartedly I admire your—"

Lenox waved a hand at him. "Is your mother not in England any longer?" he asked Leigh.

"She died two years ago."

"I'm very sorry to hear it."

Leigh inclined his head, as if acknowledging the history that went into these words. It was the first time their schooldays had arisen, even tacitly. "Thank you," he said.

Lenox paused, then said, "I was astonished, Gerald—not at the news, since I know your qualities perfectly well, but because I had not heard it earlier, you see—that you are become very great in your field?"

Leigh shook his head, frowned. "In my field? No, no. Not particularly. No."

McConnell looked about to take violent exception, and Lenox hurried to cut him off. "Well—anyhow. Gerald, if you come back to our offices in Chancery Lane, we can promise you safety, while you are in our care at least, and if anyone has come searching for you there on the strength of my card we will know it immediately."

Leigh stood up. "I am your man," he said. "Lead the way."

Lenox, a little surprised and also a little touched at this instant faith, also stood up. "Good. I wonder whether you want to retrieve your things from the Collingwood first?"

Leigh brightened. "Oh! Would it be possible? I have some papers there of the first importance, and a silver snuffbox that I acquired in the China Sea, and should be very sorry to lose. Everything else is disposable—though I haven't changed my collar in two days. If only it weren't for these villainous fellows who set about me."

For the first time Lenox observed an ugly welt on Leigh's left hand. "Anixter will go," said Polly.

"A first-rate idea," said Lenox. Polly went out to the carriage to tell the former seaman, and McConnell signaled to the barman for the bill. "Do you have anything to bring?"

Leigh shook his head. "Only a book. I had better pay for my last coffee, though—thank you, Doctor."

When he had paid, the three men went to the door of the coffeehouse. It was midday outside, and Lenox kept close to Leigh, glancing left and right as they went out.

He needn't have worried, however. Polly, bless her soul, had returned with a constable.

"This is Vickering," she said. "He'll see us to the carriage. Do you have tuppence?"

Lenox handed over the coin. He wasn't fond of the (entirely legal) ways that police constables had of making extra money by their profession, such as watching the crowds at theaters or, more innocently, knocking on doors in the morning to wake households that hadn't a clock, but he found himself grateful for it in circumstances such as this.

Vickering put them in the carriage, and as he closed the door promised to see they were not followed.

"Well, Leigh," said Lenox, turning to look at his friend across the carriage. "Let's have it, shall we? What is all this business?"

Leigh sighed heavily, as if he were unsure how to explain it all. Then he said, "Do you remember the MB?"

CHAPTER SEVEN

Chance might have thrown Lenox and Leigh together on that lengthy afternoon at the beginning of their Fifth Form year at Harrow, but they hadn't immediately become friends thereafter. The social hierarchy of a schoolboy playground is infinitely less flexible than that of a king's court, far more finely shaded in its calibration, and universal in its intuitive comprehension of rank. When Lenox's friends returned from the summer hols, in the day or two following Lenox and Leigh's long conversation, there was no question whatsoever in Lenox's mind of integrating Leigh into the group. Nor in Leigh's, probably.

Still, they had taken to nodding cautiously toward each other from time to time. Here and there they traded a word. And then, toward the end of September, chance had thrown them together again.

It was a chilly Saturday, with a blustery wind sweeping down the tall, lingering summer grasses. A mist hung in the air, perpetually a hundred feet away.

They met by coincidence at the turning to Mrs. Allison's house. She was the laundress to whom most boys at Harrow sent their clothes; she generally returned them each Monday and Thursday, but it was known that if you were caught in a bind, if you stained your house tie for instance, she would sometimes oblige you by getting it fixed before then.

This meant a walk to her little cottage, a mile from the school's grounds.

"Ahoy, Leigh," called Lenox. They were in view of the small thatch-roofed domicile. "What brings you here?"

"I've torn my only decent bluer."

"Sew it."

"I don't know how."

Lenox frowned. Every boy at Harrow knew how to sew—it was essential, given how closely the prefects scrutinized the uniforms. He saw that Leigh was holding his bluer (the standard blue jacket all the boys wore) in a limp tangle. "Have you got needle and thread? I can do it for you while I wait."

"No, I haven't."

"Mrs. Al will. Let's go."

A thin woman, passing by middle age, her gray-brown hair back in a bun, greeted them with her usual brisk friendliness, listened to their requests, and agreed that she would try to find Lenox's extra pair of gray trousers ("Spilled again, Master Charles?" she asked) before leading the boys into a sweltering kitchen, where she rummaged in a drawer until she found a spool of thread and a needle.

"It'll be a bit," she said, "while I go out the washing shed."

"Thank you, Mrs. Allison," said Lenox.

When she was gone, Lenox took the bluer from Leigh. Its right arm was in shreds—an unnatural tear, he saw immediately. "What happened?"

"I caught it on something."

"That's a fib. You'll go to hell."

Leigh looked at him stonily. "Ketchworth did it, after I got ripped in old Yardley's class."

Ketchworth was the bully of their year, Yardley their Greek professor. Lenox raised his eyebrows. "Ah."

"Can you fix it?"

"Oh, yes, no difficulty there," he said, bending down to the work.

All the boys at Harrow wore the same uniform: a bluer first, brown plimsolls, gray trousers of the exact cut and shade that Mrs. Allison was currently fetching for Lenox, and a varnished straw hat with a blue band. The only difference in attire was that each boy wore the tie of his house, while monitors, like Edmund, could wear ties of their own choice, which was considered a perquisite of inestimable worth. The key point was the hat, though. It was not a boater, a point upon which all Harrovians, even the least academic among them, could become as pedantic as a Paris doctor. It was a Harrow hat.

Leigh's own was tilted back on his head. He sat for some time in silence as Lenox worked. "By George," he said at last, "you're handy with that."

"Noonan taught me when I was in Shells. Nobody taught you?"

"No," said Leigh shortly.

By one of those happy little flukes of life, Mrs. Allison came in with Lenox's trousers at precisely the moment when he was cutting his thread. "There, done," she said, and the boys looked at each other and laughed. "What? What is it?"

"Nothing, Mrs. Allison," said Lenox, standing up and snatching his trousers from her. "Thank you! You've saved me a hiding!"

They rambled home slowly through the empty country lanes that separated Mrs. Allison's cottage from the school. Lenox found that they fell once again into easy and natural conversation. When they had gone half a mile or so, he ventured a question that had been on his mind since their last one: the identity of his fellow student's benefactor.

Leigh's people were from Cornwall. He had grown up a mile or two inland of the rocky coastline at Tintagel, known as King Arthur's castle, which many people considered the most beautiful place in all of England. Lenox had only heard descriptions, of ancient steps descending from high windswept cliffs down to a curving shore. Leigh's mother was the niece of an earl, but her father was estranged from his brother, and relatively poor, a younger son.

Leigh's father too had been poor, though of high birth, as well. He had been educated at Harrow and Caius, and had put Gerald down for Harrow at birth and begun to squirrel away money from his salary as a parliamentary inspector—a berth secured for him by a distant cousin—to pay for it.

But four years before, when Gerald had been ten, his father had been struck by a carriage near Bath and killed.

This was tragic in itself, but especially so because of how Leigh's face seemed to become illuminated when he spoke about his father. They had been uncommonly close, from the sound of it, spending hundreds of hours together on the heaths of Cornwall, collecting specimens of every kind, plant, mineral, animal. This was the source of Leigh's almost preternatural knowledge of the natural world, Lenox had deduced, a knowledge that he proved again on the walk home from Mrs. Allison's with a passing reference to the hollow-weed along the side of the road.

After his father's death, Gerald and his mother had moved to a smaller cottage and lived on their savings. Leigh had implied to Lenox in that first conversation that money was very close with them; and even now it was clear that some of his things were secondhand, especially his books and his clothes.

Harrow had become, of course, out of the question. The money that Leigh's father had put aside was needed for the basic management of their lives—his mother, the daughter of an aristocrat, niece and granddaughter of an earl, had no way of making her own. She spoke perfect French, could play a piano or draw a tree; but it was not possible to convert these attainments into cheese and bread.

But then, a surprise. One afternoon Leigh's mother had met him at the top of the road as he came from school, clutching a letter in her hand. ("She looked very chuffed," Leigh recounted glumly.) It was from Harrow. His fees for the year had been paid; they would expect his arrival as a member of the Fourth Form on the fifth of September.

As Leigh had described it to Lenox, he had known immediately that it was a bad idea. He had been thus far an indifferent student at his local grammar school; within the family, the idea was that he might make it through the age of sixteen and then lean upon that same generous London cousin for some government sinecure upon which he could found a life.

Now, of course, that plan had altered. Harrow! Ambitions spread out before his mother's eyes. None of her own family, those many earls, had gone to university.

"And I won't, either," Leigh had said, during their first conversation.

"Why don't you try harder?" Lenox had asked.

Leigh had thought about this for a moment— a trait of his, that he received every question as if he had never considered it before. "When my father died I decided that I would never again do anything I didn't want to."

"Except come to Harrow."

"Well; that's different. My mother had her heart set upon it."

"Does she know that you're—"

70

Lenox hadn't known how to bring this sentence to a graceful end, but Leigh had saved him the embarrassment of an attempt. "I've told her I won't be sitting the exams for Cambridge. Her own grandfather stopped after Eton, so she doesn't mind. She's glad at least that I'm here. Among the gentlemen."

This last word was not uttered very kindly.

After the mysterious letter from the school had arrived, Leigh's mother had sat down and written them back, inquiring who had paid her son's boarding fees. They ran to nearly a hundred pounds a year—a fortune upon which a man of the upper reaches of the lower class might easily marry and have children. (It was considered among the clerking class that a hundred and fifty pounds was the minimum sum upon which any respectable person could propose marriage to a lady. Many banks would sack any clerk who was married before reaching that salary, on the presumption that he would be tempted to steal from the cashbox.)

Harrow had promptly replied that they had been given specific instructions should such a question be asked of them, which were to say that the fees were paid by "a friend" and would extend through the remaining years of Gerald Leigh's schooling. The correspondent—the registrar, Higgins—added that such anonymous munificences were in fact relatively common, and added, did Master

Gerald intend upon taking his place at the school?

He did; he had. His mother had insisted.

Lenox had learned all of this during their first conversation. Now, as they walked back from Mrs. Allison's, each with a garment slung over his shoulder, Lenox asked whether Leigh had any idea who "a friend" might be.

They were passing through a small, enclosed field, where three horses were grazing in the chilly mist. "The benefactor? I don't know."

"Hm."

"How I hate him, though! You have no idea."

"Why?" asked Lenox.

Leigh, his expression surly as a moment of silence passed, finally said, "He's why I'm here."

"It's not so bad as that."

Leigh shook his head fiercely. "And I also have some idea it's a person whose help I don't want—a person whose face I wish I could spit in."

They had walked on, quietly, this remark hanging in the air, for some time.

CHAPTER EIGHT

From his earliest memories Lenox had found something thrilling about the idea of a crime. Perhaps it was because he had grown up in so utterly conventional a home. The most serious trespass the local village of Markethouse could offer was generally a stolen brace of rabbits on market day.

The great shining alternative had always been London, whose name he sometimes sounded under his breath in a sighing undulation, *London,* where life seemed so infinitely more complex and dangerous. Once he could recall his father returning home to the country from a sojourn in the capital for a parliamentary session, and describing to his family—and the servants around the dinner table, who were very plainly listening too—that he had seen with his own two eyes the arrest of Black Calvin, a seaman wanted for murder.

"Whom did he murder?" Lenox had asked, at all of eight.

"That's none of your business," Edmund had said. "Father, was he big?"

"He was enormous. Charlie, he murdered a fellow sailor, they say. It was quite a commotion when they found him."

"Where was he, Father?"

"In Trafalgar Square. I was walking up to my club, and he was sprinting past Nelson's Column. Apparently they'd run him to ground in a public house not far away."

"Will he hang?" Edmund had asked.

Lenox's father had frowned, his gentle face troubled. "That's not a fit subject for the table."

"None of this is," Lenox's mother had said, and the conversation had shifted on.

In his schooldays, Lenox became an obsessive reader of the penny adventure stories you could buy on the train platform. They described desperadoes in the wilderness of California, or mysterious castles in the dark reaches of Prussia, or Scottish Highlanders on the hunt for an escaped convict. There was a healthy trade in these publications at Harrow, and seemingly always a new one available. The best of them for Lenox's money was about a detective: it was called "The Murders in the Rue Morgue," and had several heart-chilling illustrations. He never traded it away. There was another story about the same character, called "The Mystery of Marie Roget," but it wasn't quite as good. According to a fellow named Mitchell in the Sixth Form there was a third story in the sequence, "The Purloined Letter," which was better than both of them. But he had lost it at home over summer holidays, and by whatever vicissitude of fate their own newsagent never got it.

When Leigh said that he had an idea about who his benefactor might be, Lenox felt a small prick of excitement in the same part of his mind that was so drawn to the stories he read.

"Why, who do you think it is?" he asked.

Leigh waved a hand. "Oh, I don't know."

"You don't have to say."

They had crossed the paddock and come within view of the gates of the school. Leigh glanced at them with obvious dread—all of the freedom of his personality sank back within him, and he simply muttered something about it not mattering anyhow.

Lenox glanced at his watch. "There's two hours till evening service," he said. "Why don't we find some tea? I'm starved."

Leigh glanced at him in surprise. "Don't you have anything to do?"

He did—he was meant to walk to town with his friends—but he felt a mixture of pity for Leigh, who was not a bad fellow and certainly not as stupid as he seemed, and curiosity about his history, which nobody else in the school had winkled out yet. "Not especially."

Leigh hesitated, then said, "You could come to my room."

"Lead the way."

By pure chance, Lenox soon learned, Leigh had an exceptionally good room. It was high up at a corner, with windows on either side, and better still had a little alcove behind a secret door. Leigh opened this door and Lenox saw a tray with a kerosene stove on it, and a teakettle on top of that. To the side were a whole host of biscuits and chocolates, along with half a loaf of bread and a plate with softening butter on it. Most boys had food, but few anything like this much. There was a pitcher of cream, too.

Leigh put the kettle on. "How dark do you take it? I like it pretty well black, myself."

"It doesn't matter to me. I say, you do yourself not too shabbily up here! I have to go down to the scullery to fix tea. The monitors are dreadful about it too, if it gets cold when you're taking it back upstairs."

"Oh? Yes. My scout is from Cornwall, as it happens. He's a very nice chap. Found me the kettle."

"And what about the food?"

"My mother sends that."

Lenox whistled admiringly. Food was one of the most discussed and beloved subjects at their school—at all schools, perhaps. "Well done by your mother."

Leigh, bent over the teacups, shrugged. "Hall is abysmal. I never saw meat so gray."

Lenox almost smiled. Somehow this fellow hadn't internalized—well, what the rest of them had, that you couldn't complain, that it was *all* bad, the studying and the smashing a ball around in freezing rain and being away from home, but that you didn't say any of that, that you got on with it. "The mash isn't bad," he said.

"Come visit home with me sometime and I'll give you proper mash. With cow's cream."

Lenox rolled his eyes. "I've had that." Then he realized there had been an invitation buried in this further complaint. "But not from Cornwall, thanks. Wretched, though, how you do your tea down there."

"No it's not!" said Leigh, turning back with an angry look. "It's a sight better than what you get round here! I would give half my term's pocket money for two decent scones with clotted cream and jam, like we get back home. Dixon would, too. His wife can't make them at all."

Dixon must have been the Cornish scout. Lenox shook his head doubtfully. "We have cakes in Sussex. I'd take that any day."

"Then you don't know what you're talking about."

But Leigh's anger didn't last. He divvied up the biscuits and the tea, and a few minutes later they were each seated, legs crossed, on the broad sills of Leigh's windows, wordlessly and ferociously consuming their repast. When Lenox's was done he sighed happily and took a sip of tea. He turned to the window. The panes were cold to the touch. Below them was a sweeping view of the school's playing fields and houses, a few people on its old paths, a beak with academic gowns billowing behind him.

"There's Ward," said Lenox.

Leigh flexed his left hand. "He caned my palm last week, the bugger."

Lenox laughed. "You have to study harder."

"They can whistle."

Lenox turned back to the slight, stubborn chap

opposite him on the windowsill. "Go on, then. Who do you think he is, your anonymous friend?"

Though neither knew it then, this was the subject that they would spend many long hours discussing in this very room over the Michaelmas term, sharing out Leigh's Cornwall-bestowed riches and sitting in these same windows. They would draw up lists, debate clues. Once or twice they would argue. Leigh never became part of Lenox's circle of friends, but at least three or four times a week Lenox would slip away and come over to Leigh's, and as best he could, he tried to draw him into conversations at hall, at chapel services, in games. It never quite worked.

But their friendship did—they told each other more and more over the succeeding months, achieving that peculiar intimacy that is possible on ships and in schools and in monasteries, places enclosed or formal, battened or strict.

Leigh started to answer the question; then, haltingly, another, before finally saying, "When my father was killed, there was no trial."

Lenox frowned. "There was an inquest, surely."

"Yes, of course. It was ruled an accident at the inquest. He was killed at a crossroads just inside the city of Bath, where he was working. He had just gotten off the coach himself."

Leigh screwed up his face angrily, and Lenox realized he was trying not to cry. Another lesson he hadn't learned, apparently: you never, ever cried. Lenox took a lingering sip of his tea. "Rotten luck," he said.

"I think it was reckless driving, you see. It was a farmer from that part of the world. I say farmer, but he owns several hundred acres, and lets out some of it to tenants."

"A squire."

Leigh shook his head. "No. He's a rough fellow—a new man. Townsend's his name. Made his money in lending."

Lenox nodded. The word "squire" had no technical meaning, but nearly every Englishman understood it implicitly. There was a single squire associated with each English village. He mattered. He held land; was on visiting terms with the local aristocrat, though unquestionably beneath him in station; might have a curacy in his hands; was expected to do good works in town, and sit in the first row at the church. His family had likely been in the same place since the Domesday Book. He was probably not much for London.

"And so?" said Lenox.

"Some of his land was in the process of being bought from the local squire at the time, Brittney, a chap who was in financial troubles. Three guesses who was in charge of the inquest?"

Lenox's heart fell. This might easily be another of the squire's duties, even if he had reduced his holdings in land. "Brittney."

"Yes. Never went to criminal court, even though

Townsend was drunk as a bishop when he barreled over my father."

"That's awful, Leigh."

"Yes, I'll say."

"But I still don't understand the connection to—"

"I think he's the 'friend.' Townsend. He doesn't want to admit his guilt, but he feels guilty nevertheless, so that is how he's handled it. I can't tell my mother. I know she would refuse it if she thought the money came from Townsend, and she had her heart set on my coming here."

Lenox widened his eyes. "Do you think so? A coarse fellow like that, caring if you went to Harrow or not?"

"Yes, I do. Who else could it be?"

Lenox pondered that for a second, taking a sip of tea. "Well," he said, "I have one thought. Your uncle."

Leigh, to Lenox's astonishment, looked as if he had never even considered this possibility, so fixated had he been upon the idea of his father's murderer paying his way here. He opened his mouth to speak, then shut it again, then opened it, then lapsed into silence.

"I say," he offered finally, "I wonder if we could figure it out?"

"I bet we could."

CHAPTER NINE

The friendship between the two boys stretched from September to January. Those were often happy times for the two of them—by a long stretch Leigh's happiest at Harrow, as he bluntly admitted. But in January, after a smoother autumn, Leigh's troubles had begun again in earnest.

Though he attempted to conceal it, it had been obvious from the third or fourth time they spoke that Leigh's single locus of joy at Harrow was Miss Emily Farquhar. This was the school nurse, a rosy-cheeked young Scottish woman with a soft demeanor and an easy, quiet laugh. He was not alone in this—there were few other feminine presences at the school, and none so becoming—but he might have been alone in the degree of his ardor.

When they returned from Christmas, it was to find that Miss Farquhar had been replaced. Engaged, was the rumor. For Leigh, who had stood at many a twilight near the chapel steps, hoping merely to get a glimpse of her as she walked the short distance to her little cottage on the school grounds, it had been a profound blow. It was already the worst time of the year, when the days seem to last only an hour or two, and the wind seems stronger than your will, the classroom a mausoleum.

One Tuesday after Miss Farquhar's departure, Leigh had missed out on all of his classes. Lenox went by his rooms to check on him—such an absence was so out of the ordinary that all of the students had noted it immediately, for all of Leigh's usual invisibility—and found his friend sitting on a rug in front of a tall fire, drinking from a bottle of stout.

"What on earth are you doing?"

"Having a day off."

Lenox had taken a biscuit and then gone and sat down in the armchair near him. "You're going to get walloped."

"Let them." Leigh kept his eyes on the fire. "Did you hear back from the solicitor?"

"Not yet. Any day, I'm sure."

They had finally settled on three "suspects," the two of them. At times Leigh seemed to take the whole thing as a lark. The MB had become a running joke, so that for instance if they were let out early from games (which Leigh loathed, other than the school's indoor racket game, squashers, at which he possessed a certain angular talent), Leigh would say to Charles with a grin, "The MB has stepped in, evidently."

But at other times he seemed to pin some obscure hope on the matter.

The first of their suspects was Townsend, of course. The second was Leigh's uncle, his mother's brother, Robert Roderick, Earl of Ashe.

When Lenox had first proposed this uncle, Leigh had been scornful. In the first place it was one of the poorest earldoms in Britain. In the second, there was a longstanding quarrel between brother and sister, dating to before their father's death, and what was more, his uncle had enormous gambling debts and all of the family's ready money was tied away from any use, his father having known his son's character.

But Leigh had gradually come around to the idea. He was fifth in line for the earldom, after another brother and his three sons. It wasn't impossible that he would inherit Ashe Hall one day. Perhaps some family feeling had awoken in his debauched uncle, in the last fifteen years?

What amazed Lenox about this was the way it showed how little Leigh seemed to care for the opinion of the other chaps at school. There was tremendous snobbery at Harrow, and if the other boys had known that he was so closely related to an earl—any kind of earl, even a modest one—they would have found space for him in the social hierarchy of the place, one way or another. But Leigh didn't care in the slightest, the same way he didn't care when he got a rip, or when he skipped class to drink beer, or spent two hours staring into a tidepool as if he didn't have lines from the *Aeneid* due the next day.

Lenox had written to the family's solicitor in London, inquiring whether it was "to the Earl himself that my friend Gerald Leigh ought to address his thanks for the opportunity of studying at Harrow School (where he is flourishing)." As he had written this letter it had seemed to him surpassingly polished, confident, and elegant, the last word in cosmopolitanism; he had very nearly been expected to receive a job offer by return post. But as yet they hadn't had a response.

Then there was their third suspect, Brewster. He was more elusive, but had become Lenox's own personal favorite candidate—an older bachelor in Cornwall, who had been paying unremarkable but steady court to Leigh's mother since she had emerged from her first mourning. The case for him was very slender: It rested upon one conversation he and Leigh had had two summers before, but a conversation that had concluded tellingly, Lenox thought, with Brewster saying to the lad something like "I hope that you know you can always count me a friend," a final word to which Lenox, deeply absorbed in his detective stories, had ascribed what he freely acknowledged was perhaps too great a deal of significance.

"No letter ever, I'd bet," Leigh said, dejectedly.

"Chin up," Lenox had replied.

"Mm."

The fallout from this day Leigh had taken "off" was immediate and ugly. He had been caned by both his housemaster and the headmaster, and warned that he was on thin ice.

"Thin ice," he said bitterly that weekend, as he and Lenox walked across the countryside together. He had asked if they might get off the grounds—a rare request—and seemed to want to give his feelings their full liberty. "You would think the whole school was built on a sheet of ice a millimeter thick, for all the times I've heard those words."

"You *are* on thin ice, though."

Leigh pursed his mouth tetchily. "Not you, too."

"You don't want to be sent down, Gerry."

"Don't I?"

Leigh stooped down suddenly after saying that. They were in a field, its ground still frosty though it was midday, the pale sun above them throwing off no warmth. Very tenderly, he picked up something. "What is it?" asked Lenox.

Leigh opened his cupped palms. Within there was a pinkish young field mouse, shivering, its eyes closed. Leigh pulled a bit of biscuit from the pocket of his hunter and put it to the mouse's lips, but the creature made no movement toward it, expressed no recognition. "My father could spot these from five hundred yards. A wood mouse, we call them in Cornwall."

"Are you going to keep him?"

Leigh wrapped the mouse carefully in his handkerchief. "Yes."

They traipsed toward the town, and after Leigh had ventilated all of his emotions about the fools in charge of the school, their talk turned, as was customary, to the three wise men, as they called their suspects for the role of MB.

Lenox would realize later that it had been a singularly incompetent investigation—but not one without energy, to the credit of his younger self. They had gone and tried to talk the school's registrar into giving them information; had inquired into whether Townsend used a London bank, since Harrow accepted its fees only from London banks or in cash; Leigh had asked in one of his letters home if his mother thought her brother might have softened and become "a friend." She had replied that anything was possible, though in a way that sounded much the same way that you might argue it was possible a gargoyle from Westminster Abbey might sprout wings and fly to Liverpool.

They had uncovered precisely one genuine clue, Lenox would later see. At half-term, Leigh had lost his Greek dictionary. When he returned there was a new one waiting for him—used, from a bookstore in Truro.

Lenox had thought of that over the years.

On the afternoon of their walk, Leigh's mood had grown increasingly dangerous. He wasn't the sort to get violently or passionately angry, but he could grow very acidic, indeed. "If Townsend is paying to send me to this hellhole, he's had it over on my family twice," he said, just as they reached the school gates.

Lenox winced. Sometimes he thought about how it would feel for four galloping horses and a heavy carriage, taking a corner at speed, to hit you. He hoped that Leigh's father—who sounded as if he had been so full of life—had been killed instantly. "You have to turn it to your advantage," he said.

"You can't take any turns on thin ice," said Leigh.

The next day the Fifth Form had Tennant's Latin. It started directly after chapel, and Leigh was late. Lenox had felt his heart fall as the minutes ticked past eight o'clock, and Leigh still didn't appear.

Tennant was a smart young buck recently up from Cambridge, who had studied at Marlborough and considered himself a great favorite among the lads—which he was, if you counted only a certain swaggering sort, who did indeed follow his style and slicked their hair to the side and dropped their gs and said "ain't" a great deal.

"Lenox, where is your friend?" whispered someone from the next row.

Lenox had scowled. "Shut up."

Tennant, at the blackboard, was writing out the page numbers they were to translate that day. He turned. He had heavy eyelids and a drawling voice. "That you, Lenox Minor? Well, where is Leigh?"

Edmund was Lenox Major. "I don't know, sir."

"Well. The paddle isn't going anywhere."

A few of Tennant's favorites snickered.

Just then, Leigh came in. Everyone gasped: for he was without his hat. The effect couldn't have been more jarring if he had come in without trousers on. The first and last rule was that you kept your hat upon your head at all times—the gates of heaven could open above, and you would clasp a hand to your hat as you ran toward your savior. They all knew that.

Tennant had reddened. At first his eyes widened, and then he got a dangerous look on his face. "Where is your hat, Leigh?"

"I don't know, sir."

"Go and find it. Don't come back until you have it."

Leigh had turned, tiredly. "Yes, sir."

Tennant, shaking his head and turning to the blackboard, had said, distinctly enough to be clearly heard, "Going to the dogs it is, here, since they started letting in these provincials."

The boys on the right side of the room had laughed. Leigh paused, with a look of pure hatred on his face. Lenox tried desperately to will Leigh to catch his eye, but to no avail. His friend turned and left.

What was maddening was that Leigh would never, ever point out to the other boys that Tennant's own people were in no way particularly distinguished, and certainly not in comparison with Leigh's—but they did have money, making the master particularly suited to the kind of snobbery he had just demonstrated.

Fifteen minutes later the door opened again. Tennant started first at the sight of what came in. All the boys had been doing their translations, but they looked up—and then, though they resisted at first, a tide of giggles rolled over the room, stifled at first, then transmuting into uproarious laughter, impossible to turn back.

Leigh was wearing four hats, one on top of another. Beneath them he had Tennant's slick hair; he was also wearing a pink tie, the master's signature, and profoundly against school rules. He had on his look an absolutely perfect imitation of the sneering and complacent resting expression Tennant had on his face.

"Get those off," Tennant said furiously. "Get over here. You need a caning."

"Shaaaan't," said Leigh lazily, in perfect imitation of the master's drawl.

"Get over here."

Lenox, who was laughing too, was amazed. Leigh had never been a mimic. "Shaaaaan't."

Tennant started toward the door, but indecision stopped him—then he said, "Right," and grabbed Leigh by the collar and jerked him forward. Leigh didn't resist. "We're going to the headmaster. Continue your translations. They'd better be on my desk finished when I return or you'll all have Sunday detention."

In that single moment, Tennant's reputation had been permanently damaged. He knew it; you could tell from the rage in his behavior. Nobody returned to their work after Leigh and Tennant had gone, needless to say. They had already begun reliving Leigh's rebellion, as they would do until it passed with almost no waiting period into Harrow's highest pantheon of myth and legend.

When his day was done Lenox ran breathlessly to Leigh's room. Nobody was there. He knocked on the door across the hall, where a large, oxlike, amiable ginger named Craycroft lived. "What's happened to Leigh?"

"Expelled."

CHAPTER TEN

Mrs. Allison had died two years after Lenox left Harrow; the news spread quickly around Oxford, where many old boys had gone on to study, bearing to its gates fond memories of her. The reported cause, given out with a few minor permutations, was that she had taken a heavy tumble at the greengrocer's, picked herself up and declared herself fine, gone home, fallen asleep, and never woken. Not the worst death by any means.

When in later days Lenox thought of school, it was often Mrs. Allison's little kitchen that popped into his mind, oddly enough. He'd gone there at least every other week for four years. Thinking of it was strangely stirring, perhaps because the kitchen belonged so firmly to a world that he had watched vanish, the world of both Mrs. Allison and of his parents. The England of his boyhood; 1845, 1846: So much had changed since then in utterly irreversible ways, much of it good, to be sure, and yet some of it, too, fraught with the tiring ambiguities of all modernization.

Take the laundress herself. She had been around sixty when Lenox came to Harrow, which meant that she had been born within a few years on either side of 1785. In those ensuing decades she had likely never traveled more than five miles from her home—almost no Briton had, then. Her husband had been a laborer on a nearby farm, where he was granted a small plot for his own use. He had also sold firewood to the school, because he had the right, bestowed by uncountable generations of tradition, to gather it from his squire's land. This he could do in one of two ways—it was strictly forbidden to cut it down, but he could fetch any dead branches from the trees with a hooked stick, or he could pick up any fallen wood with his walking staff: could gather it, as the saying went, by hook or by crook.

Their life had been simple, rural. They had kept a few pigs and chickens to the side of the house. In the kitchen Mrs. Allison had brewed her own beer, from scavenged local barley. Nearby they had cooked over an open fire, never in an oven. They had pumped water for themselves, and for the laundry. They had certainly never seen an electric light.

It was only when the rails were finished in 1850 that this had changed. Before then food, letters, and people moved no more quickly than a horse could bear them down a road.

Afterward, suddenly and without warning, it was different. You could send a telegram from London to Leeds in the time it took to have a cup of tea. Trains transported fresh fruit, fresh milk, the day's newspapers, and the catch of the Atlantic all over England by each morning's end. (In Lenox's earliest days, fish had been the delicacy of a squire's streams and ponds; by the time he reached Oxford, it had become the most popular workingman's treat in the country, when it was fried together with chipped potatoes, doused in vinegar, and served in a twisted sheath of newsprint.) Almost all at once, in other words, on the stroke of old Mrs. Allison's death, they had entered Victoria's era.

That meant progress, which was a wonderful thing. Parliament began to notice distant problems more quickly—no, of course no child ought to work in the mines or factories; yes, of course there ought to be decent schools; no, they couldn't have orphanages full of starving charges ruled over by a fat corrupt old miser. It was an unalloyed good that such things had changed. In the north, the boom of industry meant that there were continually new jobs. Above all, life became more interesting, more open-ended. You could travel to the seaside on a whim. More and more people picked up sticks and moved from their villages to the great cities. There were thrilling opportunities to be had for any venturesome youth, who in an earlier time might have seen only a few dozen faces in his entire life.

And yet, of course, something had been lost too, as it always was when one generation relinquished the world to another.

The Allisons' country existed no more. Theirs had been a small, communal life, unchanging and companionable: the church, the green, the two pubs (where her husband spent his evenings, but which she would only visit at the back door, to fetch beer), the apothecary, the butcher, the dressmaker. The midwife who delivered their five sons. The gatherings at the well whenever a person was sick or in love.

Lenox could picture their lives in full, because they were the same lives that the laborers upon his father's land had lived. It had been simpler, truly. That didn't make it better—but progress didn't make things better without exception either, and when Lenox thought of the countryside in which he had grown up, its empty lanes and enormous blue skies, the local accents ten times stronger and the beer twice, none of the noise and fug of coal, the emerald fields tilled for their eight-hundredth autumn, when he thought of these things it was hard not to think that it had been at least in some senses a more peaceable world, gentler in its pace, unrushed, milder in its ways.

It was to Mrs. Allison's that Leigh had gone when he was expelled, in order to fetch the clothes he had with her.

Word had gone around the school rapidly that he was simply waiting to be gotten by his mother. (The school, fearing he would run away, refused to let him take the train back home, though he had done it alone for term breaks.) He was now half prisoner in a little stone house next to the apiary, by Grove Wood, watched over by the ancient widow of an old master. He wasn't even seen at chapel services, and Tennant made it known very quickly that anyone attempting to see Leigh would, themselves, be in serious trouble. He had been a dissident and malign influence upon this school, Tennant told them the day after it all happened, in tones of awesome gravity.

You could have heard a fly's wings beating as he used these words, it was so silent in the room. Later that evening, Lenox's older brother, Edmund, had stopped him outside of chapel. "You're not going to try and see Leigh, are you?"

"That's none of your business."

Edmund had frowned. This had been probably the least likable six-month period of his entire life, forward and backward—full of the eminence of his position, in the first cricket eleven, sitting the Oxford exam soon enough and a cinch to pass into Balliol. "Now see here. They've told us that anyone who goes to see Leigh will be sent down. Do you hear that? *Sent down.* What would Father make of that?"

"You're lying."

"I'm not."

Lenox had shaken his head. "Tennant was beastly to him anyhow."

"I don't care. Leigh ought to have known better. He's never got on here. And your friends think it peculiar that you've spent so much time with him anyway. It's better he's gone, a chap like that."

That stung. Lenox's friends had asked him, now and then, why he saw so much of Leigh, and accepted his answers chummily enough—but perhaps it was true after all that he had been spending less time with them, and that he wasn't quite so much on the inside as he once had been.

That evening Lenox's housemaster came to his room and repeated Edmund's advice, saying, in a kindly way, pipe between his teeth, that word had been passed down that anyone attempting to see Leigh would be dealt with very, very harshly— disrespect to a master being among the most unforgivable crimes at Harrow School.

95

"I won't try to see him," said Lenox.

"Good lad," said the housemaster. "Best to forget about him—never a fit, never a fit."

Lenox had nodded, read for a little while, and then turned out his lights. He lay there, heart beating hard. Finally, at midnight, he had opened his window, shimmied down an old stone column outside of it, and set out to see Leigh.

The rules at the school were strict enough during the daytime—but to be outside after lights away, for any reason that didn't involve an immediate medical calamity, was grounds on its own for being expelled, or at the very least caned and set an infinity of detentions. To do it for the purpose of seeing Leigh was suicidal.

Still, he went, filled with an undirected anger. It was all so bloody unfair.

Perhaps God agreed: Lenox was able to slip across the D'Addison Lane with miraculous ease, not a soul in sight. It was only a few minutes' scramble to the little stone house on the edge of the Grove Wood. Lenox paused when he was in sight of it—everything looked calm enough, indeed almost eerie under the placid moonlight, the house imported directly from one of those woeful German fairy tales about a stepmother. Lenox had had tea here (a dreary obligation for all the boys) and knew exactly where the little alcove guest room would be. He went and, after a moment's hesitation, tapped on the window.

Leigh's face popped up immediately. "Lenox!" he said. He disappeared for an instant, his footsteps scrambling across the flagstones. Then he returned. "Tennant is patrolling this area. You'll be thrashed if you're not expelled."

"I brought you our notes on the MB. And your biscuits."

Leigh grinned and accepted this bounty, crumbling off a morsel from a shortbread and hovering it over the pocket of his pajamas, from which the field mouse popped its head and took the biscuit with enthusiasm. "Decent of you."

He actually seemed happier than he had in a while. "Aren't you blue?" said Lenox. "Leaving Harrow?"

"It's the best day of my life."

"What are you going to do? Go home?"

Leigh held up a copy of the *Times*. "There's a ship going to the West Indies that needs a surgeon's mate. I have a cousin at the admiralty who can get me on it, I bet. No pay but a fifty-pound signing-on bonus, and room and board and training, and we might catch a prize, you know."

"A ship!"

"I can give the fifty pounds to my mother."

"You're mad."

Leigh's face grew serious. "No, I'm not. Listen, Charlie—thank you for sticking by me this fall. You can stop all that stuff about the MB. Forget him."

97

"I'm going to find out who it was."

Leigh nodded. "All right," he said. "If you like. But it doesn't matter."

Suddenly there was a flare of light. "Who's there!" cried Tennant's voice. He had evidently been walking the lane. "Stop right there!"

Lenox darted beneath the eave of the windows and started to crawl around the side of the building, as the master strode forward, a lantern at his side.

"Tennant, you great prat, it's me," called Leigh. "You need to get a grip, man. You're boxing at shadows."

The master whirled, snarling. Lenox rose and sprinted into the woods. For a terrifying moment he was sure Tennant was behind him, and darted left, into the thickest part of the forest.

Soon he was lost. Minutes passed, stumbling through the undergrowth—until at last he came out, in sight of the school, though at an odd angle. Returning to his room would mean a long loop around.

But it had been worth it. Why did he care for Leigh enough to feel as much? He had time to puzzle it out as he walked. He had many excellent friends at Harrow, but all of them were like himself, in their way, conventional. All of them did ultimately believe in the old school tie and the old school song, even if they grumbled about them now and then.

And something more insidious: all of them believed in themselves, their right to be here, whereas Lenox sometimes had the uneasy feeling that only enormous luck had landed him in this life.

Leigh—well, it was hard to put your finger on it, but Lenox was glad to have befriended him. For a while there had been an unusual person in their midst, who didn't fall for the whole story quite so easily—who was himself. That was all. After that night Lenox wouldn't hear any word of him again at all for thirteen years.

CHAPTER ELEVEN

As the carriage passed through the Temple Bar, toward Chancery Lane, Lenox said to Leigh, "Would you describe the entire chain of events that has led you here, please? Straight through from the beginning when you arrived in England."

"Not just the attacks?" asked Leigh.

Lenox nodded. "No, the whole thing."

"Perhaps we should wait three minutes then, and see if Dallington wants to hear," said Polly. "It would give us another brain on the problem."

"Yes, that's a notion. If it's all right with you, Gerald?"

He nodded. "Of course."

Dallington was not present, however, and

according to the people in the office had yet to appear that day. Evidently his business in Parliament was taking longer than might have been expected—or else he had gone out to investigate it immediately.

The offices of Lenox, Dallington, and Strickland, London's first—and premier, they hoped, though competition was growing intense—detective agency, were centered around a large, sunny room. Its slanted clerks' desks found a pleasing reflection in the large windows of the ceiling, which slanted upward itself. The room was murmuring with activity, though everyone turned to acknowledge the arrival of Lenox and Polly. The clerks and detectives politely ignored Leigh and McConnell, being accustomed to uneasy strangers—though one or two inclined their heads toward the doctor.

There were several smaller rooms ranged around the central one, including the private offices of the partners and a larger meeting room, which overlooked Chancery Lane.

It was into this large meeting room that Lenox led his old friend, with Polly and McConnell following them. "Can I offer you something to eat?" he asked. "Or tea, coffee?"

"I'd take a tea," said McConnell.

"I never want to see coffee again after spending the night at Mr. Covington's shop," said Leigh. "But I too would take a cup of tea very gladly. What a cold day it is! There have been times in my life when I have forgotten that such weather is even possible, and got as brown as a nut."

"I envy you them."

They sat down at the polished table in the meeting room. Lenox had a notebook and there were inkpots at the center of the table; taking a nib, he wrote three names at the top of the first sheet: "Townsend," "Brewster," "Earl of Ashe." Soon tea arrived, and Leigh poured himself a cup, smelled it, and then took a small sip, sighing with contentment.

"The one thing I have well and truly yearned for in England. It can be scarce abroad. I've often thought about a cup of Harrow tea."

At school, nearly everything had been shabby, from the gloppy food to the cold and dirty baths. This was a part of the ethic of asceticism there. (If you could get through January at Harrow, the thinking went, you could send your troops over an enemy hill, endure a scorching day in India, make decisions of state.) But there had been one golden exception: tea. As if in acknowledgment that the absence of absolutely all creature comforts would have been too much for boys to bear, there had always been large steaming kettles of brown-golden tea at strategic locations around the schoolhouses, with cream and lump sugar (which could be stolen for candy) nearby.

Lenox smiled and took a sip of his own tea. "Not bad, is it."

"Now," said Leigh, "if I might ask: Isn't this the one place we ought to have avoided, since they have your card from the hotel? They seem certain to come here."

Lenox shook his head. "I hope they do. We have a former constable at the door at all times, as you saw, and with a blow on his whistle another half dozen would come. Then we would have caught them fairly easily, these people hounding you. But either way we shall find them. Go on, though, if you would, tell us what has happened. I am deeply curious, as you can imagine."

Leigh nodded and looked up at the ceiling for an instant, organizing his thoughts, then began his tale.

He was living in France presently, he said. For many years he had traveled, collecting samples and identifying species, but more recently his interest had turned to smaller animals, the very smallest in fact, which he described with a term Lenox did not know, "microbes." ("A new word," he explained to McConnell, who expressed curiosity, "from the Greek *mikros*, small, *bios*, life. Adjective 'microbial.' You see, Charles, I really ought to have been paying attention at school after all. I've had to get my Greek secondhand for all these years, and I'm still a poor fist for all that.") They could only be seen under powerful magnification.

Three weeks earlier he had received a letter from a London solicitor named Ernest Middleton.

Its contents had been an utter surprise: he was named as the heir to a substantial fortune. Middleton requested that Leigh come to London, in order to expedite the process of probate.

Leigh had been loath to leave his research, and wrote back to ask, first, of whose generosity he was the recipient, and second, whether the business could be conducted by correspondence.

Middleton had replied that he was not at liberty to provide an answer to the first question, and that the answer to the second question was no. He had offered a variety of dates when Leigh might come to London; if he found himself embarrassed, funds could be provided from the estate for his travel.

Aside from Leigh's voice, the only noise in the room was of two pens scratching, but now Polly laid hers down. "Have you heard of this Middleton?" she asked Lenox.

He nodded. "Yes. The firm is Middleton and Beaumont. Very solid reputation on estates, I believe. Beaumont was in the news some time ago because he wrote Lord Castleton's will—left it all to his gamekeeper. The will held up. Their offices aren't far from here."

Polly nodded. "That makes sense if they're often in and out of the courts."

Leigh had replied to Middleton with his thanks and named a date, the earliest one the solicitor had offered in fact, just after the year ticked over to 1877. The French were fond of New Year's celebrations. He would miss less at work by leaving then and returning before they had quite recovered from their binges.

"Is your French good?" Lenox asked, as an aside, curious.

"Quite good, yes. I was on a French corvette for three months once, off the coast of Africa. Abominable food they had, too. And it meant that I said a few words I shouldn't have in mixed company, at first—didn't know any better, you see."

Leigh had arrived in London, then, three days earlier, on the first of the year. It had been more than a decade since he spent any time in London greater than was necessitated by a transfer of trains. He had been to Cornwall several times in that period to visit his mother, and then, finally, to bury her, two years before.

In advance of this trip, he had decided that while he didn't wish to address the Royal Society, he would take advantage of his time in London to meet several colleagues with whom he had exchanged theories by correspondence over the years. He had written ahead to make plans for a dinner.

"I have no doubt your address would be respectfully received," McConnell said, sounding wistful.

"Oh!" Leigh's eyes widened. "Well—perhaps."

"But on the other hand, many of the liveliest scientific conversations occur at just this type of informal dinner, as I'm sure you know."

"That was my hope," said Leigh.

After making the crossing he had gone straight to the Collingwood Hotel, where the administrators of the Royal Society had positively insisted he stay, he said, on the provision that he offer them at least a few casual remarks on his work after supper.

"And did anything strange happen on that first day?" asked Lenox.

"Nothing at all. I slept for half the afternoon, and then I went to my club for supper. I ran into Churchill on Pall Mall, incidentally. Hasn't changed a bit."

This was an old schoolmate of theirs from Harrow. Lenox smiled. "No, he hasn't. I see him now and again."

"He had his son with him, Winston he said the boy's name was, four years old and greeted me very handsomely. Looks like a bulldog. Randolph said he certainly means to send the boy to Harrow. Fat round-faced little fellow, very jolly-looking in a navy coat two sizes too big. I said he'd be better off at the local grammar school, and Randolph said I had always hated Harrow, but that didn't mean we all had. I conceded that it was a fair point. After all, you didn't hate it."

"Indeed, I liked it."

Leigh laughed. "They tell me it takes all sorts to make a world."

The following morning, Leigh said, he had gone to see Middleton at his offices. There he had signed several papers.

The sum in question was much larger than he had expected: twenty-five thousand pounds.

This number sent a little wave around the room. Lenox whistled. Leigh hadn't mentioned this figure in the carriage, and after he did, now Lenox, McConnell, and Polly all paused, obviously commencing the rapid calculations that were native to their class, in which every girl of nine could estimate a fortune to a farthing. At five percent that would be a thousand pounds a year, a very, very handsome living. Even in the safest of investments, the consols at three percent, it would be enough to live extremely well on, keeping horses, dining out, all that sort of thing.

"Were you not shocked?" asked Polly.

Leigh frowned, considering the question. "I suppose I was surprised, yes. I don't often think about money unless I don't have any."

"And have you any?" asked Lenox, in as light a voice as he could.

Leigh smiled. "A fair question. When I was much younger I invented a small wooden box in order to catch birds without killing them. I'm not an inventor. It was only that I needed one like it and couldn't find anything—and it might have ended there, except that my mother very wisely insisted that I apply for a patent. That's brought me in a few hundred pounds a year, every year, sometimes a bit less but never nothing. I've been able to live off that when I needed to, indeed much less than that often, since I have been abroad so much. They victual you pretty well aboard a navy ship, if you dine with the officers. And it allowed me to provide for her while she was alive."

McConnell looked curious. "Which trap is it?"

"It's called the step-spring."

The doctor laughed incredulously. "My friend Exum swears by it, absolutely swears by it! You invented the step-spring? My goodness, will wonders never cease. What I find, however—"

And here for a moment the conversation devolved into a technical discussion of the merits of various scientific collection methods. McConnell's own passion was the marine life of the North Atlantic, and Leigh, though he had evidently moved on to these microbes, spoke warmly of his own experiences collecting and identifying flora and fauna there.

Lenox and Polly waited patiently, until at last Polly interjected. "And you had no idea whatsoever who might have given you this incredible sum of money? I find that astonishing."

"Ah. Well. I had a previous experience of anonymous benefaction, you see, as Charles knows." Lenox nodded an affirmation of this. "And Mr.

107

Middleton—who was all friendliness in person, after his rather formal correspondence—gave me a letter which offered, I thought, a clue. Only two words at the end, really. But there you are."

Leigh pulled a folded piece of paper from his breast pocket and passed it to Lenox, who skimmed it and felt a thrill. "Shall I read it aloud? With your permission, Leigh. Yes? Very well."

It was undated, from a typewriter with the letter *s* weaker than the rest, he noted from force of habit.

> Mr. Leigh,
> I have followed your career with admiration, and wish we had had greater opportunity to spend time together. My hope is that this money will allow you to realize your farther-reaching scientific ambitions.
> Sincerely,
> A friend

CHAPTER TWELVE

The hour had just ticked over to three, and Lenox found that he was hungry. He and Leigh had been explaining to Polly and McConnell, as succinctly as possible (which was not very) the history of the Mysterious Benefactor. He let Leigh carry on and popped out to the main room of the offices to hail one of the young boys who worked there, handing him a few coins and asking him to go out and fetch sandwiches for the four of them.

As he returned to the meeting room he saw that Leigh and McConnell had again been diverted into a scientific discussion, as Polly, ever assiduous, looked over her notes.

Seeing he had returned, she asked, "What were the three candidates' names?"

"Brewster, Townsend, Ashe."

Leigh looked up and shook his head. "Brewster died many years ago. It can't have been him."

"Your uncle, then, Ashe, and Townsend," said Polly.

Leigh looked away. "Yes."

Sitting, Lenox glanced at his own notes. "Robert Roderick was your uncle's name?" he asked.

"Yes," said Leigh again.

"What was your mother's Christian name, if I might ask?"

"Regina," said Leigh. "Why?"

"Oh—only trying to remember."

But that wasn't quite true. He could tick off one mystery: *RSR,* the embossed seal on the envelope of Leigh's letter. It must have belonged to his mother. No profit in pointing out this memento of Leigh's grief, however.

"Well, then," said Polly. "What time did you leave Middleton's offices two days ago?"

109

"At half past twelve. After that I went to the British Museum. It was upon leaving the museum that I was attacked."

Leigh explained that he had dined with an acquaintance from the staff and then stood politely for a while before Lord Elgin's marbles, while this friend deplored the Greeks who were so importunately demanding their return. (It would all be settled very soon, at least, the friend had added.) He estimated that he had left the British Museum at three.

"It was still light out?" Lenox asked.

"Yes, just. I walked through Bedford Square. It was very empty—that was the day the snow began—and very austere, with nobody about and the trees utterly bare, you know. It saved me, because I could see my assailants stalking me from a few hundred yards off, couldn't possibly have missed them, didn't like their look at all. And so I turned toward Oxford Street, where I knew it would be busy."

"Why did you think that they were after you?" Polly asked.

"It was something in their step. You would have thought so, too. And of course Bloomsbury is not an altogether savory area. At first I assumed they were thieves."

Lenox nodded thoughtfully. "They caught up with you?"

"Yes. It was very near-run—I was half sprinting

down a little alleyway and they nearly had me by the back of the coat when I stepped out into Oxford Street, and suddenly we were surrounded by people. It was a jarring moment. One of the two fellows gave me a hard shove anyway, and I stumbled down into the gutter. There was a commotion. They had vanished by the time I regained my feet, though it was only an instant. I looked around for them but they were long gone."

"And how do you know they weren't simply thieves?"

"Well, so, it was this way. After our little chase I was shaken, but not too badly. I've run into ugly customers over the years, you know—anyone who has been aboard a ship has—and after I had dusted myself off it didn't seem so bad as all that. I returned to my hotel, dined very pleasantly with my friend Lovell, then turned in and had a good night's sleep.

"The next morning I was to return to Middleton's office to sign a few more documents he had prepared—he wanted to know which bank would receive the money, when I could take receipt of it, et cetera, et cetera.

"As my cab pulled up to his street, though, I spotted none other than the two chaps who'd come so close to setting about me the day before."

Lenox raised his eyebrows. "Ah."

"Yes, 'ah,' you describe my thoughts to a very nice exactitude, Charles."

"What did you do?"

"I ordered the cab to proceed on its way without a stop, needless to say. I returned to my hotel. That was when I wrote you."

"You were interrupted in the middle of writing the letter, though."

"Yes, I had a caller. They left the name 'Smith.' I asked for a description, and it matched one of the two fellows too finely to be anyone else. As you can imagine, I was not eager to receive him. I finished writing to you, gave the letter to the bellman to post, and escaped through the back door. Or so I thought."

"Only thought?"

"In fact the other fellow was waiting there by the door for me—with a knife out. He came after me, hell-for-leather. I swear there was an unnatural ferocity in his eyes. If I hadn't thought quickly we wouldn't be speaking right now."

"Why a knife and not a gun?" asked McConnell.

"Noise," said Lenox. "There are more bobbies than civilians in that part of the West End. Leigh, my goodness! What an ordeal. This was when you went to take cover at the coffeehouse?"

"Precisely. I paid a passing boy to take word to Middleton that I had witnessed two ugly-countenanced fellows outside of his offices and that I would prefer to conduct the rest of our business by the mails, thought of writing to you but didn't want to draw attention to your house—they already had the solicitor's address, obviously—and then retired to the coffeehouse.

"At first I thought I would attempt to see you. But more and more this morning it has struck me that I had better just go. They keep a *Bradshaw's* at the counter of Mr. Covington's establishment, and just before you came I was going to consult it to find the next train that departs for Dover, and thence to France. It was a relief to contemplate leaving all of this terrible business behind me. That knife will live in my nightmares forever. It came within the width of a—of a microbe, of my eye."

Lenox leaned forward, frowning. "Did you not consider alerting the police to your situation?"

"I tried! With two constables I tried. Both of them moved me on. So I gave up."

It was true that Leigh, with his tobacco-stained fingers, in scruffy collar and grizzled coat, was not a classic picture of respectability. The average London policeman heard twenty outlandish tales a day, the majority of them designed to distract him from his beat so that some other crime could be peaceably conducted nearby.

"Has anything strange happened to you in the last few months, may I ask?" Lenox inquired.

"Nothing other than this inheritance."

"Can you think of anyone who might wish you harm?"

"Nobody at all," said Leigh.

"Except perhaps the person who would have twenty-five thousand pounds were it not for your existence," said Polly.

"Correct."

"And these two men—describe them, please, if you would," said Lenox.

"One was an Englishman, I think, and one, I believe, an Indian."

"An Indian."

"At any rate an Easterner."

"Dressed in Oriental clothes?" Polly said.

"Quite the reverse—he wore a highly respectable suit and a bowler hat. He might have been a clerk in Mr. Middleton's office."

"And the other?" Lenox said.

"The thing that stands out about him to me is that he had flaming red hair, and a beard to match it. A short beard."

Polly put down her pen and glanced at Lenox. He returned the look, but with caution in his eyes: better not to say anything right away.

Still, they both understood now that Leigh's position was more precarious than they had realized. These men were known to them, unless there had been a very profound coincidence. Anderson and Singh, they were called. Not pleasant chaps.

Lenox asked him to elaborate. Leigh had the scientist's natural attentiveness to details of appearance and typology, which made him a useful forensic witness. He remembered several small points that few witnesses would have—accent, shoes, even the length and style of the knife, which Lenox, who had made a point of studying such things, immediately recognized as being the standard blade issued by most army regiments.

As Leigh was searching for any last fleeting niceties within his memory, McConnell stifled a yawn. Lenox, remembering that the doctor had been awake all night at work at the hospital, urged him to go home and sleep.

"No, no. I'm wide awake. But tell me, Mr. Leigh—would you consider taking up residence in my guest room? My own wife and child are away in the country, snowbound, and I even have a small laboratory. I know you would be comfortable, and there would be numerous people about the place."

"It is very kind in you, sir," Leigh said, dropping into the earnest and old-fashioned Cornwall language just as he occasionally had at Harrow, "but I mean to stick to my plan. Straight back to France, where nobody has ever tried to stab me with a knife. Long may that record remain unblemished."

Polly frowned, pushing a wisp of light brown hair behind her ear. "Anybody who hopes to murder you in London will hardly be deterred by a channel twenty-five miles across."

Leigh smiled. "That's only to Calais, or Lille at best. Then they have to get to Paris."

"I only—"

"No, I understand. And I thank you. My hope is that by rejecting the inheritance I can put an end to the whole business. I have more than enough to live on—and they are very generous to scientists in France. I want for nothing. Excepting good tea, perhaps."

And excepting a new jacket, Lenox thought, and felt a surge of affection for his friend.

He was just about to tell Leigh who Anderson and Singh were, the Indian gentleman and his red-haired companion stalking him, when Dallington came in. He was holding a pair of brown gloves and brushing snow off the shoulders of his coat.

"They said you were in here! Hello, McConnell, capital to see you. And who is this?" Dallington put out his hand for Leigh, who shook it. "Not the internal revenue, I hope? Ha, only joking. I'm sure we're quite paid in. Polly, we are paid in, aren't we?"

"This is my friend Gerald Leigh," Lenox said. "He's found a bit of trouble."

Dallington's face fell. "Oh, dear," he said. "You're in the right place at least. Welcome. But I say, Lenox, Polly, did you hear the news down on the street? A shooting, only a few blocks away. He's dead, the poor soul, in his own chambers."

"Who was it?"

"A solicitor, according to the fellow who sells whelks on the corner." Dallington squinted, trying to remember the name. "Middleton, I think it was?"

CHAPTER THIRTEEN

Everyone in the room other than the deliverer of this news reacted to the shock of it at once, all of them hesitating for a beat and then breaking out into speech simultaneously.

Dallington raised his eyebrows. "Wait, wait. What do you know that I don't?"

It was Polly who answered. "That is the name of the solicitor who is supposed to give Mr. Leigh here tens of thousands of pounds."

Dallington looked understandably nonplussed, and Lenox said, preemptively, "Middleton was the solicitor of an anonymous benefactor who has left Leigh a medium-sized fortune. Since returning to London to sign the papers, Leigh has been attacked twice, and his attackers were waiting for him yesterday outside of the very chambers where, you now tell us, the solicitor has been killed."

Subtly, Polly gestured toward a line on her note-pad, visible only to Dallington, standing behind her, and Lenox. It said "Anderson+Singh" and though Dallington's expression didn't change when he read it, Lenox could sense him tensing.

At that moment there was a knock at the door. It was Anixter, there with Leigh's possessions.

"Anyone lurking about the Collingwood?" Polly asked.

Anixter shook his head, and after pausing to see if anything else would be asked of him, left the room.

"Chatty fellow," said Leigh.

But the stab at humor was reflexive. He looked rattled, as he had every right to. As for Lenox, his mind had already jumped forward: He had to get to Middleton's chambers as soon as possible, that was clear. The questions that remained were, in the first place, what was to be done about Leigh, and in the second, what kind of head start they had on Scotland Yard. It might be their means of bargaining their way inside the case if an inspector who looked unfavorably upon the agency had been assigned it.

First things first. "Dallington," he said, "what did Mr. Cheesewright say about the thefts in Parliament?"

"They want us on the spot. A case of interesting features."

"You and Polly ought to go and handle it, then."

Dallington glanced at his pocket watch. "Yes, I came back to report in, but I'm heading back. It's already three forty-five."

Polly looked at Lenox. "I'll stick with you."

Lenox shook his head firmly. "No, I'll take Pointilleux if I need anyone." This was a young associate of theirs, a Frenchman. It was important to retain the parliamentary business, and he also knew that the Yard didn't like Polly to come to their scenes, her presence a continual low-burning threat of humiliation for them. "I'll go over now."

"I can pay your fees, of course," Leigh said.

He looked pale. Lenox smiled. "Yes, I'll be sure to charge you twice our usual rates, since you're a Parisian now."

"Very droll."

"Listen, though, before I go, two things. First, what shall we do with your person?"

"I am dead set on returning to France as soon as possible now. It would be useful to have twenty-five thousand pounds, but it is not nearly so essential to me as an intact body."

Lenox nodded. "I understand. But I would counsel you to remain here for another day or two. The Yard may have questions. Better still they may have answers."

"Would you feel comfortable in Paris anyhow?" Polly asked.

Leigh conceded that he would not feel entirely comfortably there—but more comfortable than he felt here. "And where would I stay?"

"Are you disinclined to accept McConnell's

offer?" Lenox asked. "You would certainly be safe at his house."

What he knew and Leigh did not was that McConnell's house in Grosvenor Square was both well populated and well defended, because of Toto's family. Leigh looked hesitant, but then, giving himself over to the situation, said he would do it.

And what was the second question, he inquired.

"Ah," said Lenox. "That's more easily answered. Townsend and your uncle: Has either of them died recently? At the risk of sounding insensitive, it would be helpful if one of them had."

A faint smile returned to Leigh's face for the first time since he had heard the news of Middleton's death. "There's the rub," he said. "They both did."

Lenox raised his eyebrows.

Fifteen minutes later, the detective had ventured outside into the winter weather again, riding in a cab bound for the offices of Middleton and Beaumont.

The snow was driving down once more. The distinctive scarlet of a mail cart flashed by in the whitened street, its horses' shoes clicking sharply against the roads even through the powder. Lenox stared out through the window.

What had Leigh gotten himself into?

The offices of Middleton and Beaumont were on Maltravers Street, a lane so slender that

Lenox's carriage had to leave him off at the top of it, and walking down it felt like entering a hedge maze. The street was dominated by the legal profession. It was obvious instantly which building had domiciled Leigh's unfortunate solicitor—there were constables milling outside, and various lookers-on, undeterred by the cold or the snow, peering in the windows.

By chance Lenox knew one of the attending constables from a previous case. "Hello, Chapman," he said, elbowing through.

"Hello, Mr. Lenox. Been called in?"

"After a fashion. I believe I may have some information. Who's caught the case?"

"Inspector Timothy Frost, sir."

Frost was a competent middle-aged officer, with a thick gray beard. He was by no means unfriendly toward Lenox, which made his presence a positive development. "I'll go upstairs. Thank you, Chapman. Stay warm."

"Doubtful prospects of that, sir."

Lenox laughed and bade him good-bye, going to the stairwell.

Frost was upstairs. He gave Lenox a quick glance, then a longer one. "Hello, Lenox," he said. "We can't have called you in, can we? It hasn't been ninety minutes."

The offices were small but luxurious, three rooms from what Lenox could see. Frost was standing with an older man in black legal robes.

Beaumont, Lenox guessed. Behind them, two constables were looking carefully through the room.

"No," said Lenox. "But Mr. Middleton's name arose in a case I'm investigating—an assault, possibly an attempted murder. I came over because I wondered if they might be connected."

Frost took in this information. "I suppose it's possible. At the moment we have it pegged as a robbery gone wrong."

"What happened?"

The inspector nodded toward the older man. "I only just arrived. Mr. Beaumont has given his account to Constable Moss, but I was going to impose on him to give it to me again, fresh. Mr. Beaumont, this is Charles Lenox. Please consider him my own auxiliary for the moment."

Beaumont nodded. He was a stout, florid fellow, with pouches under his eyes and white hair that hung below his collar donnishly, curling down over his ears in haphazard fashion.

He started his story, and indeed, despite looking rather stunned, proved lucid in his speech.

It was no wonder that Frost had thought he was dealing with a robbery. In the first place, Mr. Middleton's inner office, to which Frost pushed open the door as Beaumont told his tale, was sumptuously decorated, a heavy clock upon the wall, painted ivory portraits around it, a silver astrolabe upon a delicate-looking French desk, and amidst it all Middleton's body, slumped heavily over the desk.

In the second, there were the circumstances.

Beaumont had left at noon to meet with a client in the courts at Chancery. His own specialty was entail, the tricky set of laws by which England's aristocratic families passed down their houses and fortunes. Middleton had been a specialist in more common middle-class wills and estates. They had joined their legal practices nine years before, believing they would dovetail well, and been satisfied in the partnership from the first moment, Beaumont said.

"It is only the two of you?" Lenox asked, glancing pointedly at an empty desk in the outer office.

"We share a clerk, Larkin, who is here on Mondays, Wednesday, and Fridays. As you know, today is Tuesday, so he wasn't in the chambers."

When Beaumont had left, Middleton had been drafting a will for one of his clients, a brewer from Lambeth. Lenox asked how acquainted the two men would have been with each other's work, and the solicitor answered that they knew each other's major clients—they kept joint books, each the other's insurance against a down year, and with enough trust between them to share equally in their partnership—but that they rarely consulted each other in much detail, due to their separate fields of legal knowledge.

When Beaumont had returned to the office, just after three o'clock, he had immediately noticed that something was amiss. The door was shoved in, the handle broken. Lenox looked over and saw that the wood around the jamb was splintered.

"I proceeded inward with some caution," said Beaumont, "calling out Middleton's name. He did not reply. Soon enough I saw why."

"Was the door to his office open?" asked Lenox.

"Closed," said Beaumont.

"And you went in?"

"Yes. I took his pulse—nothing, alas. That was when I whistled for the constable. Both of us are older men, and we keep a whistle on the door. Neither of us has criminal clients, but people grow restive, you know, and in Maltravers Street you do have the criminal element come through occasionally."

Lenox nodded. They were men of extreme caution and conservatism, obviously, Beaumont and Middleton, their practice well and solidly maintained, perhaps not astronomically profitable, he would have guessed, because of an aversion to risk, but certainly successful.

"Moss mentioned that things had gone missing," said Frost to Beaumont.

The solicitor nodded. "Yes. I looked with Constable Moss and saw that a set of gold pens Middleton received from a client were gone, along with his watch chain and watch, the former of which was set with rubies. I would have to look more thoroughly to see if anything else is gone."

"Did either of you keep ready money here?" Frost asked.

"No."

"Was anything missing from your office?" Lenox asked.

"No," said Beaumont.

"Perhaps we ought to go in and look at the body, then," said Frost. "Mr. Beaumont, we'll be with you again shortly if you prefer to remain here."

CHAPTER FOURTEEN

Middleton had been tall and bony, with a thin face and close-shorn hair. His head rested on its left cheek on his desk, his face not unpeaceful in its appearance despite the small bullet hole, with a trickle of dried blood descending from it, in the center of his forehead. A small snub-nosed pistol, Lenox guessed.

His desk was extremely tidy, nearly empty.

Lenox and Frost stood before the corpse for a moment in respectful silence. They had left Beaumont in the outer office with one of the constables. The landlady—all aflutter herself—had brought him a brandy and soda.

"Give me an account of how you came to hear Middleton's name, then, if you would," Frost said.

As Lenox offered a summation of Gerald Leigh's inauspicious visit to London, both he and Frost combed through the office, careful not to disturb anything.

When Lenox had finished speaking, Frost straightened and said, "Rum business."

"Yes, indeed." Lenox turned around once, and then said, as much to himself as to Frost, "Where did he keep his files, I wonder?"

There was no cabinet in the room, and the drawers of the desk were largely empty. Frost stepped to the door and asked Beaumont if they might have a word—then, realizing that he might not want to converse in the presence of the body of his partner, suggested that they might use Beaumont's office.

"His files?" Beaumont said, when they were in his own room, a slightly less refined but homier chamber. There was a rack of wooden pipes and an alepot over the fireplace. That red complexion had been fairly and squarely earned, Lenox thought. "He kept his current files in a valise which he brought between his office and his home. The rest are in a small locked room downstairs."

"With your own?"

"No, mine are in here, as you can see." He gestured toward a large cabinet. "Middleton didn't like to have estates upon which he wasn't currently working at hand, though. If something came up he went down to the locker."

This reply precipitated a trip down to the locker, to which Beaumont had a key, though he had to hunt it down in his desk. It appeared undisturbed. The door was locked, all of the cabinets of files locked, too.

But of course the valise was gone.

Frost and Lenox looked around the offices for another twenty minutes. Nothing of real interest presented itself; when Lenox had conferred with Frost, agreeing that they ought to meet with Leigh together that evening, he left. He wanted to return to the offices in Chancery Lane and think.

On his carriage ride—the sky dark now—Lenox realized that it was a case richer than usual with possibilities. There were no fewer than four potential points of assault upon its hidden truths: the mysterious benefactor of Leigh's schooldays; the attacks on him by Anderson and Singh; the unexpected legacy left to him; and now the murder of Middleton.

Where to begin?

The murder, Lenox thought—always the murder.

Though it was past the normal work hours, the office was busy. Their various investigators were nearly all occupied on behalf of one or more of the businesses the agency represented, which meant that in turn the clerks were busy—and also that the partners were, by and large, free to take on cases.

This was fortunate, both because it meant he

could concentrate on Leigh and because when Lenox found Polly and Dallington, they were having an intense discussion about Parliament, from which they had just come. Evidently that case was more complex than it had sounded, too.

They were in Polly's office, she behind her desk, Dallington perched on its edge, flipping a small unlit cigar in his fingers.

They greeted him and asked whether he had any news about Middleton.

"The details are emerging," Lenox said. "But I would guess it's connected to Leigh. It must be. What happened at the House?"

Polly shook her head seriously. "It's a more interesting matter than the papers let on. Cheesewright was fearfully agitated."

It seemed ages since Lenox had read about the smashed window that morning, and seen his two partners off to visit with Mr. Cheesewright, their point of contact at Parliament.

"I thought his head would spin off his shoulders," Dallington said.

"What happened?"

Dallington gestured toward the desk. "I drew the scene."

This was a new practice that Polly had introduced. It was useless for Lenox, who could barely draw a circle, but she herself was a meticulous draftsman, or, he supposed, draftswoman, and Dallington had a light, loose, telling hand. One of their clerks had also proved eminently useful; in fact, Lenox had asked him on his way into this room to go over to Middleton's chambers to draw the scene there.

He picked up the sheet. It showed a row of six large windows, squared at the bottom and ascending to a curved triangle at the top, with a long stone bench running beneath them. One of the windows was broken, an ugly jagged hole in it more than large enough to admit a man or woman.

Lenox had walked down this narrow hallway many times himself. It connected the famous chamber of the House of Commons to a secluded back office that was the privileged refuge of members of the cabinet, and anyone they might choose to invite—a most convenient bolt-hole. On the other side of the windows was a small flowering courtyard with a low fence, which then led out into the streets of Westminster. Certainly a vulnerability.

"The person was trying to get into the Commons?" he asked.

Dallington shook his head. "No—the other end of the hall, actually. Someone had tried to force the door of this back room."

Something was bothering him about the drawing, as he studied it. But he couldn't quite put his finger on what it was.

"What was in the office worth stealing?" he asked.

Polly answered. "That's the trouble—nobody will tell us. For that matter nobody will tell Cheesewright. The staff of the various ministers will only confirm that their masters had been in the office recently, but not what else might have been. We had a free hand to look around, but it was no different than stepping into any room at a gentleman's club. Soft armchairs, old newspapers, the usual detritus. Nothing that looked worth stealing. And nothing that *was* stolen, at least nothing blatantly gone."

"How does Cheesewright want you to proceed?"

"We were just debating that when you came in."

"How he wants you to proceed?"

"No, sorry—how we interpreted his request. He very definitely wants one of us on the spot tonight."

"Let Harding go," said Lenox. "Or I'm sure Pointilleux would only be too delighted." These were two of their agents. "Better still, have them station the night porter in that hallway. They must have reserve forces."

"They only have two watchmen for the entire vast building overnight. We're the reserve forces," said Polly.

Dallington nodded. "And I don't want to send Harding. I think something pretty nasty may be afoot, and we don't have a more important client. Look at all the business that their hiring of us put in our way. Short of the Queen there couldn't be a better endorsement. I'd like to go myself."

"But so would I," said Polly.

"Which I say is out of the question."

She smiled. "To which I reply that I am not interested in Lord John's opinions on the matter of my personal safety."

"To which *I* then reply that—"

Lenox pointed a finger at the drawing. "I see it."

"See what?" asked Dallington.

"Look at the glass of the window. Is this accurate?"

The young lord frowned, coming over to glance down at the picture he had drawn in the light of the gas lamp. "I think so. At least it's as accurate as I could get it. Why?"

Lenox tapped the image of the broken window. "Was there glass on the bench beneath the broken window?"

"No."

"Just as I thought. Look. The glass is broken outward. Someone was going *out* through the window, not breaking into the building through it."

CHAPTER FIFTEEN

The three partners of Lenox, Dallington, and Strickland spent a long while discussing the significance of this fact. ("Is that how you finally managed to get out of Parliament?" Dallington asked Lenox.) According to the two of them there hadn't been any other illicit entrances observed at Parliament the day before, which made this unusual exit all the odder. Was the criminal someone who had been there with permission? A Member, even? A *lord,* heaven forfend?

At last Dallington agreed that they could both return to Parliament that night. There, they could coordinate their efforts with the night watchmen and lie in wait for the vandal to return to the hallway.

Once Dallington realized that he was going to spend the night in close work with Polly, his mood abruptly changed—he sent his secretary out to Fortnum's with instructions to bring back a hamper of food and with it in particular a flask of very, very strong tea, "hotter than the devil if you please, and twice as strong."

The idea of a night sitting up with tea made Lenox realize how tired he was. When his younger colleagues' course of action was settled, he took his leave with a few quiet words, nearly fell asleep in the taxi on the way home, ate and read a novel, and then, feeling melancholy in the empty house for a fleeting moment after his head fell on the pillow, passed the next ten hours sound asleep.

He was woken only by the soft, discreet cough of Kirk outside his door. The butler would return in a moment or two. Lenox glanced at the clock— past eight. How indolent he became without Jane and Sophia here!

He stretched, rose, and dressed. When Kirk came again, Lenox was halfway into his warmest heather-gray jacket. "Good morning," he said. "Still snowing?"

"No, sir—but it is the coldest day yet. And you have a visitor, sir. Mr. Graham."

Lenox was surprised but pleased. "Graham!"

"Yes, sir. I have left him in the breakfast room with a cup of tea."

"We can do better than that—give him a bowl of oatmeal if you would, glutton that he is, and tell him I'll be down shortly."

"Very good, sir."

In truth there were few less gluttonous men in London than Lenox's quiet, watchful friend. An uncommon friendship, to be sure; for many years Graham had been Lenox's butler, though that word scarcely covered the variety of his roles, which also included those of assistant and cocounsel in his investigations.

Then, when Lenox had entered Parliament, he had been unable to find anyone he trusted to assume the role of his secretary, only to realize that the ideal candidate was in fact Graham. The trouble was that parliamentary secretaries were universally men of the upper class, bred into high families and educated amid old stones; and yet Graham had proven himself so adept at the battles of government, so brilliant in his maneuvers, that it had been only mildly shocking to political society when, upon Lenox leaving Parliament, he had himself run for a seat.

After a tough defeat, he had won, and now for two years had been a Member, still snickered at for his low birth, still invited almost nowhere, but with a sure and growing reputation among the serious men of the body.

He rose when Lenox entered the breakfast room. He was a compact, sandy-haired person, with a servant's natural impassivity in his face, a face that was now, after many years, minutely scored with wrinkles.

They shook hands. "How do you do?" Graham asked, in his inflection the word "sir" somehow still suspended just invisibly.

"My wife and daughter are snowbound in outer Romania and one of my oldest friends has two of the worst gang members of East London after him."

"Roughly as I last found you, then," said Graham.

Lenox laughed. "Yes, roughly as you last found me."

"Outer Romania?"

"Well—Sussex. And you? Are you quite well?"

"Quite well, yes." He looked tired, Lenox thought. "The House does become discouraging, time in time."

"How is that?"

"Oh—slow."

Lenox nodded sympathetically. "I remember."

"Yes, of course."

"How weary I grew of the accustomed pattern," Lenox said, pouring himself a cup of coffee and joining Graham at the table. "First a terrible story comes to light, be it the state of the orphanages or the children in the mines up north. Old soldiers starving to death for want of income. There is an outcry, a long article detailing the problem. The novelists get a hold of it. Then the philanthropists and the charitable societies. And only then does Parliament creak into motion."

"If then. The pheasants and the foxes will not shoot themselves," said Graham.

"And then a year or two later you might pass some laughably weak law, funded the Lord alone knows how, and if you're lucky six years later something begins to happen, perhaps—people will stop being poisoned because their milk is made mostly of chalk. And for all that things get done, eventually."

Graham nodded. "There is no other way, I suppose."

"It's like running a team of twenty horses. You have to turn them slowly."

"You ought to be able to go faster in a straight line, though. There are matters we should all agree on."

"I recall my own father working on the Factory Act. It was passed in 1802 to ensure that children worked no more than twelve hours a day—twelve hours! not all that generous a reprieve—and it was enforced for the first time in 1833, when they finally came around to appointing a few inspectors. Thirty-one years. Think of it."

For a long while they discussed Graham's efforts, thwarted by the Tories and by some in his own party too, to extend the vote to debtors. The story of their century had been that of the vote, in some ways, from only a select few possessing the franchise to tens of thousands more by now. About a decade before, when Parliament passed its gargantuan and far-reaching Reform Bill, John Stuart Mill had even proposed a motion to change the language to allow every "person" to vote, rather than every man—that is, to give women the vote. He had been mocked and scorned and derided, but now, very, very slowly, the idea was moving into the outer fringes of respectability. Among the political class it was considered very savvy to predict the coming of the women's vote—though likely not for a hundred years or so, they all agreed.

Kirk came in quietly with a pot of oatmeal and a bowl of brown sugar, then after a moment with a small glass of ale for Graham, a testament to the many years they had known each other as peers.

When Graham had been there half an hour, a messenger arrived with a note. Lenox recognized him as one of the McConnell footmen.

"If you'll forgive me, this might be important," Lenox said, opening it.

It was from Leigh.

> My dear Lenox,
> After a night's restless sleep I have decided to return to France after all. My heart is with my work there. I will also feel safe—the university is a fortress, and I rarely leave its grounds. Indeed my valet, whom they provided, was a member of their army's special services. So I beg you not to worry, Charlie. Please convey to Mr. Middleton's successor, whoever he may be, that I relinquish entirely my claims to the fortune that was left me. Should I need to have that statement notarized or somehow recorded by a solicitor, there are British attorneys in Paris.
> With many reservations I have agreed to return in a week's time to address the

Royal Society. If the police need my help then, I will be happy to give it. But my hope is that the whole matter will be behind me.

Even in these circumstances it has given me joy to see you again; will you allow me to invite you and Lady Jane to dine with me upon my return?

Leigh

Lenox showed the letter to Graham, and their conversation shifted over to the troubles of Leigh and the murder of Middleton.

Tapping the note where it lay on the table, Lenox said, "My fear is that he will not move so easily beyond the reaches of the men pursuing him."

"Who are they?"

"Foul creatures. Anderson and Singh, they're called. They first met in India, where as I understand it Singh came from a decent family. Anderson is from London. He was abroad with the army, and they somehow fell in together. When they came back they found their way into the Farthings as a team."

Graham raised his eyes. This was perhaps London's deadliest street gang. "How on earth could they have come to be concerned with an inheritance like your friend's?" he said.

"That's just what I don't know. And a clean, tidy

murder, like that of Middleton—that doesn't look like them, either. They got their name, as perhaps you know, because it was said they would put a knife between your ribs for a farthing."

They went on discussing the case, their hot coffee going cold, until at last Graham said that he had better be on his way.

Only after he had gone did Lenox pause to consider why he had come. The two men often dined together, but it was usually lunch they had. The month before, Graham had mentioned that he hoped to make a proposal of marriage soon—and now, reflecting on his glum mood about Parliament, Lenox wondered whether perhaps it hadn't gone as his old friend had hoped it would.

CHAPTER SIXTEEN

The next several days were busy. Lenox spent them closely tracking the developments in the investigation of Middleton's murder, consulting frequently with Inspector Frost. The death had been an attractive one for the newsmen: a safe and respectable street, a safe and respectable victim, and the tantalizing possibility of an upper-class killer. As a result many of the locals in and around Maltravers Street were eager to be interviewed by the police. Their exhaustive canvass produced no tangible leads, however.

Lenox had been in touch with Leigh by wire; he was again safely ensconced at the University of Paris, he said. Lenox tried to insinuate to him the lurking danger of his situation, without mentioning the Farthings outright. But Leigh either ignored or missed his hints.

In the meanwhile Pointilleux, their young French associate, had been picking up a far older inquiry: the MB.

He spent the better part of two days away from the offices in Chancery Lane. He returned on Wednesday evening, his enthusiasm undimmed by the frigid winds—he was only twenty after all—and eager to impart his findings.

Lenox was in his office, studying a maddeningly incomplete list of Middleton's and Beaumont's clients. ("Why Beaumont's?" Frost had asked. "It wouldn't be the first time a man was mistaken for someone else and killed," Lenox replied.) When Pointilleux came in, he pushed the list aside.

"The prodigal investigator! Welcome back. Have you struck gold?"

Pointilleux frowned. "I have struck snow. There is snow every place of this metropolis."

"On the case, I mean."

The lad patted a folio under his arm. "I think only silver. I can exclude one among the candidate."

"Which one?"

"Mr. Leigh's uncle, the Earl of Ashe."

140

"On what basis?"

"If this gentleman would to have twenty-five thousand pounds sterling, many, many parties would be interest," said Pointilleux, in his customarily roundabout English. "Not least Her Majesty Government—merchants up and down Jermyn Street and within the county of Cornwall—"

"Duchy. It's a duchy, not a county."

"What is the differentiation?"

Lenox started to speak and then stopped, checked by his own ignorance. "I say, I'm not sure I actually know."

"Well, people all over this duchy will wish to speak to Lord Ashe—should he have twenty-five thousand pound within his possession."

"Is that the sum of your evidence?"

"No. There is his will, as well. I have it here. It is of public record. The house and lands entail to his son. Any remaining monies are belonging to his sons equally. They should be able to have a frugal meal of chickens and potato, I suppose, ha, ha."

"Very amusing," said Lenox.

"In total it is probably no more than a few hundred pounds to each of them. How they will keep the house I cannot say."

Lenox felt a sorry sinking emotion—not for Ashe's sons, but because this meant that Townsend, the object of loathing for Leigh's

141

entire youth, the man who had killed Leigh's father with his recklessness, was also in all likelihood his benefactor. And not once, now, but twice.

And at the same time, this news introduced the faintest glimmer of doubt in Lenox's mind. Could his friend Gerald Leigh have killed Middleton, somehow, if his fury toward Townsend was sufficient? Certainly not, he thought—and yet, were it any other case, it was an idea that Lenox granted to himself that he would be forced to entertain. Covington's was not far from Maltravers Street. There had been a window of an hour or so in which Beaumont had been absent from the offices that day, and also before Lenox, McConnell, and Polly had finally run Leigh to ground.

"And what of Townsend?"

"That is a harder fish to fry," said Pointilleux. As was his custom when he deployed any English idiom, he hesitated proudly, with a very serious, distracted air to conceal it, before carrying on. "I think though—I think it is him."

It seemed the reason the young Frenchman had been absent from Chancery Lane was that he had traveled to Truro, the chief seat of Cornwall, a good four-hour train journey outside of London. For his troubles he had been firmly rejected in his attempts to see Townsend's will.

He had learned something of Townsend's

circumstances, however. Since Leigh's boyhood, it appeared, the man had grown only wealthier. Before his death he had controlled several disparate businesses with, altogether, a few hundred employees.

What was more, he had fallen out with his only son, who lived in London, mixing in fast society. The general opinion was that Townsend hadn't left his money to the young man, particularly because upon his death, according to locals more confiding than the courthouse officials, there had been several unusual legacies, including a thousand pounds to a disreputable old gambling friend, a few hundred to a local schoolteacher who had been cruelly jilted, and the very great sum of ten thousand to a former valet.

"No rumor of twenty-five thousand pounds to a scientist, I suppose."

Pointilleux shook his head. "I'm afraid not. But he was not local."

"Is there anything to tie Townsend directly to Middleton?"

"In the year before he has died Mr. Townsend has made several trips to London, of obscure purposes," Pointilleux said, squaring off the papers he was reading where they lay on the desk.

"Whom did they hear from about their inheritances—the old gambling friend, the local schoolteacher, the former valet?"

"A local solicitor," conceded Pointilleux. "But the affairs of Mr. Townsend were complex of the extreme. There are several attorneys involve alone in the disbursal of his firm, for instance, and I am suspecting his estate is much the same. This solicitor will answer only for a few legacies that he received the assignation to make."

"Assignment," Lenox said automatically.

"Yes, if you prefer, assignment."

They talked a bit more. Pointilleux had further lines of investigation to pursue. But Lenox felt sure already that he had the truth in his hands. Beaumont had confirmed that Middleton had become busy with a large estate about two months before, which coincided precisely with the time Townsend had died, and what was more, Beaumont recalled Middleton saying it was a tricky one. It was some severe wasting disease that had taken Townsend, apparently. He would have seen his death coming in time to make a will.

And suddenly a stray thought came to him: The letter left for Leigh with the legacy had said that it wished its author could have had a *greater* opportunity to know him. That implied some previous relationship, if only a slight one.

Lenox stood up from his desk. He had been feeling thwarted by the case, which presented so many features that it ought to have been easy to solve—except that the strands kept separating, each mystery refusing to tie into the others.

But now he was heartened. "Congratulations, Pointilleux. You have given us our first real suspect."

"Have I? Who?"

"Townsend's son."

"Why him?"

"If Leigh forfeited his claim to that money, it would by law descend to Townsend's closest living relative. His son. What have you discovered about him?"

Pointilleux consulted his notes. The fellow's name was Andrew Townsend. He lived in Soho, along a rather racy strip of territory around Lexington Street. That reference to fast company had been vague for a reason, however: Pointilleux knew no more than that several people in Truro had shaken their heads darkly when referring to the young man, and made oblique references to the racetrack and to women of loose morals.

"Do you have an address?" Lenox asked.

"I can locate it," said Pointilleux.

"Good. We'll go and see him in the morning, after I speak to Inspector Frost."

They discussed Townsend further as Lenox gathered his hat and his gloves, preparing to go home. He would have stayed longer on another day—but tonight was the night that Jane and Sophia were finally returning home, and he wanted to meet them at Charing Cross.

CHAPTER SEVENTEEN

O n his way from the office Lenox picked up McConnell in his carriage, for Jane was traveling together with McConnell's own wife, Toto, and their daughter, Georgiana.

The physician was waiting outside of his house, bundled tightly in a cloak and carrying a parcel. "What is that?" Lenox asked.

"The fossilized excrement of an African elephant. I need to post it to a colleague in Manchester when we arrive at the station. I think I shall just have time."

"What an exciting life you lead, Thomas."

"Ha, ha."

"I'm not sure how I can thank you adequately for blessing my carriage with such an exciting delivery."

"It's very well sealed. There is no odor—practically no odor."

Lenox hadn't seen McConnell since Leigh bolted for France, and it was this that they discussed as the carriage rolled through the West End and toward the train station. According to McConnell, Lenox's old friend had been philosophical about his position at supper, only to wake up having reversed himself.

"It was all I could do to make him stay for

146

breakfast," said McConnell. "But how glad I am that I did! I owe you a profound thanks for introducing me to him. The Englishman who works with Pasteur."

The name rang a faint bell. "Pasteur," Lenox repeated. "Remind me who he is?"

"Louis Pasteur?" McConnell said. "No, I suppose his name has not penetrated into the wider world. A very great man. There can be no doubt of that. According to Leigh too he has a mania for his work. Which is significant, as Leigh pointed out, because many of the geniuses in our field are idle to the bone."

"In my field, too," said Lenox.

McConnell looked curious. "Oh?"

"The most brilliant criminal mind I ever encountered belonged to a fellow named Partridge, who never shifted from the corner seat of a pub in Clapham. As far as I know he slept there. Certainly he delivered his orders from there. Jenkins and I spent hundreds of hours trying to catch him out in his schemes, mostly extortion, but we never did. In fact the only thing that stopped him was his own weight. He had a heart attack and died at his table."

"Pasteur is the very opposite case from the sound of it—scarcely sleeps or eats. And he has been rewarded. It wouldn't surprise me if he saves a million lives a year between now and the end of the century."

Lenox gave McConnell a look of astonishment. "A million!"

"Yes. Vaccination. He's not a doctor, you know, and people kicked up very hard about that. But on the other hand I have seen the studies myself. It all comes down to this theory of germs."

"Germs," Lenox said. "Those tiny invisible particles? Was that not disproven?"

"You could not be more wrong," McConnell said. "They're not invisible, and Leigh is the one among all of us who has done the most to discover their properties. Even Pasteur acknowledges that, and he is not renowned as a generous collaborator."

They had come within a few turns of Charing Cross, and Lenox asked how Leigh had been enticed to return to London in a week's time. According to McConnell, among the possessions Anixter had recovered from the Collingwood Hotel had been the calling cards of the two joint presidents of the Royal Society, Lord Baird and Mr. Alexander Rowan, begging half an hour of Leigh's time.

McConnell had persuaded Leigh to call on them at the Society in the half hour before his train for Dover departed. The doctor had gone along with him, and Rowan, he said (Baird had been away) could not have been more courteous, or more ardently committed to arranging Leigh's speech. This was flattering, given Rowan's own fame—he was only thirty-two, and his rise within the scientific community of England had been meteoric, paper after brilliant paper, a chair at Cambridge younger than anyone before him, but also, to go with it, a personable temperament, a handsome face, a fine fortune.

The entreaties of even someone so distinguished might not have tempted Leigh on their own, but he had also been offered, in exchange for his lecture, the foundation of a scholarship in his name for a Cornish boy of the board schools to either of the universities. Leigh's pick. A graceful touch by Rowan, and the one that had won Leigh over in the end.

"Is that usual?"

"On the contrary, very unusual. But then, so is a scientist who has no interest in addressing the Royal Society."

"I'm not happy about the idea," said Lenox. "Will he be safe?"

"I cannot say that. But at least I know he will never be alone. Already every man of scientific interests in London has canceled his plans for that week, hoping to be invited to the supper afterward. I myself feel fortunate that Leigh arranged my tickets. Men are coming from Oxford, Cambridge of course, even Edinburgh."

For Gerald Leigh! Lenox shook his head.

He couldn't help but feel surprised. When they had been boys at Harrow, in between their investigations into the MB, they had sometimes talked about the future. What had they envisioned for themselves? Lenox would later find that he had one burst of unconventionality in him—the impulse to become a detective—but at the time he had not credited himself even so far as that, imagining that he would go to university, marry, and then enter politics. His dreams then had all been about travel.

Leigh, on the other hand, had been a fidgety dreamer. One hour he would see himself making for America, the next he fancied becoming a farmer in Cornwall and studying the behavior of bees.

How had he come to be so highly reckoned? From McConnell's descriptions, perhaps by following that very restive instinct—the high seas, birds, then flora, then microbes, at each stage pursuing whatever interested him most, regardless of how many years he had dedicated to the last project. Perhaps that was one definition of genius: a willingness to surrender to obsession.

At Charing Cross, McConnell posted his parcel. When he was done, the two men went to platform 8 to wait for the train. The porter informed them that the first-class carriage would be the last car, so they walked down toward it, three abreast, the porter with his luggage cart, to wait. They were rigid in the extreme, the carriages of a British train: It was known that men who had made vast fortunes still almost always traveled in second class. Sometimes one had to acknowledge that theirs was a strange country.

"On Leigh, then—what progress have you made?" McConnell asked him, as they waited.

Lenox shook his head doubtfully. "It's difficult to say. On the murder of Middleton we are nowhere at all. But I believe we may be on the track of the fellow who left Leigh the legacy. I have a suspect. And we certainly know the men who attacked him."

A bright pair of lamplights appeared far down the darkness of the track's curve. "There they are," McConnell said, leaning forward.

Lenox's heart rose. "Yes."

The train slowly wended its way into the station, labored chuffs coming from its stovepipe—and then all at once the platform was furious with activity, and there they were! The two wives, the two daughters.

Lenox bent down and Sophia flew into his arms in a fashion that would, alas, be considered unladylike when another twelve months or so had passed, but which he could still enjoy now. She squeezed him tightly around the neck and he buried his scratchy face in her thick, curly hair, feeling the wholeness of a parent reunited with a child. Lifting Sophia to his side, he greeted Jane with a smile and a kiss, then made a cheerful greeting to McConnell's own arrivals. Governesses descended, servants, luggage. Somehow they sorted themselves out. Sophia had urgent news to convey, which was that there had been Scotch eggs on the train.

"Were they good?" he asked.

"They were better than cook's."

"That wouldn't be nice to tell her."

"It would be nice to have the train eggs all the time though, Father," she said passionately.

"Life is not all train eggs."

She seemed to accept the justice of this—or perhaps was just tired—because she laid her head on his shoulder, and fell silent.

When they were back at Hampden Lane it felt, all at once, like home again; he was watching Jane nervously, but she seemed herself, and they chatted late into the evening after Sophia had gone to sleep, describing the last few days to each other, eating a late supper prepared by their mediocre cook. They were in the drawing room, where all of Jane's touches came alive with her presence— the little portrait of her by Molly, Edmund's wife, the small porcelain birds in flight along the mantel, even the intricate white-and-wintergreen wallpaper.

Before he retired for the night he went into his study and jotted down a few notes. The next day he would find Townsend's son and he would go to the Blue Peter, dangerous though it might be, and see Anderson and Singh.

He wanted it all resolved before Leigh returned to London.

When he finally went up to their bedchamber, he started telling Jane about something Sophia had said. She didn't reply immediately, and he looked more closely toward where she sat, in front of her tall oval mirror, and realized, with a shock, that she was crying.

He went over to her and put a hand on her shoulder. "What's the matter, my dear?" he said.

"Nothing."

She had been upset over Christmas. They had fallen out. With a sinking feeling he saw that it wasn't over; and he still understood no better why. "Jane."

She shook her head. "It's nothing."

It was so rare for her to be anything other than the most composed person in a room—his sweet, kind, acute wife, whose emotions generally ran highest for other people. "I wish you would tell me at last."

She looked up at him in the mirror. "I don't want to, because you'll think less of me."

"You have my word that I won't."

She hesitated, and then looked down at the silver brush in her hand. "No, Charles. It's fine. A good night's sleep at home will set me right."

CHAPTER EIGHTEEN

T he next morning there was a thaw in the air, a blurred vivid sun. Across the city the sound of ice dripping away its existence. Lenox and Frost were both in greatcoats; but the day was sunny enough that these threatened to become warm.

They were walking along Cheshire Street, in the East End of London. This more modest part of town was dominated by an endless row of tiny specialty shops, which sold their wares primarily to larger and more refined places in brighter neighborhoods. There was a lace dealer, a broom and brush maker, a snuff seller, a yeast merchant, a hatter, a gunsmith, a shroud maker, on and on and on. They passed several anonymous black doors with small white ribbons tied around their handles: midwives.

Their destination was a pub. It was the Blue Peter, situated on a bustling corner of Chilton Street, and it was the central clearinghouse of all the business of the Farthings.

In spite of that grim fact, it was a jolly paneled place, with its draft beers chalked on the wall and the maritime flag that gave it its name—a white square at the center of a larger blue square— flying above its door.

Lenox's stomach fluttered as they went in. Without Frost alongside him, his life would have been forfeit when he entered the Blue Peter. He had put at least three Farthings away. They would never come to the West End for revenge—it would bring too much attention to them—but if he walked into their midst, he might easily make too tempting a target to resist.

The man they sought was as close as the Farthings had to a spokesman. He was a rather well-educated chap named Spencer, who stood behind the bar now, wiping it down with a rag.

"Inspector Frost," he said, without the slightest discomposure.

"Hello, Spencer."

"What brings you into these lawless and wicked and god-mostly-forsaken parts?"

"Anderson and Singh."

"Mr. Anderson and Mr. Singh!" Spencer grinned, revealing a gleaming white smile. Fake, of course. "Have they been paying calls at the Yard? Gentlemanly of them, I say, after how they've been treated there past times."

It wasn't Spencer that Lenox wanted to speak to. It was Anderson and Singh themselves. Frost knew that, and asked, "Are they here?"

"Here on Chilton Street? Those layabouts? No. Not for ages and ages."

"If they are, they can avoid hanging by talking to us."

"Not improved at listening, have you, Inspector Frost! Tut! I told you it's been ages. Now, then, let me lay you down two pints in the little room, sirs—I don't know you, but any friend of—yes, along through there—be in shortly."

They were hustled toward a back room. Lenox knew what that meant. Anderson and Singh would be offered the chance to speak to them; they might accept, might decline.

Frost and Lenox waited there for the greater part of an hour. Because they couldn't discuss the case—who knew what methods Spencer and his cronies might have of eavesdropping on them—they were forced to fall back upon general conversation. Fortunately Lenox found that he liked Frost, a Londoner bred in the bone, fond of noise and soot, suspicious of the countryside, and utterly at home in a pub like this one, adversarial but respectful toward its inhabitants. His great passion, it emerged, was codes and cyphers of all kinds. He corresponded with other amateur codemakers across England, and had even petitioned the Yard to allow him to form a task force dedicated to them. Approval was pending.

Spencer, meanwhile, kept bringing them fresh pints. Lenox was pouring his in the grating; he knew the barman was being so hospitable because he wanted them sluggish.

And then, suddenly, looming in the doorway, was an enormous barrel-bellied chap in a checked suit, with a bright red beard and a fleshy pink face.

Anderson. Lenox felt the menace of the man immediately. He had small, cold eyes.

"Yes? What do you want of me?" he asked.

There was no pretense in his voice, or any of Spencer's camouflaging amiability. "Did you kill a solicitor named Ernest Middleton?" Lenox asked, hoping to catch a reaction.

"Who are you?"

"A consultant with Scotland Yard," Lenox answered. "Did you?"

"I have no idea who the man is, but seeing as I have not killed anyone this side of the equator, I doubt it. On that occasion I did it for Her Majesty."

"Where is your friend Singh?" Lenox asked.

"You'll have to ask him."

"We're asking you," said Frost in a hard voice.

"Much good may it do you. Is that all?"

Frost shook his head. "No. We wish you to know that Gerald Leigh has our attention."

"Don't know the name."

"He has powerful friends—and should any harm come to him, the full force of the Yard might finally be borne in upon the Farthings. You may tell your superiors that."

Anderson studied them for a moment, and then turned without a word and left.

Frost and Lenox exchanged a glance. He had gone, no doubt, thinking that he had given away nothing. What they knew, however, and he didn't, was that from the moment he stepped outside the Blue Peter a constable would be shadowing him, and would continue to do so until Leigh returned in three days. Most of the Farthings lived in the crowded streets around this Chilton Street epicenter of their activity, but it was impossible to say where on a given night any of them might be. This had been their chance to find Anderson before he found Leigh. They had taken it. Not a bad morning's work.

Frost and Lenox took the underground west, then, climbing from it in the leafy middle-class precincts of Pimlico, home to much of London's professional class, an altogether less threatening part of town. They were here to see Middleton's lodgings.

It had taken a surprisingly long while to discover their whereabouts. Beaumont—his own partner—had never laid eyes on them and only vaguely knew their location. They weren't identified in any of the papers at the solicitor's offices.

That morning, however, a woman had written in to the Yard to say that she believed the man in the headlines had been the inhabitant of the second story of her house.

A constable awaited them outside the door there now. It was a wholly respectable street, the houses each clad in the same staid gloss of outward gentility as their inhabitants no doubt were, curtained attic windows exchanged for bowler hats.

"Hello, Chips," said Frost to the small, alert constable. "What have you found?"

"Name on the letterbox, sir."

Lenox had immediately noticed the same. "Very good. Well—shall we go in?"

Chips held up the key, which he had obtained from the owner.

The rooms were what Lenox had expected. There were four of them. One was a dark, fuggy sitting room, certainly a bachelor's—cigar ash was strewn liberally over the arms of the sofa and the floor, a heavy tranche of old newspapers on the settee, hunting prints on the walls—and the remaining three lay behind it, two of them bedrooms and one a small study.

Even a cursory examination showed that these were Middleton's rooms, but unfortunately a more thorough one didn't uncover the missing valise, which might have offered confirmation that Townsend was indeed the person who had left Leigh his fortune.

There were other prizes, however. "Here is his daily planner," Frost called from the study, flicking through a ledger. Lenox came and looked over his shoulder. "He was scrupulous about recording his appointments."

"A great deal of shorthand—abbreviations,"

Lenox murmured. "But it could be useful. I wonder if I could keep it for a night or two?"

"By all means—only let us take first crack at it, and we'll give it to you Friday or Saturday."

That was fair. Lenox nodded his thanks.

There were a few more useful finds—Lenox discovered two angry letters from a former client in a pigeonhole in the desk, which in a normal murder case would have vaulted their author, one Calum Aldington, into the top tier of suspects—and Chips followed them assiduously, double-checking everything they looked into. Also in Middleton's desk was a sheaf of letter cards engraved with his name and the address 24 Aldershot Place. That was curious: a second address, perhaps.

"Or an old address?" said Frost.

"Perhaps. He has been here nine years, however, according to the landlady. Would he keep them in his desk? It's a very tidy one. Worth sending a man to that address, if you can spare one."

Frost nodded, looking at the stationery. "Yes. We will."

It was in the spare bedroom that Lenox found something even more interesting, he thought. "Frost," he called out, "come have a look at this."

The inspector popped his head around the doorway. "What is it?"

Lenox held open a fitted pistol case, leather on the outside, blue velvet on the inside. "Empty."

"That's something. Do you think it signifies?"

"We didn't find a pistol in the office, nor have we here."

"He lost it, then."

"A pistol! Well, perhaps—or perhaps he felt that he was in danger, and removed it for his own protection."

"But in that case we would have found it."

Lenox raised his eyebrows. "Or else it was the weapon that killed him, and it lies at the bottom of the Thames. You'll note that the size of the pistol that was stored in this case matches that of the bullet found in Middleton's brain."

Frost's expression darkened. "Yes."

"Did you observe as we entered the dead bolt above the regular lock on the door?"

"No."

Lenox nodded. "Unlocked, of course, since he wasn't here—but new, I would guess, from the shine on the brass. The other doors don't have them."

Frost looked at him with an air of reappraisal, perhaps of appreciation. "Well spotted."

There was a call from the sitting room. Frost and Lenox went and found Chips by the door, with the landlady. She was holding a packet of letters. She wanted to see if they needed the mail she had held for Middleton.

Frost took the chance to ask her about the dead bolt. She had already said that she hadn't noticed anything unusual about her lodger's behavior—but now she said that yes, he had had a locksmith in at his own expense to fortify the door, about eight or nine days earlier.

As Frost questioned the woman further, Lenox flicked through the mail. Most of it was of the common sort—circulars, bills—but there was one unfranked envelope that merely said *Middleton* in a fine cursive.

He opened it, and something dropped to the floor. The envelope was otherwise empty. Chips stooped down and picked up the object. "What is it?" Lenox asked.

"A coin," Chips answered, holding it up for all of them to inspect. "But only a farthing."

CHAPTER NINETEEN

T he case was suddenly gathering momentum. After another hour and a half of examining Middleton's rooms, he and Frost separated, agreeing to be in touch later that day, earlier if necessary. Frost knew that Lenox was pursuing Townsend's son, Leigh's competition for the father's inheritance. For his part, the man from the Yard was going to speak with his bosses about the Farthings—since unmistakably now, by that coin, the unsuccessful attempt on Leigh's life and the successful one on Middleton's were linked, two known members of the gang pursuing the former, their very symbol appearing at the home of the latter.

A stubborn problem remained for Lenox, though: Why would the gang indicate their intentions with this letter and coin? Neither of them had been able to offer a satisfactory solution to that question.

He headed back toward the agency's offices. For some reason the streets around Chancery Lane were crammed, nearly impassable. At the little wooden soup stand run by his friend Ames, Lenox stopped, touching his hat.

"What is all this commotion?" he asked.

"Do you read the papers, sir?"

"From time to time. Why?"

"It's the Post Office, sir. Which, they've announced themselves so pressed in the need for telegraphs in the instrument gallery that they've said they'll accept women now."

Lenox glanced around. It was nearly all young women in the neighborhood, he realized. "There are hundreds."

Ames brandished a fresh copy of the *Star*. "A thousand, it says here. They accepted seven hundred of them. Salary a hundred pound a year, sir."

"Not bad."

"Well, the women are kicking up, because the gentlemen make a hundred sixty—but they were let go, the ones that fussed. And it only makes sense, as they're gentlemen."

"It's overdue," Lenox said. "They take ages now, the wires. And women can tap their toes just as well as men can. I have been at enough concerts to know that."

As he walked on, he watched the people milling around him. Nothing had changed life quite as the telegraph had. All of them were utterly dependent on it now. In America the change was even more dramatic—before the telegraph, it had taken ten days to send a message from the east coast of the country to the west, by the Pony Express; with the completion of the transcontinental line, fifteen years before, it now took about ten seconds. They were still to see how this closeness to distant parts of the world changed them all.

When Lenox returned to the offices, he found that Polly and Dallington were back. They had been at Parliament three nights successively, taking the days to sleep, and as far as Lenox could ascertain had accomplished quite literally nothing in that time, unless you believed they had acted as a deterrent. (He did not.) Whenever they were in the office they were laughing together, heads close, full of plans.

"I think it might be time to pass Parliament down the ladder," he said, when they were closeted together. They had come in to hear about Leigh and Middleton.

"Why?" Dallington asked.

"It's taking up all of your time, and unless I'm mistaken you still have no idea what happened. At this point I think we ought to call it a one-time event and devote less time to it. In fact, it's overwhelmingly likely that whatever was in the back room is gone now."

"We do have one lead," Dallington said.

"What's that?"

"There's a naval negotiation to begin in Belgium Tuesday next," he said. "To see the British government's plans for it in advance would be a serious strategic advantage."

"To France, Russia, any number of countries," Polly added. "And according to one junior minister, several conversations had taken place in the room."

This was serious indeed, a plausible motive. Lenox nodded philosophically. "I suppose you had better carry on after all."

Relief flashed imperceptibly across Dallington's face. "And what of Middleton, and Leigh?" he inquired.

Lenox told them about the morning's findings. Both expressed alarm about the farthing in the envelope; and like Lenox and Frost could offer no account for the brazenness of the symbol.

"If it was a warning," said Dallington, "they ought to have given him the chance to be warned before they killed him."

"Just so."

Soon enough they left Lenox's office—looking more like conspirators than colleagues—and the older detective was free to begin looking over the brief dossier Pointilleux had given him on Townsend's son.

His name was a peculiar one: Salt. Salt Andrew Townsend. He was just over thirty and had lived in London since leaving grammar school at the age of seventeen, acting first as a factor for his father's various business concerns, and then, after their falling-out, apparently living on a portion that his father had settled on him in happier times.

"Salt," Lenox muttered to himself, as he read this.

He sent out for lunch and continued to puzzle through the timeline of Leigh's case, jotting notes down as he went. Pointilleux dashed in at a little past two o'clock, only long enough to tell Lenox that he thought he would have run Salt Townsend to ground by six o'clock.

"Come to my house when you have, would you?" Lenox asked.

"Your house? Why, of course."

He thanked Pointilleux and waved him off. It was an unusual directive, but Lenox wanted to check on his brother. He left, directing his carriage to his town house.

Sir Edmund Lenox was a great man in Parliament now; he was in conference despite having only just returned to London, and though he greeted Charles with an expression of delighted surprise, he immediately warned him that he could spare but a few minutes.

"I had hoped I could give you tea somewhere," said Charles.

"If only. Two hours off the train, and I am somehow four hours behind schedule. Would that you could explain that to me."

"At any rate I thank you for taking care of Jane and Sophia longer than you had planned."

"Not at all."

He had been widowed the fall before, and since that terrible event had only been half himself, Charles thought, as if he and Molly had traded parts of their souls into each other over the long course of their loving marriage. But now, for the first time, there were glimpses of a thaw inside. "Was it taxing?"

"I wish we all could have stayed down there for the whole of January. We need to enlist some philosopher king to run this country once and for all, so that we can have a respite."

"I nominate Graham," Lenox said.

"You could do worse. Bear in mind that we have Her Majesty."

"True, very true. Tell me, did they seem mopey, snowed in like that, my wife and daughter?"

Lenox's voice was light—but his brother caught its tone. "Oh! Yes, I think so. Sophia mostly sprinted across the ballroom for five or six hours at a stretch and then would take a very civil little nap of six minutes before resuming her exercises. Jane was a perfect guest, obviously. The housemaids will be sadly lost without her."

Lenox smiled, and asked, "Incidentally, do you know who I'm working for?"

"Who?"

"Gerald Leigh."

"Gerald Leigh! I haven't thought of his name in years. Is he in trouble?"

"Did you know that he has become one of England's most famous scientists?"

"Leigh, who got ripped over and over? I always reckoned him a dunce."

Lenox frowned. "Yes, I remember that you refused to take my word to the contrary."

"Old Tennant must be vexed. He's still up there, you know, though none of us are younger than we were then. Gerald Leigh, bless my heart. Tell me, why have you begun working for him?"

They had only another two or three minutes, but Lenox explained. Edmund promised to drop in at Hampden Lane later, and they said their good-byes with a mutual clasp of the shoulder, each, perhaps, more worried about the other than himself.

CHAPTER TWENTY

In the next three days there were fits and starts of progress. Frost reported that the constables keeping watch over Anderson had observed him meet with Singh and go to King's Cross Station at the hour the train from the Dover ferry was expected on two days consecutively.

"I find that deeply puzzling," said Lenox after a moment, when he heard this news.

"Why?" asked Frost. "It seems the most obvious thing in the world."

"Does it?"

"Plainly they are waiting for Mr. Leigh's arrival. I'm inclined to arrest them now."

Lenox nodded. "Yes, it might be for the best."

"But then why are you puzzled?"

"Because it isn't clear to me how they know that Leigh is returning."

Frost started to formulate an answer, then stopped short. He thought for a moment, and then nodded, grimly. "Yes, you're right, though I hadn't seen it. Somehow they're keeping a pair of eyes on him, and know he's set to return this weekend."

"Precisely."

Frost shook his head. "That's bad indeed. We'll need to watch them closely."

Meanwhile the young solicitor who had taken

over Middleton's business, an ambitious fellow named Greyscale, without chambers himself but with a father who had long known Beaumont, informed them that he could find no papers regarding a large recent will, nor anything connected to a person named Townsend.

"The missing valise," Frost said to Lenox as they exited this interview.

"The missing valise," Lenox agreed. That was quite obviously where their answers lay. "I am not optimistic that we shall recover it."

So the days passed. On the Friday evening before Leigh was due to return, Lenox dined alone at his club. His house was off-limits—Jane was having supper with a small circle of friends, including Toto, the Duchess of Marchmain, a fair, plain, and penniless young person named Matilda Ludlow, whom Lenox liked tremendously, and one or two others.

After he ate it was very dark out, black. He went into the streets, thinking to kill time and perhaps ponder his case over a cigar, with the vague intention of stopping in at a small performance of chamber music that his friend Baltimore was hosting.

The air felt mild; above freezing, certainly. But the streets were still quiet after the storm, the sallow light of the street lamps falling on huge empty banks of melting dirtied snow, this indomitable city for once disheveled.

It was the kind of walk to make you look into your own heart—and Lenox felt a strange inkling there, and knew that his wife was still unhappy.

At Baltimore's, Lenox sat and listened to a lovely rendition of Albinoni, then, at the intermission, met a few old acquaintances and exchanged news. There was a great deal of interest in Middleton's death. He ran into his creaky but upright friend Lord Cabot, who was a father of seven.

"Would you care to see something genuinely remarkable?" Lenox asked.

"Yes. But it has been seventy-four years and I find myself waiting still."

Lenox felt in his breast pocket for a small object that had remained secure upon his person continually for two weeks now. "Look, there you are."

Cabot peered close. "What is it?"

"Why, any thickhead dullard ignoramus could see that it is a penwiper. Sophia made it for my Christmas present. She made it! Look, there, at how she has scored the edge with little daisies."

Cabot inspected the little scrap of cloth closely. "I admit that it is fine. And how well does it perform its function of wiping pens?"

"As goes without saying, I have not degraded it with the ink of a pen. It's more in the line of a *decorative* object, you see."

Cabot's eyes twinkled. "In all sincerity I think it a handsome penwiper."

Lenox folded the little bit of cloth in half and put it in his pocket again. "Yes, thank you. I will pass on your approbation to Sophia."

"These great artists do not tend to work for praise, though. It's the act of creation itself."

Lenox smiled. "Very true."

Lenox left Baltimore's before the third act started, cheered by his little burst of sociability; he and Cabot had made plans to dine together at the Travellers' Club the next Wednesday.

He walked down Pall Mall, mulling over Middleton's death.

Suddenly a thought came to him. They ought to intercept Leigh at Dover the next morning, he realized. He hailed a cab and directed it to Chancery Lane, where he found a few remaining clerks. Hard at work on a Friday night! It was to Polly's credit—she being the person who managed their employees.

A young detective they had hired from the constabulary in Liverpool was there. He was a little undernourished sprightly person named Cohen, Jewish, which rather set him apart from the common run of fellow, only middlingly clever but very energetic.

Lenox asked if he would take the morning train to Dover with a note and meet a man at the train station named Gerald Leigh; gave Cohen a detailed description of his friend; and sat down and wrote a note for Cohen to deliver, signed with Lenox's schoolboy nickname.

"Bring him back by coach, if you would," said Lenox. "Here, I have the money for it in my office desk. Is that all clear enough?"

"Clear as a bell," said Cohen in his heavy scouse accent.

"Two men would probably try to kill him if he came into King's Cross with the Dover train."

"Blimey."

"So bring him straight here if you would. Or if he kicks up a fuss, take him to his hotel—but tell him I would like to see him when I can."

"Done," said Cohen.

Feeling better, Lenox returned home. The women were still up, noises of laughter emerging occasionally from the sitting room where they were lingering over their coffee, and Lenox slipped by the doorway without interrupting them. He tried to stay awake to see Jane when she came upstairs, but fell asleep in the attempt.

The next morning he was woken early by Kirk's gentle knock on the door. He went to see what it was, and the butler told him. "A visitor, sir."

"Who? What time is it?"

"Just past seven, sir. An Inspector Frost."

"Oh. Offer him tea, please. I'll be down directly."

Frost was pacing nervously in Lenox's study,

173

and accosted the detective when he entered, still cinching his tie. "There you are. I've just had a wire. The constable following Anderson had to let him go."

"What? Why?"

"He and Singh went to King's Cross Station this morning. After a brief conference at the ticket window, Singh boarded a train for Dover."

"Oh, no."

"Yes. Anderson stayed behind. My constable decided to follow Singh. He wired from the first station to explain and apologize—"

"No, I think he did well."

"The result is that Anderson is lost. Three men are crawling over King's Cross but he's not there."

"Hell."

"Yes. They'll have two shots at him."

Lenox thought for a moment. "Can you wire down the line to tell your man to arrest Singh?"

"I have," said Frost.

"Good. Because Leigh won't be arriving back in London by train."

"No?"

Lenox explained how he had sent Cohen down to Dover to catch Leigh. He was glad he had, now, obviously.

The question was what Anderson would do in London. "The time has come to arrest them, I think," Frost said.

They had waited because it would be difficult to send either Anderson or Singh to jail without a more direct attempt on Leigh's life.

But Lenox agreed—better to settle for a short sentence and save Leigh's life. "I doubt we'll be able to smoke Anderson out again, though."

"Why?"

"He knows from our last meeting that we haven't got him nailed down. What's the point of putting his head above the ground?"

"What to do, then?"

Lenox shook his head grimly. "We have to figure out who is willing to murder Leigh for the sake of twenty-five thousand pounds. I hope Pointilleux has discovered where Townsend's son is. I would like to speak with him. As for Anderson and Singh—I have an idea. Perhaps we can set them a trap they won't be able to squirm out of."

CHAPTER TWENTY-ONE

That evening at five minutes past six o'clock, Lenox and Leigh stepped out of a carriage in front of Burlington House, the home of the Royal Society.

It was one of the most beautiful and recognizable of the enormous houses built along the north side of Piccadilly Street, in the very innermost center of London, with a long, intricate, symmetrical façade, and a squat tower rising above the central doorway.

"How dreary," Leigh muttered.

Lenox laughed. "You haven't changed."

Five or six steps, past two heavy doormen, and they were inside.

For many years this building had been in private hands, but now it belonged to the government. The Royal Academy—the equivalent to the Royal Society for painting and drawing—was also housed inside, having, a decade before, signed a 999-year lease, at the princely cost of a pound a year. Probably not the canniest bit of business Parliament had ever conducted, but a boon to the city, for now there were wonderful exhibitions here.

Lenox and Leigh walked down a colonnade. At the end was a marble door with a Latin phrase inscribed above it, NULLIUS IN VERBA.

Lenox smiled and pointed at it. "Unlike you I paid attention in Latin." That was true—he would quite literally rather have died than failed to follow Edmund to Oxford, when he was seventeen and a more melodramatic soul. "And as a consequence I can translate that."

"Can you? How splendid that must feel."

In an intentionally ponderous voice, Lenox said, "Well, you should have worked harder in school. How truly it has been observed that the boy is the father of the man."

Leigh rolled his eyes and Lenox laughed. Both of them were perhaps feeling a little foolish—sixteen again for a brief while, whatever their aging bodies might have told to the contrary, and pleased to be in each other's company.

"I think I can manage the translation of something so simple, anyhow," said Leigh. *"Take nobody's word for it."*

"Sound advice for a detective too, if it comes to it," Lenox said. "Not just for a scientist."

Behind the door was a marble-floored entrance hall, with two staircases curving up to meet each other on a balcony. An attendant took their coats and indicated that they might take either staircase.

Upstairs was a smallish but grandly appointed room with about twenty people in it, gathered in small civil groups. Lenox and Leigh hesitated at the threshold. Portraits of Britain's great natural philosophers ran along each wall, between large windows overlooking the inner courtyards of Burlington House. There were graceful touches: a terrarium sitting upon a priceless French card table, a beautiful gold-and-diamond chronometer situated at the center of various other treasures on a long oak chest. Servants moved quietly across the thick crimson carpet, offering champagne.

One head turned toward the door—then another—then all of them, and though the men here were too well mannered to accost Leigh at once, Lenox felt the room's energy drawn toward him.

A young person came forward, wiry but handsome, with curling dark hair. "My dear Leigh," he said, "how glad I am to see you. We feared we might not."

Leigh smiled. "I gave my word."

"Yes—but I know it was given reluctantly." The man turned to Lenox and introduced himself. "Alexander Rowan," he said. "Your servant."

This was the wunderkind who had finally enticed Leigh to the Royal Society. "Charles Lenox."

"Lenox is a close friend of mine from our schooldays—a detective, now. Previously a Member of Parliament."

"My goodness, a detective," said Rowan. "What a fascinating field that must be."

Lenox inclined his head. "One that intersects with your own, increasingly."

A look of disdain arose in Rowan's eyes but was immediately suppressed, gone before it had dawned. Still, Lenox was not a person on whom much was lost, and he felt irritated, as the Society's president led them around the room, introducing them. For many years there had been people of his class who snubbed him for his profession, and, now, as he was in business, they had begun to return. That he was used to. But Rowan's condescension was rather bitter—particularly, perhaps, because of the reverence with which the many distinguished-looking men to whom they were introduced greeted Leigh.

At supper Lenox had the luck to be seated next to a lively and easily amused professor from St. John's College at Cambridge, who in his spare time acted as the historian of the Royal Society. He gave Lenox charming little flashpoints about this history, now and then—how the Society had published Ben Franklin's famous experiments with the kite and the key, for instance, or how they had appointed a foreign secretary some sixty years before Great Britain got around to it.

"Mind you," he added, over pudding, "we are not always so brave. In '64 we gave Charles Darwin the Copley Medal—our highest honor—but without any mention whatsoever of his theories of evolution. And as for Franklin, the less said about that the better."

"Why?" Lenox asked.

The professor sighed. "It has long been the practice of the government to refer questions of scientific substance to the Society. That was one of our failures. Franklin was an advocate of pointed lightning conductors, while one of our own, a fellow named Wilson, preferred blunted ones. Franklin was quite clearly correct, but the Society did not endorse his point of view."

Lenox laid down his spoon, pudding half eaten—the food had been abominable, the wine excellent—and asked, with genuine curiosity, "And why did they not?"

"Think of the time. Anyone taking Franklin's side was accused immediately of pro-Americanism. Their rebellion was ongoing. And so we fell on the wrong side of science, imagining ourselves to be on the right side of history."

"I see."

"Science knows no borders. That is why I find Leigh so admirable. He has never stuck very close to England. For my own part, coming in to London is an adventure. If only he hadn't declined to give us the Croonian Lecture this year—our most famous lecture, a true event."

"Has he declined, then?" said Lenox curiously.

"Yes, alas. His lecture tomorrow night is in the smaller theater. Still, we have had Sanderson and Page step in. I received their paper today: on the mechanical effects, and on the electrical disturbance consequent on excitation of the leaf of *Dionaea muscipula*."

"I cannot imagine a more consequential lecture."

"Yes, I know!" the professor said, apparently without irony. "And somehow I am nevertheless confident that Mr. Leigh would have delivered it, I positively am. Still, we may hope that his speech tomorrow is some consolation. For my part I would like to hear about the earlier parts of his career, when he explored South America. A second Banks."

After supper there was a round of toasts, apparently a tradition at small gatherings like this.

The first was to the Queen; the second to the fellows; the third to the "invisible college" of eminent natural philosophers who had begun the Society in 1660; the fourth to Charles the Second, the Merry Monarch, with his twelve bastards and endless intemperance, who had given them their royal seal; the fifth, made by Rowan, to their guest, Gerald Leigh, and with it a long enumeration of his accomplishments. Lenox liked Rowan slightly better after this speech.

From there they retired for port and cigars into a small smoking room. Here Leigh and Lenox had a few minutes together for the first time since they had arrived.

"I sincerely hope I am not shot as we leave," he said.

Lenox shook his head. "There are dozens of exits. Cohen will take you to safe lodgings. And Anderson and Singh are out of commission."

He had filled Leigh in on these two nemeses. And on the trap they had set: At Dover, just before the train bound for London was to depart, the conductor had called Leigh off the train, with the enigmatic message added that his "party was waiting for him at the Dover Arms Hotel, where several rooms are booked."

Singh, apparently, had fallen for the ruse completely, racing off the train. Meanwhile Leigh was on his way to London—a few precious hours bought, at least. Lenox's firm and the Yard were going to provide a full retinue for his remaining time in London. And there were several people now tracking Singh.

Lenox still worried, however. Even if Leigh relinquished his claim to the money that was the cause of all this—how were his pursuers to know? Greyscale hadn't found a will. There would be one registered in Cornwall, he said, but Lenox wanted to convey to the person who had hired the Farthings that their quarry was retiring from the game. Evidently his and Frost's threat of attention for the gang hadn't been enough.

Which meant that in the morning it would be time to speak to Townsend's son. It had been some thirty years; it was time the mystery of Leigh's anonymous benefactor be solved, once and for all.

CHAPTER TWENTY-TWO

An increasing intimacy had sprung up in the past few days between Lenox and Frost. Before the murder of Middleton they had certainly been friendly acquaintances, but now they trusted each other.

The next morning—Leigh having spent the night in an anonymous Clapham hotel, chosen by Cohen entirely at random after the supper, a stratagem designed to avoid pursuit by the Farthings—the inspector again appeared in Hampden Lane.

It was the warmest day since the snowfall, and the city was dripping, the sound of thousands of drops making a sunny melody, people's gazes gradually unfreezing too.

Frost accepted the offer of a cup of tea. "I've had a note," Lenox said, pouring for him. "My man has found Salt Townsend's address at last. I mean to go and see him this morning."

"Just in time for a second suspect."

Lenox looked up sharply. "How's that?"

Frost had arrived with Middleton's oversized appointment book under his arm, and he laid it down on Lenox's dark, highly polished hexagonal breakfast table. "This is yours now, for the moment at least—we've looked through it exhaustively."

"And found something?"

"In the days leading up to the murder, Ernest Middleton had several meetings with a person initialed *TF*. The first reference is about three months old, and it has a full name, which is repeated once or twice: Terence Fells. You'll find it on the flagged pages."

"Does the name mean anything to you?"

"No. There is an Anthony Terence Fells living near Mornington Crescent, however, according to our records at the Yard. Three years ago he was arrested for public drunkenness, which is how we came to have his address."

"I see."

"And how's this—in the last reference to him,

there is an arrow drawn directly from his name to Gerald Leigh's."

Lenox frowned and took a sip of his own tea. "Hm."

This was new information to absorb. Worse luck. The narrative in his mind had been fairly straightforward: Salt Townsend had hired Anderson and Singh to intimidate Leigh—possibly, or even probably, worse—and Middleton. The solicitor had refused to give them the relevant papers from his valise. Perhaps he had pulled out the pistol he was carrying to protect himself. The fatal shot had been delivered. Anderson and Singh had vanished with the valise.

Anthony Terence Fells didn't fit into this tale.

"Who shall it be first, then?" he said. "Your suspect or mine?"

"Yours, I think," said Frost. "We can see if he gives himself up."

Fells. The name rang a soft and distant bell. It niggled at Lenox, though his memory wouldn't quite resolve into legibility. "Very well. Give me a moment to bolt an egg and a rasher and I'm your man."

Soon they left, with Pointilleux's note in hand. This offered little more than an address, though the young Frenchman added that he had not yet personally confirmed that Townsend lived there.

It was in the East End. "It's in Abbot Street," Lenox told Frost as they went outside to his waiting carriage, reading from the paper. "Number 34, third story."

Frost looked surprised. "Abbot Street. Interesting."

"Why?"

"That's in Whitechapel. Not far from the Blue Peter."

Lenox hadn't thought of that connection. "Curious," he said.

"Yes. And therefore also not far from Anderson and Singh."

When they arrived, Lenox saw that Abbot Street was a part of what constituted the more respectable part of the East End. The traffic was hectic, but temperate. Many of the men wore silk hats, none of the women walked alone, the truants were few enough. It was a spirited little avenue, too. A busy trade of newspapers and food was taking place up and down the pavement.

Still, Abbot Street was also visibly rakish in its edges—tiny alleyways with lanterns over doorways, men lounging on the corners and occasionally offering a subtle word to passersby—"ponces," the word for them was, men who lived on the earnings of their women. It was easy to imagine the avenue becoming more debauched without the sanitizing influence of the mild sun that passed above them in the sky.

They found number 34. In their company was the street's constable, whom Frost had spotted and enlisted in case Salt Townsend proved violent. His name was Esau Wakeman.

"Any notion that this chappie might hoof it?" Wakeman asked.

"I suppose it's possible," Lenox said.

"More'n possible. It happens about three of four times a day in these parts."

"Tell me," Lenox said, as they went into the building, "who lives in them, these parts?"

Wakeman thought for a moment. "I grew up two streets north, so I should have a readier answer. I suppose it's your honest poor; and then your less honest less poor."

Lenox smiled. "And what do you make of this building? More in the line of the former or the latter?"

Wakeman merely glanced at him with raised eyebrows. They had all taken in the glossy new paint on the building's rails, its well-kept shrubbery out front.

They climbed the stairs in single file. On the third story, with Frost leading the way, they met a man of roughly the age Lenox knew Townsend to be. He was a tubby person with a piggish, hard-set, suspicious face. "Mr. Townsend?" Lenox said, just in case.

"Yes," the fellow replied warily. "Why?"

As the timing would have it, Wakeman came around the switchback of the stairwell just at that moment, and of course he was unmistakably a bobby, in his high hat and blue uniform, whistle, torch, and blackjack hanging from his belt.

Townsend blanched. After an exceptionally lengthy second, he pushed past them and ran.

"Oh, hell," said Frost.

The two policemen darted ahead of Lenox— damnably slow reflexes, he thought even as his feet began to move, too much time behind a desk—and ran out behind Townsend in chase.

Their quarry turned right up the street, moving with surprising velocity for someone who didn't look as if he had ever declined a second helping at supper.

"Townsend!" Frost called. "Stop!"

That didn't work.

"Stop!" cried Wakeman, also to no avail.

People all around stared on, though without making any move to intervene. Then Lenox tried. "It's about the murder of Ernest Middleton!" he called.

All at once Townsend drew up to a juddering halt, and turned. He stood there, panting, hands on his hips. When they reached him, he shook his head and said, "The what?"

"The murder of Ernest Middleton," Lenox said—panting himself, to be fair.

"You're under arrest, you wretch," Frost said in a choked voice.

"I haven't murdered anyone. Much less anyone named Ernest Middleton."

"Then why on earth did you run?" Frost asked.

Townsend's eyes shifted right. "I had an appointment I forgot."

"Yes, that seems likely," Frost said, half bent over.

"An appointment with whom?" asked Lenox.

"That's for me to know."

"Will you come to the Yard and speak to us?" asked Frost.

"No. I want to see my attorney."

"We only have a few questions."

Townsend shook his head. "I know my rights."

Wakeman, who hadn't heard of Salt Townsend fifteen minutes before, took this as a deep personal affront. "And I've the right to stove your face in," he said.

But Townsend, with the air of a man who had been threatened by larger and more frightening men than Esau Wakeman, shook his head. "Take me in if you will, but I'll be seeing my attorney or I'll be clabbered."

Frost sighed, and he and Lenox exchanged looks. "Very well," said Frost. "You can while away your time in the station the whole week for all that I care. Wakeman, secure him in your handcuffs, if you please, while I whistle for a cab."

Wakeman clamped his man in handcuffs, and began the slow procedure of shifting him back to the Yard and fetching him his solicitor; Lenox and

Frost agreed that they would use the time to move on to their second suspect.

Thus, a little more than an hour later, they were standing in front of Terence Fells's small, handsome house in Mornington Crescent.

He was absent—but worked in the City, according to his next-door neighbor, who said that he generally returned home between five and six o'clock. There was one fleeting point that stuck with Lenox: To the side of the house, a workman was installing new copper piping. Expensive and handsome, and perhaps not entirely within the range of affordability one might generally expect to find in this middle-class quarter.

"I wish I could remember how I knew the name Fells," he said to Frost as they left.

They had agreed to return at six, warning the neighbor and the workman both to say nothing of their visit. "As do I."

The answer would have to wait; an hour having passed, Frost was going to see how Townsend had gotten along in his quest to meet with his attorney, and whether he would now deign to speak to them.

Lenox, for his part, returned home for lunch. He opened the door and halloed loudly, hoping Sophia would be there. She wasn't, but in the dining room he did find Lady Jane, Toto, and McConnell.

The doctor was beaming. "What is it?" Lenox asked immediately.

He glanced at Toto, and then said, overflowing with the happy tidings, "We're going to have a second child, it would seem, God willing. In May, they believe."

"My dear McConnell, how wonderful," said Lenox, "shake my hand."

As he strode forward, he caught from the corner of his eye a glimpse of Jane's face. In that flash, he saw that the news had already been known to her, and for the first time understood why he had found her crying the week before, at Edmund's.

CHAPTER TWENTY-THREE

Kirk brought a bottle of champagne up from the cellar, and Lenox raised a toast to their friends, who were quite obviously dumbstruck with happiness. Toto had been to her physician that morning for confirmation.

"Part of me does hope it's a boy," Toto said, her hand falling unconsciously to her stomach. "We've got George after all and we're not the Elizabeth Bennets."

"You're very far from the Elizabeth Bennets," Lady Jane said.

"My enemy Duckworth is on her seventh child already, and won't ever stop talking about it."

"To be fair I'm not sure I would either, if I had seven children," said Lenox.

"Two should at least quiet her down to a murmur, I hope."

Lenox glanced at Jane.

There were facts in life; there were things you couldn't help; it had mathematics in it. Jane was forty-three. Not quite too old to have another child, but not either young enough to have faith that she could do so without difficulty—and their particular era, Lenox had thought once or twice, was such a cruelly fertile one, families of ten and twelve and twenty, pouring into all the crevices of enormous houses. Never had a capital city been richer or more rudely healthy. To have one child could seem faintly feeble.

And how lovely it would have been to watch Sophia meet a baby brother, a baby sister.

He was suddenly struck by a long-forgotten memory of Lady Jane, perhaps because it dated to the same period of time that Leigh's sudden reappearance in his life had dredged up in his mind.

Even as a child, Lady Jane Houghton, she had been self-possessed, with an affect of slight irony. Most children would laugh at anything whatsoever—but not she, five years younger than him then as now, even when such a gap had seemed perfectly enormous.

Home from Harrow once, he had seen her at a

country ball. Perhaps it had even been her first—too young by a few years for London society, but allowed to dance in Sussex, as long as it was with a cousin or close friend.

She had come up behind him in the hall as he was leaving, just before supper, and at her call he had stopped, bowing slightly and greeting her. She was slender, with brown hair that fell in long pretty curls. "We didn't have a chance to speak," she said.

"Yes! I'm sorry for that. How are you?"

She had smiled and said not very badly. "And they say you will go to Oxford, as your brother has done?"

"I hope so," Lenox replied.

"Will you give me tea if I come there?"

"Any time."

"I'll hold you to that, Master Charles," she had said. "I know my father wouldn't mind, as it's you—and I'll die if I have to spend another winter here in the country. He'll let me go when I turn fifteen, I think, with Mother."

"Are you so bored?"

"Yes. How I wish they would let us go off to school, as you do! Or failing that, I don't see why we can't go to London and live there."

"Your father is important in the county," Lenox pointed out.

"I suppose." A maid had come in then, looking for Jane. "I think I ought to go. Good luck at Oxford!"

"And good luck leaving Houghton. You look very lovely this evening."

She had blushed and thanked him, and Lenox had realized, with true amazement, that she had perhaps some romantic admiration for him—that perhaps, as in a novel, he was her faraway ideal, a slightly older chap, away at Harrow.

He had forgotten that for all these years. He would have to ask her if she remembered.

They gave McConnell and Toto lunch. Just as they were drinking their small glasses of sweet wine afterward, Sophia emerged from the nursery, bleary-eyed and tender following her nap, to say hello. When Lenox went off into the afternoon again it was with a feeling of warmth for all that he did have.

Leigh had spent the morning at the Royal College of Surgeons, delivering an informal lecture on his experiments on certain victims of alkali poisoning a decade before, near the Strait of Magellan; with him for protection were Cohen and a constable of Frost's. Lenox met them at around two o'clock. There had been nothing peculiar about their day, fortunately.

"Have you seen Anderson?" Lenox asked Cohen when they had a private moment.

"No. No large red-haired fellows at all, sir."

"Singh?"

"One Indian gentleman—a valet here, it would seem, brought back from the East by a scientist who trained him as an assistant. He's widely known, however. Not Singh."

"Good. Keep your eyes open. And after the talk tonight—"

"A hotel I've never heard of, neighborhood randomly chosen. Yes, sir."

Lenox nodded. "Good."

Having checked in on his friend, Lenox hailed a cab and directed it to Scotland Yard, where he met Frost.

They walked together along an inner corridor, returning from the front courtyard to Frost's office. "Has Townsend consented to speak to us?"

"Yes—with his attorney present."

"I suppose we could do worse. Are we going there now?"

"I thought we might."

Townsend was waiting for them in a holding cell, the remains of a desultory lunch on a tray nearby—half a bottle of wine the only thing that looked to have been consumed entirely. With him was a small, ferret-faced sharp in a cheap suit, one of the jobbing attorneys who lurked around the courts, none of them stupid. He introduced himself as Chisholm.

"You understand that your presence here is a courtesy?" Frost asked him.

"I suppose so, sir," said Chisholm. "Then again I could tell my client to hold his tongue and we could wait you out."

Frost gave him a hard look. "And we could come and have a look at your other clients, and instruct the bailiff not to let Mr. Townsend order such luxurious foodstuffs—if you want to play that game."

Chisholm shrugged, as if it was a matter of very little consequence to him, and then with a calculated degree of insolence began to pick at his teeth. Frost looked black with anger, but Lenox, sensing the futility of playing an attorney's game with an attorney, said, "We are concerned solely with the death of Mr. Ernest Middleton of the Temple Bar. It occurred on the fourth of January. Does your client have any knowledge of it?"

"None," said Chisholm.

"You may answer yourself, Mr. Townsend, if you have nothing to hide," said Lenox.

Townsend glanced at his attorney and then said, echoing him, "None."

"The name is unfamiliar to you?"

"Yes."

"You were never in the offices of Beaumont and Middleton in Maltravers Street?"

"Never."

"Mr. Middleton was not your father's solicitor?"

For the first time Townsend looked thrown. "My father?"

"Did he not execute your father's estate?"

"My father's estate! What in heaven are you on about?"

Lenox looked at him narrowly. "Let us retreat farther back. Did your father die in 1876, sir?"

"He did, but I cannot see what that has to do with the price of tea in China."

"You were not a beneficiary of his will?"

Chisholm held up a hand. "Salt, don't answer that. What is this line of inquiry about, gentlemen? We have told you that Mr. Townsend had nothing to do with the death of Mr. Middleton. They were not acquainted."

"And we are suggesting that they were," said Frost.

"I can help you there, then. I wasn't. He was not my father's attorney," said Townsend.

"Who was?" Lenox asked.

"He had three. Two in Cornwall and one in London, Mr. Josiah Dekker. He's a fool, but he's not dead. At least as far as I know."

Lenox felt a creeping uneasiness. He thought back to the stairwell at 34 Abbot Street, when Townsend had run from them. No doubt he had run at the sight of a police constable for dishonest reasons. But he had also stopped at Middleton's name, genuinely surprised at the cause of their chase.

Fells, he thought grimly.

"What were the terms of your father's will?" Lenox asked.

"Not your concern," said Chisholm, slicking his very thoroughly greased hair, which Lenox hoped never to see again, down his temples.

"Mr. Townsend, you may exonerate yourself if you tell us the answer honestly."

Townsend paused, then, with a gambler's air of feeling content to throw his freedom on a toss of the dice, said, "Well, why not. There were a few small bequests, and the balance came to me—in trust, worse luck, since it means that I can only spend the interest. Fortunately I've dissolved the businesses, so the interest is still a tidy income."

"Our investigation indicated that you and your father were not speaking."

"It's true that we weren't on close terms, but I never doubted for a second that he would leave it all to me. He was proud of the Townsend name."

A misplaced pride, on the evidence of father and son, Lenox thought. Leigh had grown up without his own father because of this man's—and now the son was engaged in some malevolent practice or other, whether he was involved in this business or not. "Are you certain that he might not have left a separate amount, through Middleton, unknown to you?"

Townsend shook his head. "No. Impossible."

"How can you be sure?"

"Because all of it was in the businesses, bar a few hundred pounds of ready money. Dekker's book-keepers went into very great detail determining just how much they were worth, and every penny was accounted for by the end. And except for a few thousand pounds it's mine, thanks be to God."

CHAPTER TWENTY-FOUR

The English custom of driving on the left side of the road had practical origins.

It had started in medieval days, when genuine knights had traveled the high way between villages. A knight kept his sword to his right as he rode, in order to have his strong hand toward the middle of the road in the event that he should cross paths with thieves or other highwaymen. To ride down the right side of the road would have meant fighting with a weaker left hand closer to the middle of the road; a possibly fatal disadvantage.

In America, that newer country, they drove on the right—and this decision, too, had a logic, for there, with the huge teams of horses required to move across the vast land, it was necessary to drive with a very long whip. By riding on the right, the drovers could keep it to the outside of the road, so that if they passed another team they would never cross whips or inadvertently strike a fellow driver.

At the Royal Society that evening, Leigh stood in front of an overflowing and rapt audience and began his lecture with this cryptic little piece of trivia.

Soon he had opened out into a larger discussion

that explained it, however. First he gave them a subtle and humorous delineation of all the manifold ways in which scientific process was necessarily different from country to country—just like driving!—and then he delved into how it was different specifically, in all the innumerable places he had been during his travels. Finally, losing Lenox but evidently winning over the rest of the room, he had gone deep indeed into his own investigations into the microbe.

At the very end of the speech, he returned to America and England. "As a going concern they will surpass us in the next century, I have no doubt, the Americans," he concluded, "but in science our tradition cannot be bettered. I am proud to join its history this evening, even if I am only a far-flung particle in the greater body."

In the period of questions that followed there were a great many detailed interrogations into the nature of the microbe and the research of Pasteur. One questioner did return to Leigh's final line: impossible to imagine a capital more powerful than London, he said angrily, a nation whose interests were so intricately tied to those of a hundred million souls across the globe—why, in shipping alone—

Leigh listened patiently, and then replied. "Yes, I have heard about whether or not the sun sets on our empire—that it doesn't—but I do think it will be the States that matters more in 1976 than Britain."

"But, sir—"

Leigh plowed ahead. "That is for two reasons. The first is that they have the common schools, which we have been foolish in the extreme not to build. I myself see four or five of my old schoolmates here this evening"—there was a brief smile at Lenox as he said this—"and understand that nobody could be better educated than our landholding class. But as long as we do not educate our lower orders, the Darwin of 1976 is bound to be from a farming family in, say, Missouri.

"And then, the second reason. They have land. Which is a thing that every time I return home here to England I observe that they have laid down no more of—and which is more or less infinite there. I have seen the birds across the plain, and as they thundered past you would have thought it was nighttime, though it was noon, so many I thought they would never end, so wide that I couldn't see the edge of the flock. It is a large, large place, gentlemen."

There were a few more questions, but Lenox's thoughts stayed on this striking image, and when Leigh had finished, though there was applause, the mood in the room seemed to have stayed there too, something slightly melancholy and queer in it, as claret was passed out on trays in this room at what they had all believed twenty minutes before was the center of the universe.

At the supper afterward, Leigh sat, by his own

request, with Lenox and Lady Jane—women were welcome at the Society, an enlightenment most such establishments had not yet achieved—at one of eight small tables under a beautiful ceiling tiled with a black-and-gold map of the heavens. Rowan, the wiry president of the Society who had been so desperately eager to bring about this evening, was also with them, beaming and accepting congratulations.

At regular intervals gentlemen would stop by to meet Leigh and leave a card with him. The first was a bald-headed gentleman named Parkes, a metallurgist who had discovered, Leigh said, a very promising and pliable new industrial material. ("He's had the abominable taste to name it Parkesine," Leigh added, after Parkes had gone, "though I am pleased to say that people are not using the name. Rowan tells me they generally call it 'plastic' instead.") Close on his heels was Prince Alfred, one of the Society's three Royal Fellows, a dashing thin fellow in a blue coat with dark moustaches and a twinkling smile—the Queen's son.

They all rose as he approached the table. "America, then!" he said, but laughed. "I shall have to tell Mother."

"No country could exceed hers during her lifetime or yours, Your Highness," said Rowan, bowing.

"Indeed not. And I must take issue—for we are

acquiring new land almost continually. It simply happens to be in other countries."

Leigh smiled and nodded. "Very true, Your Highness."

"As for the microbes—damned interesting." The prince looked around at the seven other people at the table (he was seated, by his request according to Rowan, with a certain group he favored from the Jockey Club) and his eyes alighted on Lady Jane, to whom he inclined his head. They had met several times, though it was clear he could place only her face. "How is our Miss Phillips?" he asked.

Apparently he did remember that Jane was somehow associated with Toto, who in distant days had been a part of his set. "Exceedingly happy, Your Highness," said Jane. "A very proud mother."

"Please give her my best, would you? Is it a girl or a boy?"

"A girl, Your Highness."

Nearly six, too. "I shall send round a rattle. That's what's done, isn't it, Rowan?"

"Or a cup, as the case may be, Your Majesty."

"Nonsense. It must be a rattle." Prince Alfred, standing there with his gloves in his hands, beamed at them, a creature without anxieties. "Congratulations, Mr. Leigh! I thought your speech very interesting—for all that you have rejected our generosities."

After the prince had gone, the little table buzzed with happiness, even the least impressionable among them there rather excited at this visitation from the vaults of heaven. Lenox turned to Leigh. "Their generosities?" he murmured.

"Oh, they tried to knight me."

"And you declined? Shouldn't you like to be a knight?"

"No."

Lenox smiled.

It was truly rare for a married couple to be seated to supper together, and Lenox and Lady Jane took the chance to have a long conversation with Leigh. It was hard not to feel a little proud, watching him so guarded with every other member of the party, and so open and happy with them—so immediately prepared to make a friend of Lenox's wife, finding delight in her company without any hesitation or prompting, though even his great ally Rowan could not elicit any very strong reaction from him in other moments of conversation, and the palace itself should be denied.

Baked mullets came out to the tables; rissoles, and roast fowl, and macaroni with parmesan cheese, and sea-kale; for dessert there was a laudably enormous charlotte russe placed at the center of each table, with vanilla hard sauce trickling down its sides. Every table made its way through wine and wine and more wine. It was a merry evening, and that before the toasting had even begun.

"What was Charles like in school?" Jane asked Leigh as they ate dessert. "I know my own memories of him, but I am curious to hear yours."

"I have never met anyone who grew up in the country and knew less about plants."

"That's not fair," Lenox said. "If you'll recall I taught you how to whistle with a blade of grass during field day."

Leigh flashed a smile. "I had forgotten that. Yes, it's true."

"He was a scoundrel, then," said Lady Jane.

"Oh, no. On the contrary, even then he was a personage of the utmost respectability. I seem to recall him reading adventure stories at an impossible pace—and doing very well at Greek, less well at Latin. Better than I did in either. Refused to sport with the beaks. I disliked his older brother."

Lady Jane looked amazed. "Edmund!"

"Yes—but I was a truculent specimen in those days."

"And Edmund was rather high-handed," Lenox said. "He was chased and dunked in the fountain at Christ Church during his first week at Oxford. It taught him a world of humility."

"By whom?" asked Leigh.

"A gang from Winchester."

"Miserable sods."

Lady Jane laughed. "Were you dunked, Charles?"

Lenox laughed. "I wasn't hobnob enough to be considered. We had a lovely time as undergraduates, though. And meanwhile Leigh was sailing across the world."

"And that, was that a lovely time itself?" asked Lady Jane of Leigh.

"I cannot imagine a better one, my lady," he said, sitting back with his thumb in the watch pocket of his jacket, and smiling as he reflected upon it. "The splendid open water, birds and fish to study, good fellows everywhere around you, just enough in the way of excitement from a storm and a cannonball. I only rue that I am too old now to be a surgeon's assistant. Sometimes I am tempted to go out under a false name and sail without any responsibilities at all, preparing tinctures for some drunken old sawbones on a ship bound for the Horn."

"You would grow restless."

"Never. If anything I have grown restless in Paris. With that money, you know, I had it in mind to hire a ship and go to India, to stop wherever I wished, to hug the coasts. I am almost done with the microbe."

"Just as you are uncovering its secrets!" interjected Rowan, who had been eavesdropping.

"Others will do the rest."

There was a footstep behind Leigh's chair. He

turned, expecting, Lenox could see from the polite set of his face, another set of congratulations. But it was Cohen.

"A letter, Mr. Leigh," he said, "left with the porter."

Leigh opened the letter, frowned, and passed it to Lenox. "What do you make of that?"

Mr. Leigh, I hope you will meet me in the upper courtyard at a moment of convenience. What you hear there will be to your benefit. Please come alone.

CHAPTER TWENTY-FIVE

A trap," Lenox murmured. He turned to Cohen. "Do you have your revolver?"

Cohen patted his jacket pocket, where evidently he kept his weapon, the snub-nosed Webley that Dallington, a good shot, had selected for all of their investigators. "I do."

"The constable and I shall go then, if you lend it to me. You must wait here with Mr. Leigh and Lady Jane, please."

Jane put a hand on his arm. "Will it be safe?"

"Oh, quite safe," said Lenox. He leaned across her toward the Society's president, who was engaged with the fellow on his right. "Mr. Rowan, I wonder if you could tell me whether there is a less-traveled corridor with access to the upper courtyard."

Rowan frowned. "The main staircase will not do? The porter may be able to guide you there by some other route. I'm afraid I do not know one. And I should warn you too that the toasts are about to begin."

"I hope we shan't miss them."

A servant in a swallowtail coat met them at the door as they left. Lenox turned back, hesitating. Was it a ploy to leave Leigh alone—a double trap? But no: an attack inside of this room would be both treacherous and certain to fail.

The servant did know an alternative route to the upper courtyard. Leading them through the kitchens quite tranquilly and without any questions—perhaps these scientists were eccentric masters as a general rule—he brought them to a small half door.

"Through here, sir," he said.

Lenox's nerves were on edge. "Blackjack out, I think," he said to the beefy constable behind him.

"Yes, sir."

He pushed through the door silently. It was a small terrace that he came out upon, gleaming in the snowy moonlight, and in its center stood a tiny, very upright figure, hands behind his back, gazing up at the sky.

"Don't look much," murmured the constable.

Indeed, the man, as he rocked on his feet, came

into clearer view, and it was obvious that he was well beyond seventy, perhaps even touching eighty. White hair curled around his temples, and he had little half-moon spectacles that sat delicately upon the tip of his nose. He wore a heavy coat and a thick wool scarf.

Lenox scanned the terrace. It was empty, and offered nowhere to hide except perhaps the small row of columns from which they themselves were emerging.

"How do you do, sir," Lenox said in a sharp voice, stowing the pistol behind him.

The man turned without any appearance of undue concern and peered at Lenox and the constable. "Who are you, sir?"

"Who are you, sir?"

"I am a person desirous of speech with Mr. Gerald Leigh."

"And I am a person desirous of knowing why you are desirous of such speech," said Lenox, though he did just smile, to soften the edge of his words.

"Because I have his best interests at heart—and I cannot presume that everyone does."

Lenox frowned. Was this man someone who knew about Anderson and Singh, or about Terence Fells? "You had better tell us what you mean," he said. "I am accompanied by Constable Watkins, as you can see, and Inspector Frost may be fetched here very quickly. There have been attempts at violence upon Mr. Leigh, and if we find you have been involved in them it shall—"

"Violence!" The old man looked alarmed. "Only an intellectual violence, sir. Violence!"

Lenox was nonplussed too, in his turn. "Intellectual violence?" he said.

The old gentleman glanced from Lenox to the constable. "I heard Mr. Leigh's speech this evening. I am a fellow of the Society, sirs. One of the few amateurs remaining in that company. I wanted to tell Mr. Leigh that I believe there to be unscrupulous parties who may be willing to take advantage of his work on the microbe, without the due correspondence learned men owe each other."

Lenox, confused, said, "I'm sorry—can you be clearer?"

"Theft, sir. Mr. Leigh indicated several promising courses of inquiry this evening that may be taken advantage of by our very own British scientists, like it or not, should he fail to take steps to protect his intellectual property. I am also a solicitor, you see, sir—though a botanist in my free time, which has increased since my semiretirement."

Suddenly it all became clear. Lenox breathed a sigh of relief. A solicitor. "I see," he said, "and may I ask your name?"

"Joseph Bartram, sir. What is yours?"

"Charles Lenox." The detective passed the old man a card. "I'm sorry to say that Leigh is extremely busy at the moment. If you call upon me this week, or write me, I give you my word I will convey your concerns to him."

The old man looked at the card. "The utmost secrecy is required in matters of scientific endeavor, when the—"

"I understand. Believe me."

Bartram looked him in the eye and then nodded. "Very well. Thank you."

The amateur took his leave through the main stairwell, Lenox watching him go with a powerful sense of reprieve. A false alarm. He would be happy when Leigh had returned to Paris the next evening; the Farthings frightened him.

Lenox was as good as his word to Rowan, returning in time to catch the toasts to Leigh. At the end of them, the honoree rose and gave the audience a well-placed joke, and thanked them. Thus the evening was concluded.

Rowan urged them to come to his club for a whisky. "It's only two streets away," he said, a last effort after his offer had already been declined several times.

Leigh smiled ruefully. "I still have that faint buzzing in the base of my skull that I get after speaking to a large group of people. Anyhow it is late, and I am pleased with the evening's work."

"Oh—so am I," said Rowan gamely, though he looked disappointed.

"And there is always lunch tomorrow," Leigh added.

"Yes, true," said Rowan, acquiescing. "Still—it did go well, I think."

Lenox walked downstairs with Leigh and Lady Jane, their coats waiting for them in the arms of a porter. He saw Leigh and Cohen into a cab—the fourth or fifth at the cabstand, chosen at random, a usual precaution—and then, with an unburdened feeling, found his own carriage, ready to return home with Lady Jane.

It was late, and she laid her head against his arm as they rode through London, shutting her eyes. For most of the journey he let her rest, but then, when they were close to Hampden Lane, he said, "Tell me, did you know Toto was going to have another child when we were in Sussex?"

"Yes," she said.

"And is that—"

"Yes," she said, and after a beat squeezed his arm, as if hoping that he wouldn't pull away.

He put his hand over hers. Trying to think what he could say, at last he came up with a commonplace. "Sophia will be five this year!"

"Astonishing, isn't it?"

"I wonder what she shall be like when she's our age."

"Better at spreading jam on toast than she is now, I expect."

He thought for a moment. "It will be 1917."

She smiled, eyes still closed. "Imagine that."

"And we shall be very old."

"Or gone."

"No, not gone," he said decisively. "But very old. And she will have her own family. Probably with uncountable numbers of grandsons and granddaughters."

"That's true," said Lady Jane, struck by the thought. "I wonder where they'll live. Heaven preserve us from a military husband. I cannot imagine having to wait for them to post home on holiday from Calcutta."

"No, she'll marry someone a street or two away."

Lady Jane laughed. "Now you are daydreaming."

"And you and I will still live in Hampden Lane."

"Will we?"

"Oh, yes. We shall be there in 1917. And I will love you and Sophia just as much on that day as I do on this one."

"Will you?"

He nodded. "Yes. Possibly more."

They were turning onto the very lane under discussion. She opened her eyes, and kissed him on the cheek. "That's a nice thing to know."

"I think so."

"And if we aren't here?" she asked, looking into his eyes.

He smiled. "Then I shall love you wherever we happen to be."

"All right," she said. "Good."

CHAPTER TWENTY-SIX

At just before eight the next morning, Frost and Lenox stood in Scotland Yard's long tearoom, the former moodily stirring a cup of charred-black tea that he had just poured himself from a tall polished urn. Lenox followed his lead—there were stacks of chipped cups and chipped saucers next to it, as well as a colossal tray of biscuits, underneath a sign that said, with the compliments of the women's relief society.

Lenox took a custard cream, silently blessing the Women's Relief Society. "The hellish thing about it is I was so sure Townsend was our man," said Frost.

"He's still in custody?"

"No. We had to let him go. Chisholm was threatening all manner of suits against us. Noisy enough in the end to have Townsend sent home. With a strict warning not to leave London, but— you know."

Lenox did, and for a moment he wondered whether they had merely been fooled by two accomplished actors the day before. "And Anderson and Singh?"

"Choirboys. The jig is up after Dover. Neither has moved from the Blue Peter. All we've done is give them a vacation."

"And kept them from murdering Leigh, in fairness." Lenox thought for a moment. "We had better think of who their next team is, the Farthings."

Frost brightened. "That's a stroke. You're quite right. It would probably be the Pole, Wasilewski. An ugly character. English mother."

"What does he look like? I'll warn Cohen and Leigh."

"Very pale, watery pink eyes, rather like a rabbit, fair hair. Dresses inconspicuously."

"And after him?"

They went through a roster of possibilities, Lenox taking notes. At last, sighing, he said, "And then, Fells."

Frost sighed, too. "Yes. Fells."

The inspector had arrived at the house of Terence Fells at six o'clock sharp the night before, while Lenox was at the Royal Society. Fells had been home, according to Frost's description a tall, curly-haired fellow whom one could spot from a mile as doing what Londoners called "black-coated work," something in the clerking or bookkeeping or accounting or banking lines, respectable, not manual.

Frost had mentioned Middleton, and Fells had denied any knowledge of the name.

Even from the last week's papers? Frost had asked.

Fells replied that he didn't read the papers.

He had never brought Middleton business?
Never.

But Frost had seen something in the young man's face, and had begun to hammer away at him, asking over and over in every way he could think to ask whether he might have run across Middleton and not remembered it. He offered Fells all the dates from Middleton's ledger that were marked with his name—though without mentioning this fact—and waited patiently as Fells got his own datebook and answered for his whereabouts on those days.

Then Frost had begun expanding the reach of his questions, asking about Leigh, about Anderson and Singh, about the East London gangs. Here Fells had seemed genuinely perplexed.

"Though it is possible," said Frost, stirring his tea morosely, "that by this stage he had merely braced himself for all my lines of questioning."

"Just so," said Lenox, who could sympathize.

At that moment someone behind them called out Lenox's name from a distance of fifteen or twenty feet, and both he and Frost turned to look who it was.

"Oh, hell," Frost muttered.

Lenox turned fully and smiled at the young gentleman who approached them, a chipper fellow named Huntington. "Hello, Huntington," he said.

Huntington looked delighted. "Lenox, my dear

chap, what brings you into these quarters—this prosaic old place!"

"Oh, a case, as usual."

Huntington shook his head with good-natured consternation. "It really is beastly, isn't it? And the swill they serve as tea. Hullo, Frost."

Lenox, in his Harrow days, had been unique among his acquaintances in his obsession with the police and with crime. Now he had been joined by a more generously peopled younger generation of enthusiasts—Dallington was not the only junior aristocrat in England who wished to be a detective, a change that Lenox attributed to the enormous spike in popularity of detective fiction, following Mr. Poe's innovations. In particular the novels of Wilkie Collins, *The Woman in White* and *The Moonstone*, had made every impressionable young adolescent of the 1860s a connoisseur of the detective novel.

Now they were beginning to pop up around the metropolis. Huntington was one example. The son of an unimpeachably lineaged Hertfordshire nobleman, he had been to Eton and Cambridge and then at the age of twenty had arranged, through high-powered friends, to be placed in a favorable position at the Yard, and more egregiously still on what was called, within these walls, the murder squad, which was generally home only to the most accomplished inspectors.

On the one hand this was an admirable choice—

Huntington hadn't any need to work at all, and had very probably wagered his annual salary from Scotland Yard on a single hand of whist at the Beargarden only the night before. On the other hand he was incompetent, lazy, and grandstanding, and worse yet never let go of the fact of his astonishing choice to become a detective, moving about in perpetual awe at his daring, reminding everyone he met of it, most particularly the new colleagues to whom he condescended so impossibly.

Lenox had hopes that he might grow—he was young—but at the moment this particular young aristocrat was not a credit to his class's involvement in police work, alas.

"Tell me," Huntington asked confidentially, "is it about Middleton?"

"Can't say," Frost replied quickly. "Forrester's orders."

That was their chief. "Ah, too bad. Tell me, Lenox, has Johnny Dallington left Parliament yet? I heard he had pitched up there with your—other partner."

Lenox felt a flash of irritation at the intonation of those last two words, which Huntington delivered as if Polly was somehow disreputable. "I'm not sure. I've been occupied with other matters."

"Mm, yes, Middleton." Huntington sighed. "A nuisance, no doubt, in and out of the courts where he worked, all of that. Say, Frost, are you close?"

This was the single worst question you could credibly ask a fellow detective, of course, and Lenox saw, with a mixture of mirth and pity, that Frost was hard-pressed not to give Huntington an earful. "Very close," Frost said with bitter irony. "A matter of hours. Possibly minutes."

"That's excellent!" Huntington was generous, at least—he wanted to like and be liked, he enjoyed good news, he wished nobody failure. "Let me know if I can help. I'm on rather a run of form, I fancy."

"I'll be sure to knock on your door."

"Good, good." Huntington had poured himself some tea, and sighed again. "Well, no rest for the weary, gentlemen. A milliner in Hampstead has been stabbed. Off I go, if I can choke this down first."

Frost looked after their departing friend murderously, then turned to Lenox. "Tell me, are we 'close'?"

Lenox laughed. "Close to getting Leigh out of England. I shall be happier then."

Frost shook his head. "I would find it funnier if he were assigned to a department that didn't matter."

In fact, though, Huntington had given Lenox a thought. "I do wonder about what he said, though—the courts."

"What do you mean?" Frost asked.

"Twenty-five thousand pounds is an enormous sum of money. Middleton cannot have been responsible alone for its passage from one person to another. What happens to it when he's gone? Who's in charge of it? For that matter where is it? Where are the documents pertaining to it, other than in that blasted valise?"

"Hm."

When Lenox thought of the chancery courts, he pictured an enormous, cathedral-sized archive, with hundreds and hundreds of rows of shelves, each hundreds and hundreds of feet high, all of them stuffed with hundreds and hundreds of spilling files and records, paper, paper, paper, and occasionally some hapless and benighted fellow worriedly wandering the aisles, taking snuff to steady himself in his search.

And yet it couldn't possibly work so inefficiently as that. "You know what—I'll have one of our fellows go over to the court and look into it."

"A sound idea," said Frost. "I feel stupid not to have thought of it myself. I wonder if I ought to send one of ours, too—to give it an official gloss."

"Yes, perhaps. They could work in concert. Though I don't know that the court is obliged to turn anything over."

"My junior can be persuasive. Nobody likes to be on the wrong side of the Yard."

They paused, contemplating this, as they watched Huntington, across the room, give some earnest advice to a man of three times his age and thirty times his experience, then depart. "You had better catch him if you have any questions about how to proceed," Lenox said.

Frost scowled. "I have some ideas."

"What do you intend to do?"

"For some reason I haven't been able to track down Beaumont for a day or two," he said. "I'd like to ask him a few more questions about Middleton's last days. He might have remembered something else. I suppose I'll go to his home, since he hasn't been appearing in his chambers."

"Mm."

"Then I'm going to visit the Blue Peter again, if only out of sheer frustration. I want to rattle the cages of Anderson's and Singh's superiors. They know something. Would you care to come?"

Lenox shook his head. "I'm going to send someone to the courts—you can push your person along with me if you want—and then I'd like to take a look at that ledger of Middleton's. I know you looked at it already, but—"

"No, no, two sets of eyes are always better."

"After that Leigh has his luncheon at the Royal Society. If we can get him through that without being attacked, he may leave these shores safely after all."

CHAPTER TWENTY-SEVEN

Their lines of inquiry had been thwarted, and yet Lenox felt a certain familiar vitality which he knew, from long experience, meant that he was getting closer, not farther, from the truth. Back at Chancery Lane he sent Pointilleux to the nearby courts, in company with Frost's junior inspector, Phelps.

When this was done he went to Dallington's office, whose door was shut tight and from which voices had been emerging at a muffled but loudish volume for some time.

They came from Dallington and Polly, facing each other across a desk. They looked up when Lenox came in. "Ah," said Dallington after an awkward moment. "How are you getting along?"

There was an aspersive atmosphere in the room. Lenox paused for a moment, then said, "What is on your ankles?"

Polly burst out into an unkind laugh. Dallington reddened, and glanced down at the twinned gaiters hanging daintily over his shoes. "These are my spatterdashers, thank you."

"Your spatterdashers?"

"It's as muddy as the road to Canterbury outside, and my tailor tells me these are very fashionable.

Spats, he called them, for short. Why, look at your shoes!"

Lenox looked down at his boots, and saw that it was true they had been cleaner. "Never mind," he said. "How are you two getting along with the matter in Parliament? The broken window, and the naval treaty?"

The tension, which had dissipated a little bit after he came in, quickly returned. "We think we've discovered what happened," said Polly. "The only trouble is that we now disagree on what course to take."

Lenox was curious. "What happened?"

"It's no great affair of state, I'm sorry to say. Only the usual sordid mess."

The truth, it emerged as Dallington and Polly told him about their previous several nights' work, was that the small room at the end of the corridor had been in semiregular use by one of the cabinet ministers as a place of assignation.

"Who?" Lenox asked.

The answer was Lord Beverley, Polly said. Lenox knew him, a junior minister with a wife and seven children. Polly said that the woman had been, alas, the wife of a colleague, Mr. James Winslow. According to what they had pieced together from the charwomen and footmen who had been nearby, the angry husband had, on a piece of anonymous advice, been going to the private chambers to confront his wife and the young lord.

Beverley, cut off from any other route of egress, and with the sense of entitlement that a lord might be expected to have, had smashed the window and taken the gardens out.

"And Winslow?" asked Lenox.

"Found his wife there—she had told him she intended to dine out—and they had a furious row, apparently. She said that she was as surprised as he was to find them both there. She had received an anonymous note asking her to be there—and from what we hear," Dallington added, "very prettily turned the matter on him."

"There would certainly have been a duel between Beverley and Winslow," said Polly. "There may still be. The involved parties are not of dovelike temperament."

Lenox sighed. A duel would mean a quick trip to the fields of Belgium or Germany, where such barbarism remained legal, and likely neither party would have thrown his shot away. Polly was right: the usual sordid mess.

"Then what is the debate between you two?" Lenox asked.

"Ah. That. Dallington wants to go back again and catch them."

"And you don't?"

"I see no profit in it for us."

Lenox looked at the young lord. "They'll scarcely return to the same spot this time, after all that has occurred," he said.

Dallington looked as if he had handled this objection thirty or forty times already. "I think they will. People are fools, and Beverley has the room reserved nightly with the porter. I would wager the only thing holding him back is the common knowledge that Polly and I are there. This time I mean to conceal myself."

"To what end!" cried Polly. "Even if you catch him, there is nothing to be said to him, nor anything to be done."

"He can be shamed."

Polly looked at Lenox and threw up her hands. "Dallington is on friendly terms with this Winslow."

"No, my father is. But he's a thundering good chap," said Dallington angrily.

Lenox knew Winslow vaguely, an older, very conservative, utterly responsible landholder, certainly selfless in his public service. They had never exchanged more than a civil hello. "What does Mr. Cheesewright say?"

"He is satisfied with our answer," said Polly. "And added specifically that we should at all costs avoid embarrassment to the Members. Of both the Commons and the Lords."

"Then I must side with Polly," Lenox said to Dallington. "What business is it of ours?"

Dallington shook his head. "Something about it is off."

"What?"

Polly, with an exasperated gesture, said, "He's being a fool."

That was a harsh word, and harsher still from the person you loved. There was a long and awkward silence.

Lenox, wanting to pad out the space between it and them, started to prattle—he could see both sides of the matter, he was conscious of their duty to Parliament but also of their duty to the truth, perhaps they should speak to Cheesewright again.

But the poison would not draw. Dallington stood up, and said, very politely, "I'll manage it in my spare time. Excuse me, please."

When he had gone a look passed briefly across Polly's face. In it were regret, frustration, and, Lenox thought, a thwarted love of her own. She and Dallington had become so intimate; and yet without taking the final step that Lenox had expected they would. What did she feel? They must have been so difficult for her, these years of widowhood, London talking about her with its usual reckless cruelty. For some reason her anger with Dallington had come to its knife edge now, but he saw that she already wished she hadn't— there was a certain softness even in her astringent words to him, a certain lovingness.

She composed herself, however, and asked Lenox, "How are matters progressing with Leigh? Cohen is with him?"

"Yes, through today. Pointilleux is at the courts

for me now. I hope to find something out soon."

She grimaced, looking down at the large index she kept on her desk of the current status of all their detectives and staff. "It's a great deal to devote to a case without the prospect of payment."

"He'll be back in France by this evening."

"Good," said Polly.

Lenox returned to his own office. It was now nine o'clock, and he decided that he would dedicate a good hour's work to Middleton's ledger.

It was an oversized volume bound in red leather, with a flexible spine so that it lay flat to each open page. It contained a three-year calendar, covering 1875, 1876, and 1877. Poor Middleton had only made it two days into the third of these years, though as Lenox leafed through he saw that there were numerous appointments filled in for the months to come.

The solicitor had written densely in nearly every entry, with the exception of a two-week stretch in August that said only "Scotland" in each space. This began on August 11, and Lenox knew that Middleton had been a hunter of grouse. Every year on the "glorious twelfth," as its participants called it, the season opened, and those first few weeks were their apotheosis. Special train lines ran through Scotland and Ireland in those weeks solely to carry the hunters from moor to moor.

Though Middleton was a detailed planner, his

system was penetrable. Many of his appointments were "IC," which Lenox quickly concluded meant "in chambers." Others were out, many at hotels (most often the Savoy, occasionally Claridge's, but Lenox saw even trips to Leigh's own smallish Collingwood Hotel), which he guessed was because men of substance visiting London would use the occasion to see their solicitor.

Here was Terence Fells, too, and with a little chill he saw that Frost had been correct: a line from an entry that had Fells's initials to Gerald Leigh's name, which was shortened on the next page to GL, and later appeared again (*"letter to GL Paris"*), including on the very day of Middleton's death, when he had been appointed to meet Leigh again, to discuss the case.

The work was absorbing, a thicket of cross-references. Lenox took profuse notes on a pad of paper. Why had Middleton been so eager to track down a "Mr. Wallace" in the last month, always writing the name in that singularly full and formal style? Who was the increasingly frequent "AR" of December, or the "PQ" that had been scheduled for so many appointments in the coming month? And why did every entry feature some small sum of addition or subtraction? Were those legal fees that he had totted up?

No doubt Frost and his men had deciphered some of these answers with Beaumont's help, and the resource of Middleton's files. He would ask.

At a quarter past ten, Pointilleux knocked on the door and pushed it open. He was holding a piece of paper. "Hello," he said. "We have a result."

"So quickly?"

"Immediately," said Pointilleux. "They are a model of efficiency."

So much for Lenox's vision of the endless aisles in the courthouse, the lost papers. "And?"

Pointilleux and Phelps, the young man from the Yard, stepped fully into the office. It was the young Frenchman who laid down a sheet of paper before Lenox.

Clerk: Robbins
Name queried: Leigh, Gerald Leigh, G. Leigh, G. R. Leigh, Roderick Leigh, G. Roderick Leigh
Years: 1876, 1877
Results: None

Lenox read it and then looked up. "What does this mean?"

Pointilleux shook his head. "It mean that there is no bequest register to Mr. Leigh in the past two years at the London courts of chancery."

"So—"

"This bequest—it does not exist."

It was rare for Lenox to be truly astonished, but now he was. "What?" he said. "Nonexistent?"

"None-existent," confirmed Pointilleux, with some justified pride.

"And it would have been registered in London? There is no question of that?"

"Yes, certainly—all wills are, and in more particular our clerk knew Mr. Middleton," said the young Frenchman. "I cannot say the how come, but it is deception. There is no money. Mr. Leigh was left no money."

CHAPTER TWENTY-EIGHT

This was one of those facts that changed the complexion of the entire case. (Just the sort of enormous discovery, ironically, that thirty years before Leigh and Lenox had been desperate to uncover in their amateurish investigations of the MB, when they had sat in Leigh's rooms, spinning tales for each other. What if his real father was an Assyrian prince? What if there were 999 identical students sprinkled over the British Isles, and some bizarre philanthropist was playing the same game with all of them at once?)

"And both of you feel certain that there is no way this is merely an error?" he asked Pointilleux.

The younger man glanced at Phelps, a hunched fellow with uneven teeth and wide eyes, rather Dutch in appearance. It was he who answered. "I should have said that the clerk, Robbins, was extremely competent. Sober and reliable. I don't think there can have been a mistake."

"Or a circumvention of the courts?" asked Lenox.

Pointilleux frowned at the long word, but Phelps shook his head. "Unless the money was in ready notes or gold, no. All banks, no matter how small, are obliged to register any transfer of property, and certainly a solicitor such as Middleton would only have worked on a will that was legally registered."

"I see."

"To quote Mr. Robbins, the system has no gaps except cash."

Lenox tilted his head, thinking. "Yes, and Middleton specifically referred to a banking transfer to Leigh."

"There you are."

"You are off to see Frost next, I assume, Mr. Phelps?"

"Yes, indeed, Mr. Lenox."

"Pass him this note, would you?" Lenox quickly scribbled a letter telling Frost where he was going to meet Leigh. "Thank you."

This new information exonerated Salt Townsend. That much was clear. What about Terence Fells? He remained an unknown.

And without the motive they had presumed this whole while—a second beneficiary, eager to knock Leigh out of contention for that fortune—the case opened up in a dozen new directions.

Lenox already had one strong idea.

What was clear was that he needed to discuss the matter with Leigh. Unfortunately his old friend wouldn't be at the Royal Society for another hour.

Lenox put on his coat and hurried out, lifting a distracted hand to Polly, who had given him an inquiring look. In the street he was greeted by an icy wind; there were no cabs, and he realized, walking up Chancery Lane, that he was starved. He stopped at a cart where a husband and wife stood, selling skilly—porridge's London cousin—from a huge vat over a burning wood fire. For an extra penny the wife threw in a generous scoop of currants. He ate as he walked, the hot concoction making him feel a little warmer in the cheeks, a little thicker between the ribs of his coat. When he had finished, he gave the bowl to a passing boy, who thanked him, running off to hand it in at the cart, where he would be able to redeem it for a serving of his own.

At home in Hampden Lane there were bright lights on, and as Lenox entered the house he heard Lady Jane and Sophia, with the nursemaid nearby, discussing lunch. He would have liked to stay to eat with them, but instead he gave each a hurried kiss and then went to his study, where he hunted down a volume of his old notes. He had an inkling that this was where he had written Terence Fells's name once. But he was frustrated in his search, and finally, in a rush, changed into a new collar and tie and left by carriage for the Royal Society.

Nearly the first people he saw there were Leigh and Lord Baird (Rowan's copresident), sipping champagne, and Lenox realized that in the back of his mind, he had been worried throughout the night. But here was his slight, smiling friend, greeting him. Cohen stood at a respectful distance nearby.

"Lenox!" said Leigh. "We were just discussing a mutual hero of ours, Lord Baird and I were."

"Who is that?"

"Francesco Redi," said Baird.

"A painter?"

Leigh shook his head. "A natural philosopher of the 1600s. I wish more people knew his name. Aristotle, the fool—"

"Come now!" said Baird, an old and distinguished-looking specimen.

"Well—in this matter, at least, I mean, a fool, but otherwise passably intelligent—Aristotle put forward a theory called 'spontaneous generation,' and somehow or other it endured for nineteen centuries. He thought that living matter simply appeared from nothing."

"Most misguided," said Baird, shaking his head.

"It was Redi who doubted that a rock could produce a bug. One evening he put little morsels of his supper—meat loaf!—in three glasses, one sealed, one covered with gauze, one open. As you might guess, maggots appeared upon the latter within a few days. The sealed glass generated none. Very consequential meat loaf!"

Baird laughed, and Lenox joined in politely, though he would probably have agreed, two hundred seconds before, that any theory other than spontaneous generation was claptrap, had these two men averred it.

After a few moments he was able to get Leigh alone. "Listen, Gerry," he said. "Something strange has come up."

"What?"

"Frost and I asked two men to go and find out who left you that money in the courts—approaching it from the other end, you see. They returned with some odd news."

"Well?"

"Nobody left you any money at all."

Leigh looked perplexed. "What?"

"There was no inheritance."

They were standing in the rotunda, drawing glances from the men who were entering, all of them looking forward to Leigh's informal remarks, no doubt. "But . . . Middleton," he said.

Middleton. Lenox nodded, grimacing. "Yes. I have been thinking about him all morning, and I suspect we must move him in our minds from one category to another—from victim, to conspirator."

"Conspirator! He was so eminently respectable."

"Precisely his utility, perhaps. He convinced you that there was a legitimate bequest to you. The question that you must answer now is a much broader one. Why create this odd pretext at all? Who wishes to do you harm, and for what reason, if not over an inheritance?"

Leigh shook his head. "I cannot think of anyone."

"You have no enemies? Nobody whose interests you have trampled, or whose progress you have prevented?"

Leigh looked bewildered. "Must it be such a sinister causation?"

"Yes, I think it must. Because if there was no bequest: What was the motivation of Middleton's actions? There can be only one answer. *To bring you to London.* Hence his insistence that you could not sign the papers he had through the mail."

"Hell."

"All morning I have been considering what you told me of your life in France. 'The university is a fortress,' you said, and that you rarely leave its grounds."

"That's true."

"Your very valet is a member of their army's special services."

Leigh nodded. "They needed me on open

ground, you believe, to make their attack. But who? Who?"

Lenox shook his head. "We are behind in our investigations—fatally behind—because of this charade with the inheritance."

Leigh glanced at his pocket watch. "I can scarcely believe I have involved you in all this. And I have to give this blasted speech now."

Lenox shook his head. "The sooner you are back in France, the easier I will rest. I can continue the investigation here. What will your movements be for the rest of the day?"

"I'm meant to take the train to Dover at six past five."

"You must hire a special."

Leigh nodded. "Yes, of course. Between now and then I shall always be in company—I have promised to go down to Rowan's lab in the east, and look over his own work on the microbe, and after that he and I and Baird have arranged to have tea at the Collingwood. I had hoped I might pay a call on Lady Jane before I left. But I find that I am a contaminated sample at the moment—not fit for use."

Lenox shook his head. "As long as you are not alone. Keep Cohen and the constable with you. Look, there, I see Frost coming in. He and I will figure this out. Search your mind, though, Gerald. Can you think of nobody who bears you enough animus to kill you?"

Leigh thought for a moment. It was a hard question, to be sure: murder! How out of the run of common things. But he pondered it carefully, before at last saying, "Honestly, I cannot. I still feel as if it must all be some sort of cosmic error, and the truth, when it comes out, should we all remain safe until that time, will look almost comical."

CHAPTER TWENTY-NINE

C ould it possibly be as simple as that: an error? The luncheon was a tedious, long-winded affair, at least in Lenox's nervy mood. In a different temper he might have found it more congenial. As it was, the chore of being pleasant to his neighbors, sawing through his cut of meat, and attending the various sonorities of the fellows who rose to speak together made for almost more than he could take, given that all he wanted was a moment to think in complete silence.

But this was difficult to come by. As Lenox looked despairingly on, fellow after fellow rose to praise Leigh—and Rowan, for enticing him to speak—in their toasts. Most also paused to take credit on the Society's behalf for something that likely would have existed anyway, Lenox thought, first Neptune ("I am proud to say that we predicted it in 1843, confirmed it in 1846!"), then cholera ("we're close to ending it!"), then Galen ("He died in the year 199, but I think he would have found us a happy company, gentlemen.")

Amid these encomia, Leigh was at a raised table, with several illustrious figures around him. Just as coffee was being served, Lenox checked that his friend was still installed in his chair and that Cohen was nearby, then excused himself.

He found a little alcove near the bathrooms. There was a leather bench there, between two doors, and low yellow lights in a pair of sconces above it. With a sigh, he leaned back upon the bench and closed his eyes, promising himself two uninterrupted moments of contemplation.

What they had to go on was an odd nexus. Both Ernest Middleton, a wholly respectable solicitor, widely known in the courts, and Messrs. Anderson and Singh, two of the most violent, conscience-less men in London, a blight upon the city's claims to peaceable civility, were involved in a conspiracy to harm Gerald Leigh: an inoffensive, not espe-cially wealthy British scientist living in France.

What could have united the interests of those two parties against those of the third?

It must be money. Leigh couldn't think of a single enemy he had who was bitter enough to have stretched himself to these outlandish efforts, and the Farthings were motivated by little but financial gain, unless you counted revenge.

And yet, and yet . . . Lenox, sifting the facts in his mind, could almost discern a pattern. It was like looking at the reverse of a Persian carpet as it hung to dry—in the threads there was the ghost of its true shape, the hint of a figure, the contours of an outline, stippled in ragged white strands.

"Lenox. There you are."

He snapped his eyes open and sat straight up. It was Frost. "You caught me thinking."

"Anything useful?"

Lenox shook his head, troubled. "I'm groping in the dark. And yet I know it's there. I can feel it in my hands."

Frost nodded, familiar with that feeling. "I thought you should know that we just picked up Wasilewski three blocks from here."

Lenox felt a flutter. "The Pole who replaced Anderson and Singh."

"The Pole who replaced Anderson and Singh. I had instructed my men to arrest him before he got any closer, and they did. Took him by surprise, I'm pleased to say. He had a pistol and a knife on him. No doubt he meant to use them on Leigh."

"That's damning."

"He protested that he always carried them—they were in his line of work."

"Which is?"

Frost smiled thinly. "Wallpaper hanger, by his own previous account. But he forgot that he had told us that the last time he was arrested and said just now that he was a night watchman at a factory in the East End."

"Not impossible. The Farthings own several."

Frost nodded. "Yes. Regardless, I'm pleased to get him off our tail."

Lenox was more than pleased, he thought. It was possible that his idea had saved Leigh's life.

On the other hand, the tenacity of the gang's interest was disturbing. "Phelps found you?"

Frost nodded unhappily. He had his pipe out, and clamped it ruminatively in his back teeth, unlit. "Yes."

"The field is wide open now, I'm afraid," said Lenox.

"Could you grope any faster?"

"Let's both."

They walked out toward the luncheon, whose speeches were still audible in a muted drone from two doors away, and Frost said, "We've found something else."

"What's that?"

"Do you remember the stationery you spotted in Middleton's desk—at home, not in his chambers—which had his name and the address 24 Aldershot Place printed upon it?"

"I do."

"This morning we finally sent someone there. It's a gambling parlor, as it happens. A very high-end one, Milton's."

Lenox saw the link immediately. "He was in debt."

Frost nodded, surprised. "We think he might well have been, yes. How did you guess?"

"If he gambled there frequently enough that Milton's gave him complimentary cards—to correspond with his fellow players, I'm sure—then he cannot have been ahead over the course of his career. What did he play?"

"Hazard."

Lenox winced. The game involved not even the mathematical skill of the card player—it was one of pure chance, in which the dice were cast again and again, until they came up two or three, "crabs," or in the new parlance occasionally "craps," and the player was out. "How bad was the debt?"

"We do not know, except that they would no longer extend him credit from the start of last summer."

"And he stopped playing there?"

Frost shook his head, "On the contrary, he was away only a few weeks after they closed his house account, according to the steward. He returned with ready money."

"Did you ask Beaumont about this?"

"We still haven't managed to find him."

That was odd—and anything odd attracted Lenox's eye, at this point. He nodded, thinking. "I wonder if it was a secret from him, too. They were financial partners."

"It doesn't seem like it, if Middleton had the stationery of 24 Aldershot Place, after all," Frost pointed out.

"Yes, but no doubt only to communicate with his fellow gamblers, as I said. It's quite customary. Sometimes these men don't want each other to know their home addresses."

Frost nodded. "Yes."

"Classes cross at a place like that. The Duke of Beckham used to play penny faro at a brothel, according to the rumors of the ballroom."

"Middleton's stakes were very much higher."

Lenox nodded. Suddenly he had a thought. "I can guess where he got his money."

"Where?"

"Do you remember telling me that Terence Fells's name was connected to Gerald Leigh's, in Middleton's ledger?"

"Of course."

"You assumed, reasonably, that because Fells's name and the initials *TF* began to appear at the same time, it was one of Middleton's usual abbreviations—they're all over the ledger. But I think they may be unrelated."

"Why?"

"Because *TF*—it could stand for 'The Farthings,' couldn't it?"

Frost stopped and turned to Lenox, whistling a low whistle. "You think a man of Middleton's position would go to the *Farthings* for money?

241

That would be madness. And well out of his usual sphere."

"If he was a bad gambler, he might have exhausted all other avenues of income. Think of Charles Fox—one of the most distinguished orators in the history of Parliament, and a hundred and forty thousand pounds in debt over cards. Or Byron's daughter, the Countess of Lovelace, who used her mathematical abilities to devise a system for betting horseraces and ended up penniless."

They had arrived just outside the doorway to the luncheon room, and a burst of applause broke out. "The Farthings must have decided that he was more use to them alive than dead. Until—the contrary."

Lenox nodded slowly. "Yes. I still have my doubts about that."

He was about to elaborate when there was a soft cough behind them. A porter whose jacket had the seal of the Royal Society on its breast was standing with a letter on a silver tray. "Mr. Lenox?" he said.

"That's me."

"A letter, sir."

Lenox took the letter, which had his name upon it in a bold hand, frowning. "Who delivered it? Nobody knows I'm here."

"I don't know, sir. My apologies. It was left upon the front desk a few moments ago, just when the porter had stepped away to assist a gentleman with his luggage."

Lenox tore open the letter in a ragged strip—and as he did so a small object fell with a ping onto the marble floor.

A farthing.

CHAPTER THIRTY

Even before the coin had struck the ground, Lenox felt a coldness grip his heart. For a moment he and Frost both stood and stared at the coin where it had landed, and then Frost stooped down and picked it up, rising with a shake of his head. "Too far," he said immediately.

Lenox's thoughts were with Sophia and Lady Jane. "I have to go and tell my wife," he said. "Don't leave Leigh for anything. I'll be back shortly."

Frost grabbed his arm. "It would be unwise to go off alone after such a message, Lenox. Wait, would you?"

"No, I can't."

He made it home, looking over his shoulder the whole way for a trap but finding none, and discovered Lady Jane in her drawing room, writing letters. She looked up at him curiously when he entered. "Home already?"

"Where is Sophia?" he asked.

"Upstairs in the nursery. Why?"

Just at that moment there was a merry cry, with what he could never have mistaken for anything but his daughter's joy in it. "Thank goodness."

"Why, Charles?" said Jane again.

He told her. She had been thrown out of her daily schedule by some threat to Lenox more than once, but now that they had a child she grew angry at these intrusions of his work into their life. With justification.

"Will this never end?" she asked, standing up.

"My idea is that you should go to Toto's for the night," he said. "That will be no hardship. Sophia will like to sleep in George's nursery. And there are already men going directly to the Farthings' chief to arrest him, including the superintendent, if I have my way—I wrote him, through Frost, and used Edmund's name."

"Charles."

"Nothing will come of it all. You have my solemn word."

He felt sick, though, as he kissed Sophia's cheeks ten minutes later. "I shall be over to see you this evening, love," he said.

When they were gone, he was alone again. He stood for a moment—away from the windows, he noticed, fearful of bullets—and let his thoughts run.

Why had they targeted him now? First Middleton had been sent this message of the solitary farthing;

then an amateur detective. Was it because Frost was too powerful a figure, embedded within the official body of Scotland Yard, to menace?

But then—why send such a message at all? Why not strike, if you intended to strike? It was this question that puzzled him most, and had before that day, too.

Sophia and Jane, at least, would be safe at McConnell's heavily fortified house on Grosvenor Square, a place that would offer protection both in numbers and in concrete physical ways that not many other private houses could.

He left by the back gate, coat up around his ears, eyes darting left and right. There was a threat in every face he passed; at the corner he felt a heavy hand on his shoulder, and turned, violently.

Only Pargiter, the newsman. He looked surprised. "All well, Mr. Lenox?"

"Oh—fine, yes."

"I thought you might want the afternoon papers."

"Later, Pargiter, later. Thank you."

It was only when he was sunk low within the anonymity of a London taxi a few minutes later that he felt safe again. He directed it back to the Royal Society.

Frost greeted him in the marble rotunda. "Family safe?" he asked.

"Safe," Lenox confirmed.

"You'll be happy to know we've been busy here. There is a large group going to the Blue Peter. At least twelve men, including, I believe, Superintendent Gilbert."

"Good."

"Yes, I think so. There are fifteen of these gangs—any one of them that we really turned our attention to could be gone in a week, and they know it. The trouble is another would pop up. But it would be worth it to keep you and Leigh safe. As I said, it's gone too far. Let them kill each other—but not us."

"Thank you, Frost."

The inspector nodded seriously. "Don't mention it. I've instructed one of my men to return here as soon as possible with a report on the arrest— they may begin coughing up what they know immediately, the scoundrels."

Lenox puffed out his cheeks, very modestly reassured. "Thank you," he said again. He had fewer friends at the Yard than he once had. His dear friend Jenkins was gone. But here was a new one. "That's decent of you."

"Not at all."

To Lenox's amazement, lunch was still, after this interruption, somehow a going concern, the gentlemen in the room having loosened their ties, poured out brandies for themselves, and lit cigars, and the room whirring with amiable clubroom chatter. (One word rose above the noise again and

246

again, eliciting a laugh almost every time. In the American state of North Carolina forty or fifty years before, Rowan had told them over lunch, some particularly fatuous politician had made a speech, immediately derided as unctuous and full of airy sophistry; it was delivered in the county of those parts called Buncombe, and almost immediately, in that mysterious way of slang, that name had become a byword for just such nonsense—soon making the transition from its proper form to the more generic "bunkum," or, as the men of the Royal Society had taken to shortening it in their appropriation of the word, to indicate friendly disagreement during a post-prandial conversation, "bunk."

"I think *they're* bunk," Frost muttered at last, watching them.

Leigh was in deep conversation with a slim red-haired young man, very earnest and it would appear very engaging, too.

"Nothing off?" Lenox asked Frost.

"Nothing."

They were standing on the periphery of the room, watching the luncheon. Lenox hadn't taken more than a small glass of wine—he wanted a clear head—and Frost's eyes didn't leave Leigh. Nor did Cohen's; he stood close to the room's other entrance.

Lenox's old friend eventually noticed them, however, and beckoned his young red-haired friend to come and meet them. "Lenox, Frost—this is Mr. William Shandy. A man after my own heart: untrained."

"How do you do?" said Mr. William Shandy, untrained.

Lenox and Frost introduced themselves. "An amateur, then?" asked Lenox, civilly, despite the anxiety that still gripped him. "What is your field?"

"I propagate ferns, sir."

Instead of saying "how infinitely dull," Lenox nodded politely, and inquired about the ferns; yes, they were easy to grow; no, they had few predators in England; yes, there were interesting facts about their inherited traits.

"This is the glory of England, this kind of thing," Leigh said, beaming. Lenox hadn't seen him so happy that day. "You must remember that Darwin studied medicine and divinity, nothing else. He became a natural philosopher simply by attempting natural philosophy over and over! Which is how we shall launch an aeroplane into the heavens, one day, I imagine, no matter how many of us have to fall down first."

"You cannot believe that rot," said Lenox. "Mr. Shandy, do you?"

Shandy looked both scandalized that Lenox had spoken to Leigh in such a way, and uncomfortable that the discussion had moved on from ferns. "I cannot say, sir. I really cannot say."

Leigh was immediately approached by another

fellow of the Society, who drew him into a conversation about the microbe (Lenox hoped never to hear the word again) and had soon induced one or two other men to join their colloquy. The word "bunk" came along, and Lenox wondered how much longer he would have to endure the interminable gathering.

Frost pulled a flask from his breast pocket. "You look as if you could do with a sup, after the last few hours."

Lenox took the flask, a much dented and tarnished old pewter object, inscribed with lettering too darkened to read, and said, "If you absolutely insist."

The liquid inside was fiery—every time he visited a workingman's pub, he had to admit his tastes had grown genteel in the years since university—but its results were as gratifying as the finest Jura malt could have provided, filling him with a warm calm.

He asked what it was, and Frost said, "A London mash."

"Not for the faint of heart."

"Ha! No."

"Your flask has been through the wars."

Frost looked down at it in his hand. "Oh, yes, quite literally. It was my grandfather's. He had it in Crimea—he wore it over his heart, trusting that it might stop a bullet. Instead he got shot in the upper leg, like a common poacher, he always says. He mostly sits with the leg up in Lambeth now, where he has one of those new stores you've probably heard of. A nice little business, paid for by his pension."

"New stores?"

"Have you not been? You serve yourself. The shopkeeper does nothing but sit behind the cash register like a grandee." Frost sighed and capped the flask. "Someday I'll do it myself. I only hope I don't have to get shot in the leg for the pleasure. Granddad gave me the flask when I joined the Yard—said perhaps it would catch a bullet for me, even if it hadn't for him."

"Not today, I pray," said Lenox.

"No—not today, I quite agree."

CHAPTER THIRTY-ONE

It was fifteen or twenty minutes later when Frost's man Phelps returned, coming straight to report to them. "Checking in, sir. Nine arrested at the Blue Peter; a squad of four remaining to scrabble out any others lurking in the shadows; statements being taken at the Yard as we speak."

"Fast work, Phelps, well done. Did Superintendent Gilbert accompany you?"

"He did, sir. Came in his coach and four—like a hound from hell he was too, reading them the warrant himself."

"Who was the highest up of the gang?"

"Spencer, sir"—that was the deceptively friendly figure behind the bar at the Blue Peter, with the vulpine face—"and Smith. Assorted other lieutenants. One odd thing, though."

"Oh?"

"All of them swear, separately, that the Farthings would never, ever send a farthing coin in an envelope, for any reason, to anyone. Impossible, they said. Outright impossible."

"Not as intimidation?" asked Lenox.

"No, nor as any kind of oath of revenge or the like."

Frost furrowed his brow. "And you believed them?"

Phelps cocked his head, raising his eyebrows, as if to say it was difficult ever to know what to believe, but then nodded cautiously. "I did, rather, sir. They seemed properly outraged by the very idea."

The act had never made any sense. "Which of them seemed outraged?" Lenox asked.

"All of them, sir, as I said. Starting with Spencer."

Lenox glanced at Frost, who had a hand on his cheek, scratching his thick gray beard distractedly. "What do you make of that?"

"Peculiar."

"It might have been the bright idea of someone lower down," said Lenox. "Anderson and Singh, for instance."

Phelps shook his head. "I don't think so, sir. Spencer said something odd. 'The first rule is to leave no trace.' The moment he said it he looked as if he wished he hadn't—only he was so hotted up at the accusation that it slipped out."

"Did you ask them about Wasilewski?" said Frost.

"Yes, sir. Nobody admitted even to knowing the name."

"Mm. To be expected."

At long last, the luncheon appeared to be breaking up. Standing at the edge of the room, Lenox, Frost, and Phelps watched as various men took leave of Leigh, who was polite with all of them, though slightly distant, too, Lenox observed.

When Leigh broke away he came over to Lenox. "It has just been observed to me by an informed gentleman that if you were somehow able to conjure your way back to the year 1500, you would be dead within two days."

Lenox frowned. "Murdered?"

"Murdered! Heavens, no. You must take your mind off murder."

"Of what, then?"

"Of disease, at least according to him. Every man and woman who reached their majority in medieval London had already passed through a gauntlet of diseases that it would chill you to your marrow if I named them. When I say that the bubonic plague and typhoid fever are two

252

of the nicer ones it gives the picture, perhaps."

Lenox, to whom a protracted battle with typhoid fever seemed only marginally less pleasant than remaining at the Royal Society as these scientists slowly stumbled themselves back out into the world, far too drunk to do much of anything on behalf of British science for the rest of the afternoon, nodded, and said, impatiently, "But really, hadn't you better be going? It's already nearly three."

"Is it?" Leigh frowned, glancing up at the clock. "Worse luck. I shall have to skip Rowan's—but I will sit to a cup of tea with him and Baird. It's only civil, after all they've done for me."

As Leigh waded again into the room to find these two, Lenox wondered if he ought to leave, and go report to Jane that the full force of the Yard had landed on the Farthings. The trouble was his uncertainty about who was behind the farthing after all. Should he send them into the country, Sophia and Jane?

He was about to tell Cohen and Frost that he had to go, when suddenly something struck him, however. It came of glancing at Cohen, who was standing with Leigh's small brown leather weekending bag. The sight of it took Lenox back to where this had all begun, at the Collingwood Hotel.

Strange to see that name in Middleton's appointment ledger, now that he thought of it. Most of the hotels there were large, but the Collingwood was small, only twenty rooms.

Why did it bother him all at once, that reappearance?

Lenox looked around the room, eyes narrowed, thinking. He tried to recall what else had stood out for him from Middleton's journal. The initials, certainly: *AR, PQ*. He tried out the names of everyone he could recall from the case, trying to squeeze them into those initials, but without success.

Where was Beaumont?

He felt intensely vexed, closer and closer to some essential truth, still too far to hold it within his grip.

At that moment the same porter who had brought him the envelope with the farthing in it approached again. Lenox and Frost both turned to him with something like displeasure, and he shrank back slightly, repentant already.

"Yes?" said Frost.

"My apologies, sir. Another letter for Mr. Lenox."

Lenox and Frost glanced at each other. "When did it come?"

"Not five minutes ago, sir. Once again when the porter at the front desk was occupied."

"Christ," said Frost. "What are those constables doing? Phelps, go and speak to the men stationed outside and ask them who has been in and out."

Lenox was staring at the letter on its salver, and felt his heart beating heavily in his throat. There was a small circular shadow lodged in the lower left-hand corner of the envelope. He didn't need to open it—but he did, more carefully this time, not letting the farthing inside drop to the ground.

He held it in his palm. "Twice," he said. "In two hours. That's very peculiar."

Frost looked at him with a face traced with guilt, perhaps because he was glad that it was not he who was the target of these messages, whatever they meant.

It was hard for Lenox not to feel as if there was a pistol trained on the back of his neck—and he wondered what he could possibly do to feel safe.

What if the Farthings had been lying? And this was their second threat?

Jane and Sophia would have to leave London; that much was clear.

Phelps returned from his rapid inquiries: Nobody had been seen coming into the building, or leaving a note. Plenty of men had left in the last twenty minutes, of course.

"But that means . . ." Lenox thought for a moment. "Could someone from inside be leaving these notes?"

"Within the Royal Society?"

As Frost glanced around, Lenox slowly revolved, studying everyone he saw with new eyes, down to the inspector himself. His initials were *TF,* after all, Timothy Frost, a fact they had joked about more than once.

And then suddenly he realized, with a start, that someone was missing from the scene: Leigh.

"Where is Leigh?" he asked Frost.

Frost glanced back into the emptying room. He scanned it quickly and looked back at Lenox. Both of them had the same thought simultaneously: they had lost him in the muddle of receiving this second letter.

Lenox turned and sprinted for the building's exit. He had to push his way among several small groups of departing fellows, none of them sober, until he could run out into the chilly air of the outdoors, praying that a bullet didn't greet him there.

He stood close to the constable on duty there and looked left and right.

His eyes alit on Cohen, and seeing his sturdy, intelligent face, Lenox felt relieved. "Cohen," he said. "Where has Leigh gone?"

"He and Lord Baird went ahead in a carriage, according to the porter. I know Leigh went of his own accord, saw him go."

"Thank heavens."

"It was only a two-person fly. I wouldn't fit. I'm waiting for a cab to follow on. An address in Chilton Street, where Lord Baird's laboratory is housed. They've a plan to meet Rowan at the rail station—to have tea in paper cups, an idea that tickled his lordship no end."

Lenox nodded, a little puzzled that it was suddenly Baird's laboratory, not Rowan's, to which they were headed. He turned his gaze up the street, waiting for a cab to appear. "I'll go with you," he said.

"Of course, if you wish," said Cohen.

Except that then, suddenly, an alarm sounded in Lenox's mind. He whipped his head back to Cohen. "Chilton Street, you said?"

"Yes. Why?"

Lenox felt the blood drain out of his face. "Christ," he said. He turned up and down the street, looking without hope for a cab. "A two-person fly. Come, we have to go now—a cab, I need a cab, Cohen. My friend's life depends upon it."

CHAPTER THIRTY-TWO

Cohen, to his credit, didn't ask any questions. He removed a whistle from his pocket and blew it loudly, hoping to attract a cab. Lenox had started to sprint toward Piccadilly, in case it didn't—there would be a cabstand there.

Then he pulled up. A better idea had occurred to him, and he reversed his path some ten or fifteen steps, turning down a side street that housed, he thought he remembered, a coaching inn. Cohen followed him.

He found it just where he had recalled, with some fleeting satisfaction in the distant part of his brain not consumed by dread.

He ran up to the chest-high lower door, whose top half was swung open. "Give me a horse," he called. "A pound for a horse—a guinea—I only need it for thirty minutes."

This was such an astounding offer that six or seven faces popped up at once, and within a minute a horse was being led to him, saddled and bridled. She was a bay mare, brown all over save a black nose and one black foot.

"Is she fast?" said Lenox, vaulting into the seat.

"Lord no," said the boy who had brought her.

"Damn," he muttered, but he had already spurred the beast out into the cobblestoned street, leaving his purse behind with Cohen, to pay and to give the stable his address. The junior detective had instructions to follow him to Chilton Street in a cab when this was done.

The mare might not have been fast, but she was fast enough. In Lenox's boyhood it had been common to see men on horseback in the streets, but now it was rare, and in many places outright illegal, because it caused confusion and traffic among all the other horses needed to keep London moving—the cart horses bearing everything from carrots to silks, the cab horses, the carriage horses.

But there was nothing to beat it for speed. Lenox wove in and out of the rutted paths that the teams followed. He had forgotten his gloves at lunch, and soon his hands were stinging; he wrapped them more tightly around the reins, leaning forward to urge his horse onward.

The buildings flew by. For a brief, singing moment, as he turned down Oxford Street, he had an uninterrupted stretch of several hundred yards ahead of him, and he took her down it pell-mell, the horse snorting and straining, moving faster than she must have in many years. Lenox had always felt supremely natural on horseback, and even in these circumstances he registered the physical joy of riding.

In the East End of London, the streets became dense, stopping abruptly, forking off into tines without warning, the dark tenements concealing all but a thin ribbon of sky above. Lenox took his turns slowly, in part so that he didn't break his neck, in part because his horse, no doubt unaccustomed to such strenuous exercise in the cold, was panting and trembling.

His only hope was that Baird was taking the turns slowly, too.

Chilton Street. It was entirely possible that he was wrong, and this trip to the laboratory an innocent excursion, marked by minor coincidence—as no doubt all of life would appear to be, had one sufficient information.

On the other hand, on the other hand . . .

As he rode, somewhere in the back of his mind he thought of all that he knew about the president of the Royal Society. It didn't add up to much. He was well-born, that was clear, and in his manners well-bred. Had he been at Oxford? Lenox thought so.

Was he a murderer? Lenox would have said, flatly, no. He had seemed nothing but jolly, all throughout lunch. And what could his motive be, old Lord Baird, at the end of a distinguished career?

But Chilton Street—a stone's throw, literally the distance of a stone's throw, from the Blue Peter.

After the coincidence of Middleton's visits to the Collingwood, it was too much.

Lenox turned onto Chilton Street with a last burst of speed. He had to cross several avenues until he approached number 80, which Cohen had been dead certain was the address he had overheard the porter giving the cab driver. Thank goodness for the small habits of attentiveness all detectives picked up.

Ahead of him was a small conveyance. Was it the right taxi? Lenox's horse, with white lather on her flanks, the poor beast, he spurred on harder, just as the fly pulled away from the pavement. As he got closer, Lenox saw it was empty.

"You!" he called. "Did you just leave two men here?"

The driver turned back with an unpleasant look. "Who's asking?"

Lenox reached in his pocket frantically and held up a shilling. "Well?"

"Yes. Number 80."

Lenox flicked the coin at the man. "There's another if you hold this horse for ten minutes. And another for each ten-minute period after that. I have your cab number if you steal the horse. Tie her up at the least."

He was already down from the saddle as he delivered this speech, running for the door.

Motive, he thought wildly, his mind still working on the problem. What could the motive be? Not money. But then, what?

His mind flashed upon the queer little encounter he had had the night before with Mr. Bartram, the amateur scientist, in the moonlit courtyard below the Royal Society.

He reached the door and found it bolted tight.

Ought he to knock? He looked up and down the façade of what he saw now was a large, rather lovely white house, out of place in this makeshift neighborhood.

He saw that there was one window slightly ajar, halfway down the long row of them. He ran to it—but it was barred.

He looked through the bars, and saw, inside, Leigh, with his hands up. Lenox's heart lurched. And behind Leigh, pointing a gun at him casually, the other hand lodged in the pocket of his jacket, was the president of the Royal Society.

But not Lord Baird. Alexander Rowan.

Of course. A misdirection: that was why the plan to visit Rowan's laboratory had changed so suddenly. It wasn't Lord Baird behind all of this trouble. He wasn't even sure Lord Baird *had* a private laboratory. It was Rowan.

And in a flash it returned to him, the ardor with which Rowan, not Baird, had worked to entice Leigh to return to London for a second time. A scholarship for a Cornwall boy to the university of his choice! It was such a canny offer: attractive to Leigh's sense of honor, his pride.

And then, since Leigh had been back in London, every attempt to isolate him—Rowan's absolute insistence that Leigh stay at the Collingwood, and then his repeated and equally insistent, indeed nearly desperate, invitations for Leigh to come after supper and have a late drink at his club. Then, finally, this trip to the laboratory.

All of them, opportunities for the Farthings to do their work.

Except that they had tracked Anderson and Singh, while Wasilewski was down in New Scotland Street, no doubt refusing, in sullen silence, to answer questions.

Which had left the thwarted Rowan to do the job himself.

It took ten seconds, perhaps fifteen, for all of

this to connect in Lenox's mind. He watched, in that time, as Leigh turned and then sat in the small wicker chair to which Rowan had gestured. It was like watching a play: the same impossibility of joining in, the same sense of tragic inevitability.

Then, out of the corner of his eye, Lenox saw something—next window over, there was a lone little ledge with a box of juniper bushes along it. If he climbed that, he could maybe, just maybe, reach the second story.

He went and tried to pull himself up. No luck. He put his foot on the bars of the window, but it slid down sideways. Then he had an idea. He removed his coat and slung it over the juniper box and pulled.

It held his weight. He walked very slowly up the side of the building, his arms straining, and then lurched to a seat on the windowsill. His body was trembling, hot despite the cold air. He turned to the window and checked it.

Locked, too.

There was nothing for it but to wrap his jacket (a present from Lady Jane—torn and muddied now, but if it saved Leigh's neck!) around his fist and break the window, hoping that he might muffle the sound enough that Rowan missed it.

He did this, scraping himself lightly on the wrist as he reached in and turned the brass knob from the inside. Then he was in.

It was a shadowy room with mismatched

furniture and a dark, squeamish smell. Lenox could tell immediately that this came from next door: the laboratory, he imagined.

How could he approach them without being seen? How could he dispossess Rowan of that gun?

Middleton's gun, in all probability.

He was saved from answering these questions. "Turn slowly," said a voice behind him.

The detective turned and saw Rowan, with Leigh a step ahead of him, hands up again. "Rowan."

"Sit there," Rowan ordered. "You, too."

"You scoundrel," said Lenox.

"Sit, I said." When they had followed his instructions he studied them for a moment, then said, lifting his gun so that it was pointed directly at the center of Leigh's chest, "I suppose two will fit into my story as easily as one."

Lenox shook his head. "No they won't, if a third knows."

Rowan considered this, then shrugged. "We shall see," he said, and fired the pistol.

CHAPTER THIRTY-THREE

Time stopped; then it resumed.

The bullet had flown wildly wide of Leigh, splintering a wall.

All three men were equally taken aback. The gun had been directed straight at Leigh's sternum, and Lenox couldn't believe the luck of it, the sheer improbable *impossible* luck.

Rowan's reaction was to stare down at the firearm. It was obvious what he was thinking: Perhaps Middleton had had its sights adjusted oddly?

Lenox rose, almost involuntarily, and Rowan, coming to himself, said, "Sit, I warn you!" and cocked the pistol. "I shan't miss again!"

"Rowan, for heaven's sake, remember yourself," said Lenox. He obeyed, though, sitting, hands hovering above his shoulders. "Why on earth should you want to go to prison?"

"I don't."

"Then why kill us?"

Lenox was only talking. His heart was fluttering as furiously as a leaf snagged on a rock in a stream. He glanced over at Leigh. Rowan stared at both of them. "I should have thought it was obvious. I am an ambitious sort."

Lenox, evenly, said, "Ambitious."

"Yes."

"But my heavens, you are preeminent in your field, Rowan. The president—the president!—of the Royal Society!"

"Ah," said Rowan ruefully—and now that he had collected himself, he was utterly steady, in gesture, in tone, in every aspect of his person besides the gun in his hand, the courtesy of the drawing room lingering in his movements. "But that job requires only that you be tactful, brilliant, agreeable, fair-minded, gentle in manner, firm in decision, friendly, and intelligent."

"My God! And is there anything else?"

"Yes," said Rowan shortly. "Genius."

There it was, Lenox thought—had time to think, even in the pressure of the moment. Two scientists. One a genius, and one not.

Rowan lifted the pistol with a straighter arm, aiming now just left of the center of Leigh's chest, to accommodate for the swerve of the last shot. "Bartram!" shouted Lenox.

He had only been trying to buy them a moment, but Rowan glanced over at him, for the first time a real irritation flaring into his aristocratic features. "Bartram! What has that little toad been telling you?"

"Well." Lenox appeared to be contemplating the question, but really he was calculating. If Rowan fired again, Lenox gave himself a fifty-fifty chance of survival; he would vault at the man in the moment, praying to overpower him before he could fire again. His slackness of reaction in chasing Townsend blazed up vexingly in the back of his thoughts. Older now. "He says that there has been fraud committed against Leigh."

"Fraud?"

Lenox glanced over at Leigh.

And in his old friend's face he saw—something strange.

It was not mirth, not delight. But confidence. Suddenly, as sometimes he was wont to do in pressured situations, Lenox flashed upon a distant and irrelevant memory: Leigh's devil-may-care confrontation of Tennant, the Harrow hats stacked upon his head, defiance in his eyes.

Leigh spoke. "I suspect that Mr. Rowan has decided to claim my work. I submitted several papers to the Society late last year, the first I have chosen to publish on the microbe."

"And your work involves the microbe," said Lenox to Rowan. "Gerald trumped you, I take it?"

A bitter, half-mad laugh escaped Rowan. "Trumped. That is a word."

"I fear our Mr. Rowan is not a scientist of original thought," said Leigh, sounding genuinely sorry. "The first thing in his singularly blessed life that has not been his to pluck down ready-made from the branch."

Both Lenox and Rowan stared at him, Rowan's face darkening, and Lenox, desperately, trying to tell Leigh not to antagonize their murderous adversary.

But it was too late.

"More fool you," said Rowan.

He lifted the gun, and fired it once more, both Leigh and Lenox rising in concert from their chairs in the millisecond that it was clear he was going to act again.

There was an odd explosive sound, quite unlike

a gunshot. Lenox, in the confusion of the moment, saw only a bright red burst of light, immediately gone, and then Rowan recoiled, dropping the gun, falling to the ground with an agonized cry.

"Quick!" said Leigh. "The gun!"

Lenox was ahead of this piece of advice, already having covered the ground to Rowan. He picked up the gun and pointed it. "Don't move."

"Don't fire it!" Leigh said.

But as they caught their breath, it became clear that Rowan was no longer a threat. He was writhing on the ground, clutching his arm underneath him, moaning incoherently.

"What on earth has happened?" said Lenox.

"I did it in the cab Rowan forced me into," said Leigh. He was heaving breath, like a ship bailing water. "A little wad of paper from my day's program, jammed in the flintlock. I had a second, less than a second, when he was standing up out of the fly—but I slotted it in there as perfectly as you could wish. I saw it slip in. I've never been happier."

"How—how?" said Lenox, unequal to the articulation of his many questions.

Rowan, beneath them, was whimpering pitifully. Leigh, still breathing hard, shook his head, as if he couldn't believe the luck of it himself. "It's one of the first things you learn on board a ship, for some reason," he said. "Thank God it was an old-fashioned pistol."

"And that was why the first shot went wide," said Lenox. "Of course."

"Yes."

And why Leigh had borne on his face that strange look of confidence. "You've saved us, old friend."

"I knew if he shot once it would be wide; twice and it would explode, in all probability. I didn't want to risk being wrong, however, and charge him."

They were both looking down at Rowan, who had gone quite pale. "I think we had better bandage him, and get him care," said Lenox.

They stooped down to do this. Rowan's hand was a disaster: huge chunks of it missing or stripped away, blood everywhere. He had sustained a wound in his stomach, too. He tried feebly to push them away.

They wrapped a dishcloth hanging from a nearby laboratory table around the wound as tightly as they could, and then Lenox stepped to a nearby window, opened it, and called out for a constable in his loudest voice. "Police! Police needed!" he called.

Below him he could see the man who had driven Leigh and Rowan here, still dutifully holding Lenox's horse, bless his heart.

For a second the full exertion of the last half hour rose up in him all at once and he laughed, and then realized he was shaking, too. Shock.

Cohen would arrive soon—must. Behind him, Leigh was sitting back on his haunches against the wall, gazing at Rowan, who had fallen into exhausted silence. On the table there was a typewriter, and Lenox, for want of anything better to do, typed the word "assessment" on it, having to hunt for each letter. The exercise gave him the confirmation he had been looking for: This was the typewriter with the weak *s* that had been the source of the original letter written to Leigh concerning his fictitious bequest.

"Who is this Bartram?" asked Leigh.

Lenox shook his head, recriminating with himself. "I should have told you. He wanted to speak to you about what he believed to be some kind of theft of your ideas."

"How could he have known?" asked Leigh, frowning. "I myself never would have suspected Rowan—never, in a million years. A more generous fellow had rarely come across my path, I would have said until fifty minutes ago."

"I cannot say. We must find him, clearly."

"Or ask Rowan."

Lenox looked down at their foe. "He will be up before the Queen's Bench. I don't know how forthcoming he will be."

"No."

"Meanwhile we are left with a question."

"What is that?"

Lenox found himself laughing again, though

more tiredly this time, the shock of the situation wearing off. His muscles were still tremulous. "The same one we have been asking for thirty-odd years. Who was the MB?"

CHAPTER THIRTY-FOUR

Leigh was not destined to make it back to France that evening.

Cohen arrived in Chilton Street. He hailed a wagon from the local station and they were transporting Rowan to the surgery at the Yard. All the blood had drained out of the man's face; but he had recovered consciousness, more or less.

From his stretcher, Rowan made a final gambit, though it cost him an enormous amount of energy. "You mustn't let Gerald Leigh claim credit for my work!" he cried. "He's a thief!"

It was hard to say whose benefit this was for—the constable did not look like someone who kept closely abreast of the latest researches into the nature of microbial organisms—but perhaps Rowan only wanted to plant the seed.

Lenox wanted to harvest one, meanwhile. "You sent those letters with the farthings in them, Rowan?" he asked. "To Middleton? Two to me today?"

Rowan, gazing at him impassively from the

stretcher, didn't reply. But a swift flicker in his eyes, before they moved away, told Lenox the whole story. The first farthing that morning as a threat; the second to distract Lenox long enough that he could isolate Leigh and lure him away from the protection of the crowds at the Society.

After Cohen, Frost arrived. "What, then?" he asked. "Mr. Rowan? I'm baffled, I have to say."

Lenox nodded. "As am I."

"I have rarely met a more solicitous man. You believe he killed Middleton?"

"I do."

They were in the solicitous killer's drawing room, just beyond the front door of the residence. "Why?" Frost asked.

Lenox explained the scientific ambition which had driven Rowan to madness. "The proximity of this place to the central turf of the Farthings cannot be an accident," he said. "It must be how they came to be involved as Rowan's hired intimidators. He couldn't have guessed that we would be able to identify Anderson and Singh from their descriptions so easily."

"They ought to separate those two," said Frost reflectively. "Too easy to spot when they're together."

"Don't tell them and I won't."

Frost chuckled grimly. "No. Certainly not. And yet—I cannot imagine such a distinguished man living here! Who *is* this fellow?"

Across the room, Leigh, who was reading a book, glanced up. "Here you are," he said.

The book was *Who's Who*. Leigh had it open to Rowan's entry.

ROWAN, Alexander George; *born* 1834, *2nd son of* S. Wellington Rowan *and of* Elizabeth Wright, *daughter of* Windsor Wright *of* Calamine Manor, Hants.
Address: 28 Green Park Terrace, W.1.
Educated: Eton College; Peterhouse College, Cambridge.
Recreations: Historical research, botany, chemistry, hunting, chess.
Clubs: Beargarden; Boodle's; Carlton; Oxford and Cambridge; White's.
Arms: Ermine, 3 Rowan Trees Courant, argent; motto: Floreat Rowanensis.

Lenox read this out loud, and then said, "You can see that his listed address is in the West End. This was his private, secondary place."

"Do you know anything of the family?" asked Frost.

"I have always understood him to be very well-born," said Leigh. "I'm sure he was elected copresident of the Royal Society partly on the back of that public school accent I loathe so much."

Lenox sighed. "Well—certainly the Wrights are

well-known in Hampshire. They are connected to the Windsor earldom, which must be how his grandfather came by that name. I do not know anything of the Rowans, but all the signs are there. An aristocrat; pressed by his own ambition, and his own inadequacy, into this mad course. For more information I think we must speak to Bartram."

That was not his first priority, however. He wanted above all to see Jane, and tell her she was safe.

As Frost and a small contingent stayed behind to investigate the contents of the house for information, Lenox wrapped himself in his coat. He had sent the fly and horse home long before, and wondered whether he would be able to get a cab—but Cohen, seeing the question in his face perhaps, informed him that there was a cabstand just around the corner.

"Shall I go with you?" Leigh inquired.

"By all means. Unless you want to stay here?" asked Lenox.

"I see no reason to."

Frost, listening from across the room, only asked Leigh to remain in London so that they could speak with him again soon, and before long the school friends were in a rickety taxi bound for Grosvenor Square.

"Tell me something," Lenox said as they started on their way. "Did you ever confide in anyone else but me about the Mysterious Benefactor?"

Leigh cocked his head, thinking. "I suppose I have over the years, three or four times. In any event I have never been secretive about it."

"Any of them in the Royal Society?"

"No, I think not." Leigh pondered this for a moment. "Wait—yes! I was once on a long trip to Java with a fellow named Milstone. A surgeon, an indifferent lepidopterist, too. We were the only two English-speaking men in a Dutch company— many long hours together, though each of us picked up enough of their language to make do at the officers' supper table. I did tell him of it. I recall that distinctly."

"And do you think he kept the secret?"

Realization dawned on Leigh. "Do you think he told Rowan?"

"I don't know."

"He was no great friend, Milstone, weak in many of the usual ways you find among seafaring gentlemen—a braggart, a drinker, lonesome at bottom. Decent company. I believe he's in Plymouth now, grounded. But he might well have encountered Rowan in London a dozen times since our voyage."

"I wonder, then," said Lenox, "if Rowan has been inquiring after you since last fall, looking for a point of pressure to draw you outside of your Parisian university. That would explain how he knew that you might give credence to such a bequest."

"Yes."

"And of course, too, the use of that phrase: 'a friend,'" said Lenox.

"How devilish. Yes, I would have told Milstone about those words. No doubt of it—they have always stayed in my mind."

"Mine, too."

London was quiet in the soft night, inwardly drawn, cold. When a case had concluded, Lenox always felt a certain melancholy. The futility of the crime was often part of it. The prospect of going without work, too. He dreaded his return to the papers and records of Chancery Lane. He half wondered if Dallington wanted a companion at his solitary vigil in Parliament.

But this was a happy day, he forced himself to think: Leigh was safe, Frost had agreed that the Farthings were both far too scared and too self-interested to pursue a vendetta outside of their own precincts, and especially with Rowan now decommissioned. Indeed, it wasn't even clear whether they knew of Lenox at all. London was safe for him again.

At McConnell's house, Lady Jane, whose face was stony when Lenox first appeared, greeted this news by relenting slightly: a promise kept! Leigh, for his part, immediately sat down cross-legged opposite Sophia and Georgiana McConnell and became engaged in the small construction project they had undertaken.

"This is the portcullis," he said. "Very nicely made."

"Yes, that's the portus to be sure," George agreed seriously.

Sophia glanced nervously at her older cousin, and Lenox felt a huge torrent of tenderness for his daughter, who didn't want to reveal her ignorance of this piece of architecture. But Leigh had moved on, and soon the girls were explaining every element of their castle: where the princess lived; where the princess's father; where the dragons were to be docked.

"I'm having a sister," said George.

"Well, she won't fit in this castle."

The little girl nodded. "No."

Standing above them, Jane said, "Incidentally, Mr. Leigh—where are you staying tonight?"

Leigh looked up. "I hadn't thought of it. Not the place I stayed last night, anyhow. Nor the Collingwood."

"You must stay with us, of course."

Leigh looked prepared to offer some polite cavil, but at that moment Sophia leaned her head against his arm, absorbed in connecting two locking blocks, and he looked up, laughing. "Very well," he said. "That would suit me perfectly."

CHAPTER THIRTY-FIVE

The three of them had a quiet but happy supper at Hampden Lane, all filled with delight to be alive, Lenox and Leigh replaying the scene in the laboratory over and over, correcting each other, filling in each other's memories, Lady Jane a rapt audience of one. There was a cassoulet to eat, and a fine joint served with a mellow French wine, and for dessert, best of all, one benefit of this cold time in the year, a lovely ice cream, flavored with chocolate and with mint from the gardens at Lenox House. It was a day to appreciate how nice a small thing such as this one could be.

As they were sipping coffee, two visitors came by. Both were close friends of Jane's: the Duchess of Marchmain, who was Dallington's mother, and Matilda Duckworth. The hour was an unusual one for a visit, but they both wanted to be sure that Jane was still alive.

"We are, yes," Jane said, "little thanks to my husband."

"*Some* thanks, if I might be permitted to correct you," Leigh put in. "Though mostly it was my ingenious little wad of paper. I wish I could have taken it back in the aftermath of our encounter. I would have treasured it like the grail, whatever old crumpled state it was in—kept it under glass, and made a totem of it."

This enigmatic statement required, of course, a retelling of the afternoon's events, which horrified their guests but had now been told over so many times that there was almost room for something like amusement in Lenox's and Leigh's voices as they described it.

"I know Mr. Rowan's cousin," said Matilda Duckworth. "She is a very sweet girl. I think he's meant to be very rich, Mr. Rowan—more than averagely rich."

Matilda, recently orphaned, was more than averagely poor, and as such judged these matters keenly. "Is he?" asked Lenox curiously.

"From what Effie says, yes. All the parts of London that the Duke of Westminster doesn't own are Rowan's father's—Bethnal Green, Bacon Street, Chilton Street, Liverpool Street, the East End."

Lenox glanced at Leigh, who took a second longer but then slowly realized the import of these words. Chilton Street. Was it possible that Rowan was a very landlord to the Farthings?

Who held the gambling debt of Mr. Ernest Middleton. That would close the circle cleanly.

Their visitors had hoped to entice Lady Jane to come to a musical evening they were attending— but she declined, pleading fatigue, and though it wasn't yet nine o'clock when they had gone, all three of the remaining party agreed that they were very tired, at the end of this very long day. Lenox, for his part, felt as if his body was all at once loaded down with wet sand; he could scarcely wish Leigh a civil good night, and as he went upstairs he heard the blessed sound of Kirk extinguishing the candles of the forward hall. The surest sign of a day's ending.

He slept through the early sunlight of the morning, waking only when two deliverymen in the street outside began to argue. He let his eyes open slowly. A bright day, luxuriously little to do, the prospect of a good breakfast ahead of him.

He went and enjoyed this, divvying up the newspaper with Leigh—Lady Jane, more enterprising than either of them, was already out visiting—and reading it in pleasant silence, broken only occasionally by a passing comment.

"Nothing of Rowan in a single paper," said Lenox.

"How would word have spread?"

"There are informants at the jailhouse, always interested in a boldfaced name. But I wonder if Rowan was able to spend more than the tip was worth to keep the papers silent."

Leigh frowned. "He cannot hope to emerge from this with his reputation intact, can he? Though I suppose it is only our word against his."

The idea troubled Lenox, too. He had been on

the end of that pistol, as well. "We must go and see Mr. Joseph Bartram."

Lenox still had the amateur scientist's calling card. It listed an address in Holborn, not far from his own offices in Chancery Lane. They set out fairly soon after breakfast.

They found Bartram in his office. He answered the door himself. "Mr. Leigh!" he said. "This is a signal honor. I enjoyed your speech immensely. And Mr. Lenox—how do you do?"

"I'm pleased to meet you again," said Lenox.

They followed Bartram into a cozy little room, with a fire blazing, a bookshelf lined with specimens and little framed drawings and silver instruments, and a strong smell of tobacco. There was a very old beagle on the rug in front of the fire, who looked at them and then yawned. "You are fortunate to catch me. In general I only spend the hours of ten to twelve here, to receive visitors, before dining at the Royal Society and passing my afternoons there."

"You are much involved with the Society, I take it?" Leigh asked.

"It is my passion. I told you I was semiretired, Mr. Lenox—nine-tenths retired would be more honest."

"What is your field, sir?" asked Leigh.

They conversed for a few moments, Lenox catching most of it, he thought. Bartram seemed more given to the organizational work of science, classification, organization, than to original research, but Leigh responded to his descriptions of these projects with real warmth, and they were soon discussing minor technical points that threatened to venture beyond Lenox's ken.

At a very brief pause, he said, "But if you could resume this conversation later—Mr. Bartram, we are very eager to know about your suspicions."

Bartram, a thorough but not a rapid thinker, blinked through his half-moon spectacles. "My suspicions? Oh! Ah! My suspicions! Yes, Mr. Lenox—I am glad you have brought Mr. Leigh—I would have forgot—my suspicions, yes."

"You have heard that Mr. Rowan was arrested last night?"

That caught Bartram's attention more quickly. He looked astonished, and then quickly accepting, and then, to Lenox's surprise, heartbroken. "Rowan, was it?" he muttered. "Our president. How very, very sad for the Society—what a stain. But not unexpected, I suppose—no, not unexpected at all, if I think about it."

"Come, Mr. Bartram," said Leigh, "let us in on your thoughts."

"Oh? Ah! Yes." Bartram sighed again, and settled back into his armchair by the fire, putting a hand down to scratch his dog behind the ear. Lenox and Leigh, waiting on a sofa opposite, attended him closely. "The situation arose three months ago, perhaps a little longer. It had to do with the periodical library at the Society."

"Pray go on."

"The library is the clearinghouse for all the papers received as submissions to the Society's journal. They are registered, noted down by our librarian with author, name, and précis, and then left in orderly stacks, where they may be consulted by any fellow of the Royal Society. Recommendations—primarily endorsements—may be left with the librarian. A small committee, which I took a turn serving upon in the year seventy, decides in consultation with the editor which pieces will be published. It is a very profound honor, as Mr. Leigh knows.

"Many fellows go months and years without setting foot in the periodical library, of course. Probably fewer than two dozen take an active interest in the outstanding submissions. Of these, I think I may say that I am exceptionally active. One of my great pleasures in life is to survey the new submissions—to see what discoveries have flowered in our country, recently. I am there every weekday afternoon; I am intimate with the periodical library's contents."

The old man stopped and removed his glasses, rubbing them against his sleeve. "Has this to do with Leigh's papers, then?" asked Lenox.

Bartram nodded. "We received three papers by Mr. Leigh at the end of September. A treasure trove, given that he has not published with the

Society before! May I ask why you decided to, now?"

Leigh shrugged. "I had been invited several times that year by the Society—both to speak, and to write. I think finally I decided it would be well enough to do it."

"I see. As it happened, I nearly missed your papers. There were three of them, and only because I happened to be present when the mail arrived, one day, did I see your return address on the envelope, and, as it was opened, the three separate papers. The next day, they were gone."

"Gone!"

Bartram nodded. "Yes. It was the librarian's clerk who opened them for his master—a boy of fifteen, without any scientific knowledge—and between his opening them, in front of me, and leaving them on the librarian's desk, and the librarian's return the next morning, they had disappeared."

"How very strange."

"And yet not so strange as this: two days later, one of the papers reappeared, and was duly entered in the ledger. In fact it formed the bulk of your recent speech, Mr. Leigh. Your initial discoveries, but not your farther-reaching ones."

Suddenly Lenox saw a partial answer to a question that had been bothering him: Why Rowan was so keen for Leigh to speak.

Leigh, too, looked as if something was dawning

on him. "Two weeks ago, when I was last here, Mr. Rowan warned me not to reveal the contents of the remaining two papers I had submitted, though he assured me that they would be published."

Bartram leaned forward. "Did he! They are not shelved in the library—have not been passed to the committee."

Leigh shook his head slowly. "I took his advice. He said there might be unscrupulous Continental scientists present. That didn't bother me—any man may turn his hand to my work, if he pleases—but as it happened, I hadn't time to address them fully in my speech, anyway. The first paper was more than enough to begin with."

Lenox nodded. "I suppose he was content for you to have credit for that one."

"It was a breakthrough—but it is the third paper, on the growth of microorganisms, that I think may have reverberations across Europe. Rowan asked me to return and speak about it in two months, upon publication."

"By which time you would have been dead, had his plan succeeded," said Lenox, "and he would be the author whose name was appended to them. So that is how he meant to steal your work. Piecemeal, convincingly."

Bartram looked as if he had been thrown into deep waters. "Dead!" he cried. "What is that?"

Leigh grimaced and then explained, to the old

gentleman, the nature of Rowan's misdeeds. Bartram, in his turn, described his own search for the missing papers. He had never spoken to Rowan directly about them; the librarian, meanwhile, had become convinced that there was only ever one paper, which had been briefly mislaid. But Bartram had stubbornly maintained what he had seen, leading to his secretive request for a moment of Leigh's time at the Royal Society's supper two nights before.

It was around noon when the two old Harrovians found themselves at last taking their leave, having consumed a pot of tea and a plate of gingersnaps, and Leigh having promised to dine with Bartram later that week.

As they walked out into the street, Leigh said to Lenox, "Well, there. We have an answer of how Rowan planned to do it." Then putting on his gloves, he added, "You know, that man is the glory of my field."

"Joseph Bartram?"

"Utterly disinterested—utterly fair-minded— committed, generous, honest. He has, I would venture, the precise quantity of brilliance that Rowan does, a modest quantity, that is, more than a layman but not of a sort destined to achieve greatness—and yet how well one turned his abilities to use for our greater good, how pro- ductively, and how evilly the other! Men are strange, Lenox."

"Yes, they are."

"I cannot understand it."

"Because you are gifted," said Lenox. "You have that fortune."

Leigh shook his head. "I suppose so."

"You would hate my work, if you are so easily dispirited by the depths of behavior to which our species can descend."

CHAPTER THIRTY-SIX

Lenox's desk at the offices in Chancery Lane was guaranteed to be a demoralizing vision, and he approached the offices with some gloominess. But it was necessary. Leigh had taken the carriage onward, going to see Frost and provide a more complete accounting of their adventures the day before.

As Lenox entered the sunny main office, he observed immediately that there was a hushed nervousness in the air. A moment later, as muffled but obviously angry voices rose from behind Polly's door, he understood why.

He said a few mild hellos as he walked through the little neighborhoods of the room, wondering whether he ought to go to his own office and leave well enough alone. But curiosity—or concern, if he were more generous with himself—turned his steps at the last moment to join his colleagues.

He knocked on the door, got a very curt invitation to enter, and found himself with Polly and Dallington. Both of them were standing, both, plainly, upset.

He realized that he had a card he had not played—already Rowan's villainy was settled news for him, but he hadn't been to the office again, and they would have had no way of learning of what had passed. "Leigh was shot at yesterday," he said. "I was about a foot from him. Very close quarters, too!"

The anger dropped out of both of his friends'—his partners'—faces right away, and each began at the same time to express their concern and anxiety. "But what happened?" asked Dallington, speaking for both of them.

"We have caught the fellow who killed Middleton, and wanted to kill Leigh, I think," said Lenox. "It was Mr. Alexander Rowan. The president of the Royal Society."

A dozen questions ensued from this declaration, simultaneously again, and by the time Lenox had begun to answer them, detailing the events of the previous afternoon, all three were sitting, Polly in her usual high-backed chair before the large windows of her office, looking out at the smoky chimneys, across from her Dallington and Lenox.

It took some twenty minutes or so to unspool the tale. "Can you make it stick to him?" asked Polly at last.

Lenox shook his head. "We shall see. I fear it may be difficult. It is our word against his."

"There are two of you, at least. Both reputable."

"Yes, true." Then he said, turning a cigar from Polly's desk over in his fingers, hoping they were pacified, "And may I ask how things have been here?"

Immediately an angry guardedness returned to Polly's face. For Dallington's part, when Lenox glanced at him, there was only a resigned look. He was the one who answered. "We have had a letter from Lord Sumlin."

"Who is that?" said Lenox.

"I can't believe we have found someone *Debrett's* knows and you do not!" said Dallington. "A Member of the House of Lords. Dear, dear. What will Lady Jane say?"

"Well? Who is he?"

"He's a lord."

"I had grappled my way that far into the matter, complex though it might be."

"And he is not often in London, living mostly on the Continent—but when he is, I suppose, he doesn't like to have his private use of the back halls impeded. He has written an angry note to Cheesewright because I very gently inquired who he was and why he was visiting the cabinet's private office—the one at the end of our corridor with the broken window, you know."

"I see."

Polly held up the letter. "Direct rudeness," she said. "That is a quotation."

"What an old maid," said Dallington dismissively.

She looked dangerously angry. "You are threatening to leave us two thousand pounds short a year—and our most prestigious standing client. I would beg you not to treat it so lightly."

Lenox frowned. "Can Lord Sumlin's word carry very much weight with Cheesewright, if he is not often present at Parliament?"

Dallington and Polly exchanged a glance. The former tilted his head, then admitted, "Cheesewright is getting rather itchy. Finished business, he says."

"And you disagree."

"It isn't finished business. We still don't know exactly what happened—and right at the heart of the Commons!" Dallington said. "Fifteen feet from the chamber in which you yourself sat for several years!"

Polly looked close to standing again. "We have had this out already for an hour, Charles—the better part of ninety minutes—and I cannot abide the answer Lord John deigns to give me. He is not a free agent. Let us put the issue to a vote. I say that he gives the inquiry up and returns to work. Neither of you has earned a penny for the agency in the last week."

She reddened, perhaps realizing her infelicity so

close to Lenox's brush with death, but said nothing more. Dallington sat there looking neutral. He was never prone to confrontation—and Lenox saw, in his face, almost wholly concealed, a pain, which must have originated from it being Polly who was so angry with him.

But all he said was that he wished to continue.

Lenox weighed his thoughts, and then said, "I think Polly must be right, John. It is not that I do not admire your tenacity—but that I think if Mr. Cheesewright is satisfied, we must be, too. If Lord Sumlin can make matters tenuous for us, imagine what some greater figure, a cabinet minister, could do?"

Dallington looked between them, and then stood up. "I am going to continue for a night, anyway," he said in a mollifying tone, his face etched with irenic apology. "Something is amiss. It has all come too easily, and been too fine, and now they are pushing us away? No. I am not settled in my mind about it."

"John—"

Dallington shook his head, soft in manner but resolute. "They may fire me—or of course you may—but I must follow through on the matter, I fear, for my own conscience."

"When did you develop a conscience?" said Polly.

There was a horrid silence.

The blow, coming from her, had struck too deep—all three of them saw that instantly.

"Excuse me," said Dallington, and picked up his hat and cloak from beside his chair.

Polly and Lenox looked at each other, regret already in her eyes, and then Lenox, after a beat, stood up to follow Dallington. But only long enough to see him ducking out of the office and down the flight of stairs into Chancery Lane.

They did not see him again that day. Lenox—as he had expected—had an interestingly unsteady mountain range of papers along his desk, and three of their inspectors needed urgent help, one of them necessitating a meeting at a local pub with a man named Randolph, who for two pounds and an open bar tab running through midnight sold them the name of an embezzler. (He would vouchsafe the name only to "that Member of Parlyment what works with you.")

As a gesture of conciliation, Lenox, before he left, sent over to the Houses a basket containing a few bites to eat and a bottle of Médoc; if Dallington meant to keep his vigil, he might as well be provisioned.

When he returned home he found that Leigh and Lady Jane were playing cards, laughing over something. Both looked so full of happiness to see him that his heart, hardened by the afternoon's work, immediately softened, and he settled down with a sigh into a third chair, asked Kirk to bring him something to eat—anything, it needn't be hot—and then took up a hand of cards himself.

"The news of my day is that I am to be brought suit against," said Leigh. "By Rowan."

"What!" said Lenox. *"Rowan?"*

"Yes. I have been stealing his work for years, it emerges."

"That is nerve, I must say. Can anyone believe it?"

Leigh shrugged. "I hope not. The scientific trail does not bear him out, and he could not re-create my results were Isaac Newton himself to come and garland his brow for the achievement—but any man may say any word he likes, in a court of law, and test the credulity of his fellow citizens."

"You seem awfully calm."

Leigh looked mystified. "I? Oh—well, I know it to be false."

He had always been a fellow out of the ordinary way, Lenox thought, and with a shake of his head laid down a knave atop his wife's four.

The next morning was genuinely warm, chasing the last banks of snow down a foot before ten, watching them vanish, in full retreat, into the watery, bright streets by noon. It made the city more cheerful.

And yet not the office at Chancery Lane: Polly was in a fearsome temper, querying old expenses to their benefit, shouting at Anixter, while Lenox snapped at one of the clerks that he needed half an hour, an hour, without intrusion. The mood was sour. Dallington was often gone—but then, he was often there, too. He was more than a talisman, but his good cheer, his idle words, his neat appearance, Lenox realized, were essential to the happy workings of the agency. When at lunchtime he left to go see Frost and Leigh, he felt their absence himself.

CHAPTER THIRTY-SEVEN

Frost was in equal parts pleased and frustrated, Lenox found, arriving to meet him at Scotland Yard—pleased to have found the murderer of Middleton, frustrated that he could not extract a confession from him. A careful search of both Rowan's home and his laboratory on Chilton Street had turned up no incriminating papers.

"Even if we found Leigh's missing articles," Frost said, "they aren't enough to convict him of murder. Some scientific papers, in the possession of such a man. What jury could find that unusual?"

"Was there nothing at all out of the ordinary?"

"Nothing. And yet we now definitively know that he *owns* the building that houses the Blue Peter, the very public house of the Farthings itself! We are leaning mightily upon the gang's members we have in custody to implicate him, but they are holding steady, filthy, gap-toothed, knockabout lot that they are."

"Hm."

"Sooner or later we shall have to let them go. Meanwhile Anderson and Singh may well have murdered a woman in Cheapside last night. Unconnected. A baker's wife." Frost sighed. "Ugly, ugly, ugly."

Leigh was present again to offer his consultation, and he and Frost and Lenox went through the case point by point, searching for the moment when Rowan might have exposed himself. There was the typewriter, but that was weak proof; Middleton's meetings at the Collingwood, but those were highly circumstantial; Beaumont, who had finally returned, looking, according to Frost, as scared as a schoolboy who had seen a mouse, could not attest that he had ever seen his partner in conversation with Rowan. The connection to the Farthings had existed for years.

Leigh grew graver as this litany of misses was stated. "What is our recourse, then, gentlemen?" he asked.

Frost and Lenox looked at each other uncomfortably. The courts were odd. Many a sixteen-year-old boy had been hanged on slender evidence; but on the other hand, a well-bred person, testifying on his own behalf, without more than another man's word against him, always stood a chance. Then there was the slippery matter of juries, which so stubbornly followed their own logic. Lenox had once attended a trial at which a boy of thirteen, who had stolen a horse in plain sight of twenty-five people, was convicted of stealing a bridle—the horse following along quite incidentally, the jury explained, which happened to free them from the responsibility of sending him to the gallows. Very sensible, their prevarication, in that case.

But it showed the unpredictability of the thing. In three months' time Rowan might easily be free.

Frost and Lenox explained the situation to Leigh, who listened carefully. At last, he said, "I think it is my turn to play detective again, then, since you have had yours, gentlemen."

"What do you mean?"

But he wouldn't be drawn out; saying, only, that he had to pay a call to the Royal Society.

At Chancery Lane again that afternoon, Lenox was surprised to receive a call from Graham. He appeared, with his small unflappable smile, at around three o'clock.

"You're most welcome!" said Lenox. "Here, sit. Will you take a cup of tea?"

"I would, very gratefully," said Graham.

Lenox popped his head out and asked their landlady to fix it. Coming back, he said, "I am surprised to see you here. Parliament is in session this evening, is it not?"

"It is. I am to speak."

Lenox smiled. "It has been too long since I came

and sat in the gallery. But then, it has been a busy time."

"Have you had a case?" asked Graham.

"Indeed I have—the one to do with my old friend Leigh, which I mentioned when we dined."

"And is it resolved?"

"It is—for now."

Lenox told the story once again, and Graham, as he generally did, asked a few probing and thoughtful questions. He was extremely curious about Rowan; the father, he said, had several seats in the House at his command, and held one for himself on the Tory side, though it was rare to see him attend. This was the kind of political trivia that had once been at Lenox's own fingertips, but now he was surprised to hear it.

When they had exhausted the subject of Rowan and Leigh, however, Graham said, "I am here on other business."

"Business? Are you?"

"There are strong motions under way to release this agency from its post in Parliament."

Lenox, taken aback, repeated, "Motions?"

"Yes. I have heard of it several times today already—and given our particular affiliation, I feel certain I am not hearing the worst of it. Word has been spreading. Too intrusive; too little use. One of the gentler terms I heard was 'incompetent.' It feels like a campaign against you."

Lenox ought to have been disturbed by this

news, but instead he was confused. "Incompetent," he said. "And yet we have resolved the most recent cases Mr. Cheesewright has put before us. As for an intrusion—I know Lord Sumlin—"

"Not a serious person."

"He has been complaining. But I cannot imagine Dallington affecting the daily interactions of any of the House's Members. I don't doubt you in the slightest, you understand—I am only taken aback."

Graham's lips tightened in thought, as he considered this. "We know that there are Members who wish you ill."

"Monomark."

The agency's old partner, LeMaire, had become a rival, under the unscrupulous patronage of Lord Monomark, an eagle-eyed and vindictive press baron. "There are also people you voted against— the average rub of disagreement that you find in politics."

"They have held their tongues till now, if it's them—the Wickstroms and Killingsworth-Smiths of the world."

"Perhaps they have found their moment," said Graham, shrugging.

The tea came in. The old friends passed an amiable twenty minutes drinking it, and yet Lenox saw that something was amiss in Graham, and when the latter departed, offering as his apology for visiting so quickly the evening schedule of

Parliament, he felt again that Graham must, perhaps, have been unlucky in love. Lenox had invited him to Hampden Lane to dine the next night—offering Leigh as an inducement, "a capital fellow, you know"—but Graham regretfully declined, busy as ever.

When he had gone, Lenox, sipping the sweet final ounces of his tea, had a realization that should have been obvious but struck him as significant: Rowan must have an office at the Royal Society, in addition to those at his home and in Chilton Street.

He sent a note asking Frost to meet him there, and at a little after six o'clock they were again in the building's large and charming rotunda.

Rowan's office was in an aerie overlooking London's smoking rooftops. There was a large appointment book on the desk, and Frost and Lenox both made a beeline for it. In the event it was rather drear—tidy inked reminders of very specific duties at the Society—but Lenox was intrigued to see that the day of Middleton's murder had an appointment not far from the solicitor's office in it.

"Perhaps that is our angle," he said to Frost. "Tracking his movements upon that day."

"I'm going to fetch his secretary to see what he can remember. It was scarcely a week ago."

But the secretary was gone for the day, and as the light failed Lenox and Frost had to examine the room alone. They found nothing resembling Leigh's papers—many, however, in Rowan's own hand, describing various actions of the microbe. Were these the plagiarisms? Lenox put them in his valise to show to Leigh.

They left, each a little discouraged, but agreeing that they would return the next morning to speak to those who had been closest professionally to their quarry. A tacit agreement had emerged in the conversation between them, somehow: They couldn't leave it to an amateur scientist to find proof of a murder in the very heart of London, their city.

That evening Leigh was out, and Lenox and Lady Jane had the kind of old, happy supper that he remembered so well from his bachelor days, when they were only neighbors, and yet near enough that neither needed an invitation to enter the other's house—days when their love had been unspoken, perhaps even unrealized, and yet, like a spring within the earth, moving with cautious ceaselessness toward the day it would surface. When he went to bed, it was in a state of contentment.

A voice woke him in the dead of night. "Sir," it said, low, but urgent, from the doorway. "Mr. Lenox. Sir."

Lenox struggled up to his elbows, still half away. He glanced at the dark lavender light behind the diaphanous curtains. The late calls of a detective had skilled him in guessing the time over the years. Just three o'clock, he would have said.

"What is it, Kirk? Is Sophia all right?"

"She is, sir." There was an unwonted note of sorrow and sympathy in the undemonstrative butler's voice. "It's Lord John, sir. Mr. Cheesewright has sent word for you. His Lordship has fallen from the roofs of Parliament—three stories— altogether deprived of consciousness—may not live the night."

CHAPTER THIRTY-EIGHT

Prostitution was not illegal in London. One could be arrested for it, to be sure—but only on some auxiliary charge. "Annoying passersby," for instance, or "public drunkenness." It was one of the stranger facts of their judgmental age, which in most matters of morality condescended dreadfully toward England's prior eras—the highwayman lawlessness of Queen Elizabeth's time, the libertinism of the Restoration, the debauchery of the Regent's reign.

Lenox thought of this very Victorian paradox as he saw, from his carriage window, the night's women ranged along the periphery of Green Park. It was awfully cold, and they were huddled around barrels of fire. It filled his spirit, already heartsick over fear for Dallington, with something like a mortal sorrow. Like the majority of his friends, and in fact many of his more sincerely Christian friends too, he could never fault these women for their choice of work—money was scarce and allocated unfairly, gin and bodies were cheap and allocated without much partiality at all—and yet he might wish such a different life for them than this. Was the law the answer? Gladstone had gone into the alleys to preach to them; Dickens had founded a house where they might retire, these women; and yet here they were, along Green Park, waiting out the hours of the night.

What a vale of tears the world could seem at the wrong hour, in the wrong place, and particularly when you had heard the wrong news.

In the instant after Lenox had absorbed Kirk's information he had been out of bed. "Get the horses up, please."

"I gave the order immediately, sir."

"Thank you. Was there a note?"

"No, sir. The messenger came only with word. Lord John is in the Parliament's infirmary."

"Very good."

"Can I offer any assistance, sir?"

"Send for McConnell. Go round yourself if you must."

Kirk nodded. "Immediately, sir."

Lenox was dressed in under a minute, down-stairs in four long strides. Kirk, waiting in the front hall, handed him his coat, gloves, and hat. Through the narrow band of window by the door, Lenox saw Rackham perched unmoving atop his box, the little orange glow of his cigar occasionally intensifying and then fading.

"Wish him luck, Kirk."

"I will, sir. Give His Lordship our very best—all of us, sir. The finest gentleman."

The finest gentleman! That was not Dallington's reputation, of course; London was quick to name a person, and devilishly slow to unname him.

The cab moved quickly through the silent streets. Down Whitehall, the enormous gray buildings stood alone, without sentry. Always a strange experience to see nature's light in a city— a reminder that humans, for all they had built, were not automatic, were not essential, were not indispensable.

There was a low lantern slung above the visitors' gate of Parliament. Lenox stepped down from the carriage and knocked on the door.

A night porter was there. "Who is that?" he asked.

"Charles Lenox. You must remember me from my own days here, Drinkwater."

"Of course I do, sir, of course. A differing context is all, sir. Of course I do. If you are here for Lord John Dallington, he is in the infirmary."

"Have you seen him?"

"Yes, sir."

"How is he?"

"I cannot say, sir. Not being in the medical line myself at all."

And yet Drinkwater's face had answered the question. They walked quickly through the back corridors. "Who found him?"

"The other night porter, sir, Wilson."

"Where?"

"Directly beneath the south gate. There was a crash."

Lenox thought of this: just beneath the knee-high crenellations that made Parliament appear so beautiful from the opposite side of the river. His stomach turned over at the thought of it. He had been on that roof. Could one survive a fall from such a height?

The infirmary was one of Parliament's little peculiarities. It was in a room canted just so over the river, and was provided for emergencies like this one, rather than for lengthy care—though Lenox had heard of it being used most often when a Member was dead drunk, or, in the more generous parlance given out to the press, "tired and emotional." He could picture it from his first tour of the building, small, with a single cot and a medicine stand in the corner. He hadn't been back since.

He tracked Drinkwater's squat, hurried gait through various slender hallways, up two stairwells, down the reverse of a small hidden corridor. "Who is with him?" he asked.

"The physician we have on call from Harley Street, Melman, and his assistant. Along with Mr. Cheesewright, of course."

"And what has Melman said?"

"Nothing to me, sir."

They came to the door. Drinkwater tapped gently upon it, and pushed it open.

Inside there was the low light of a single candle, flaming back at itself from the window, growing large and small in its own shadows against the wall as it quivered. Three men were standing toward one side of the room, Cheesewright among them.

Lenox looked at Dallington and gasped.

He had been expecting a calmly comatose patient—but here was carnage, devastation.

Dallington's left leg was elevated. The pants were ripped back to reveal a huge, open wound, and the sickening white gleam within it of bone. The arms were folded over his chest, hands enrobed in bandages, one of the elbows horrifically out of joint.

And his face, his poor face—a mass of red and black, the hair shorn away in huge uneven swaths, cuts crossing it.

The doctor was in shirtsleeves. He looked at Lenox. "Family member?"

"Yes," said Lenox.

"Virtually," said Cheesewright.

"Will he live?" asked Lenox.

Melman looked him directly in the eye. He was a large, ruddy man, with huge hands. "I don't think so."

Lenox felt his heart cave in. "No?"

The doctor shook his head. "The damage to his internal organs is severe. There is blood in them. He has not regained consciousness—is concussed, certainly—no. He will not survive this fall. We will attempt to keep him alive. We have sewn him and patched him where we could. But I do not think he will live to see the dawn."

Lenox looked at the window. Already there was some paling in the sky.

He went and sat on the small stool by the bed. His inclination was to reach out and touch Dallington's brow—how young he looked!—but he reached for his hand. "I'm here with you, John," he murmured. "Just so you know."

There were perhaps two or three minutes of silence. Finally, the doctor said, "There is fever, sir. We must apply the cold compresses."

Lenox nodded and stood. He and Cheesewright stepped into the hall. "What happened?" asked Lenox.

"I don't know. There was this note at his station, however."

Lenox saw an envelope with his own name on it—again. Polly's was next to it. He grabbed the envelope and ripped it open. Inside, in a desperately quick hand, was a line from Dallington.

306

Nothing to do with lovers. It's Labrenz. Giving chase.

Lenox stifled a gasp. Labrenz was a Prussian spy, wanted throughout England. He'd been thought dead for nearly a year now.

They would never have even imagined a connection between him and the broken window. But now, his mind racing, Lenox wondered what the truth of the business in Parliament had been. Was the story of the lovers' quarrel a red herring, designed to lead them off the scent of the real reason Labrenz was there—something to do, presumably, with affairs of state, after all?

It had come too easily, that information about the affair, even Polly had acknowledged that, the chattering servants revealing without any hesitation what had supposedly gone on between Lord Beverley and Mr. Winslow, all of it second-hand, their sources perhaps not in on any particular lie, but only too happy to gossip it forward. He, Polly, and Cheesewright had all been too credulous. Only Dallington had felt that something was off. And meanwhile, a spy had been lurking around Parliament, the true cause behind that broken window.

Which meant—he realized—that it was eminently possible that Dallington had been pushed.

As he was reckoning with this information there

was a footfall in the hallway behind him. Wilson, the other porter, appeared, leading McConnell.

"Lenox!" cried the doctor. He was carrying his leather bag. "For Christ's sake, what's happened? Kirk came to my door."

"It's Dallington," said Lenox. "He fell from a great height. The physician—a man named Melman—says he won't live two hours."

McConnell pushed forward without hesitation. "What utter nonsense. Melman is a fool. Let me see him."

CHAPTER THIRTY-NINE

Dallington made it into the morning hours of the new day, long enough that, had he been conscious, he would have heard the world awaken and begin its gradual reclamation of its daylight routines: deliveries first of all, daily servants second, then slowly the workers, and then the clerks, a ceaseless processional in the streets of black jackets and furled black umbrellas. Last of all, mingled in among them, and not looking so very different, the Members of Parliament.

And yet McConnell was worried—too worried to move his patient. Melman's dark prognostication, Lenox could see, had perhaps not been so cynical that it could be declared wrong outright.

McConnell called in help immediately, first a

friend from the surgeon's college, then another from Harley Street. They passed the hour of seven o'clock in grave conference, phrases falling from their mouths that Lenox misliked: compound fracture; hemorrhage of the kidneys; concussion; damage to the cranial hemispheres; and worst, far and away the worst, "ease of passage."

At last McConnell turned to him. Cheesewright had gone, as had Melman and his assistant. "We cannot move him. My colleagues and I agree."

"Will he survive?"

One of the men's faces said no; the other said it was difficult to say. For his part, McConnell nodded firmly. "If he makes it past noon, which he will, then he will survive. Yes."

"What is wrong with him?"

"Generally—everything. Acutely—there is internal bleeding."

"And how shall you handle it?"

"A great deal depends upon his constitution."

The news went out that day. Edmund was the first to stop by, having heard from Cheesewright, and then Jane, evidently having been apprised of the news by Kirk. She wished to know how Dallington's parents were to be informed. Lenox didn't have any idea. When she said, steeling herself, that she would do it, he felt grateful, realizing that he had been anticipating the horrible task as his own—and then, chiding himself, offered to do it.

But she was close to Dallington's mother. Jane reappeared together with the duchess an hour later, this older lady, always so comfortable a figure, transformed into one instead of terrible austere grief, streaks of tears lining her face. She was as set upon her son's bedside as an arrow upon its target, ignoring all the people nearby, including Lenox. She went and sat beside her son, brushing his hair back. Thereafter she didn't move.

The minutes crept by. There was a crisis just after eleven o'clock, a convulsion rising in Dallington's body. His color was suddenly awful, something like a very pallid sea green.

"Christ," said McConnell, and without ceremony pushed Dallington's mother aside. "He's having a seizure."

They were all expelled from the room except for the duchess. Her husband appeared, deeply grave.

At the same time, Lenox was being pulled away by a series of increasingly alarmed officials. All of them wanted to hear it for themselves: Labrenz? At noon, he went up to the roof with Drinkwater and a diplomat named Barkley. This was a difficult part of the building to gain access to from the inside, and yet, a flaw, not terribly difficult from the outside, provided you could do a bit of climbing.

They looked down. Two sets of footprints; no others.

"This is where he fell," said Drinkwater.

They all peered over the edge at the flagstone court below. Lenox felt a wave of nausea—a visceral terror. Hell, to fall that distance, just long enough to register the pain that you were about to experience. There was a disturbance in the muddied snow below, and he saw, amid it, even from this distance, a crumpled red flower—the carnation that Dallington always wore in his buttonhole.

Up on the roof, one trail of footprints continued on toward the east side of the building, hardened in the icy snow. It left off by a drainage pipe. Barkley had seen all he needed to. "Thank you, Lenox," he murmured. "I must go now."

"And Labrenz?"

"If he is in this country, he will be found. The danger is that he is not."

"Papers are missing, then?"

Barkley was no fool—a young man with hair parted slickly to one side, endowed with heavy responsibilities. "We cannot yet know. It would be of immense value to hear His Lordship's account of last night's events."

Lenox nodded, agreeing; though the significance each man would find in such a conversation differed.

At one o'clock Polly arrived. Her cheeks were colored, her bearing rigid. "Is he in there?"

"Yes."

She went in, and Lenox followed her—but while

the impulse of her body, he saw, was to move toward the bed, Dallington's mother was in the way, and so she merely stood, upright and silent, watching.

In the hall again, some time later, she asked, "Will he live?"

"I think so."

She gave him a searching stare. "And it was Labrenz."

Lenox nodded. "I think so."

"Then John was right." She looked away. "It came too easily, I see now, all the information we received—the misinformation—about the cabinet ministers' private room."

Lenox nodded. "And the foolish complaints about Dallington's presence. Their side, again."

Polly looked as if she could hate herself. She took a moment, piecing through the information she had. Then she looked up and said, "I must ask if you will go and organize the office."

Lenox frowned. "But—"

"I know he is your old friend. But only one of us is going to marry him when he wakes up."

He nodded. "I'll go now," he said. "Please tell his family I'll be by again this evening."

Time never passes, until it does. There was the slow, agonizing night, during which Dallington had another seizure, one that this time almost finished his life. A cot was brought into the infirmary; McConnell slept there. The next morning went. A few small swallows of water were imposed upon the patient, and one of broth. An afternoon then; and another night, more stable.

Lenox, true to his word, made the office his business: with two of them gone there was a great deal to be delegated that had never been delegated before, and Pointilleux became an indispensable ally, assuming more responsibility than ever he had theretofore.

And yet Lenox was back at Parliament whenever he could be. His brother came up regularly, bringing food and wine to those assembled outside of the small room.

It was on the fourth day that McConnell felt just enough confidence in Dallington's condition—it had been two days since his body last seized, his fever had declined slightly, his broken bones were expertly set, and his body was already regenerating the skin around his wounds—to move him. He was taken to his parents' house. It was more awkward for Polly to go there; and yet she did. It didn't fall to her to keep vigil at his bedside, but she was the one who brought in flowers, who brought flasks of beef tea to McConnell and his satellites, who made herself indispensable. Lenox had never seen a person so determined.

Meanwhile Dallington's final encounter continued to obsess the governmental officials Lenox saw more and more of. Labrenz was not in the capital, that anyone could determine, and gone with him were papers of significance.

"And yet," said Barkley, who checked in daily to see if Dallington had awoken, "many fewer than would have been taken otherwise—only one of the drawers forced open, and the rest still locked. Your friend did well."

Had done well; and also did well, his fever improving further, his color also, and something ineffable releasing itself in his body, a tension that had been held there from the first moments Lenox saw him, as if only now had he truly fallen into a deep rest.

"I think the worst is past," McConnell said on the fifth day, in a subdued voice, standing in a dim hallway. "But I feel I ought to warn you, so that you may inform the duke and duchess, that now it is all up to chance. He may wake up ten minutes from now. But it is also possible that he will die in the morning, or that he will be in this coma a year, a decade. His entire life."

"What seems most likely?"

"I cannot say, sincerely."

McConnell looked crestfallen, and Lenox put a hand on his shoulder. "You have been a hero. Thank you."

"Give it a week, and see how that word 'hero' becomes revised." McConnell sighed. "He is the finest of fellows, Dallington. And he is so amiable in his manners that I'm not sure who ever remembers to tell him so."

CHAPTER FORTY

McConnell gave Lenox this word of warning at a moment when Dallington's many friends were heartened by his apparent progress. Ten minutes had seemed a more likely horizon for his wakening than ten days, certainly.

And yet the tenth day came and went, and Dallington had not awoken. McConnell passed the case to a specialist in such matters—concern having shifted now to deterioration of the muscle, nourishment of the body, rather than sheer survival.

The attendees at the young lord's bedside were loyal but more intermittent. All except two: Polly, and his mother, both constantly near him.

All manner of rumor crossed the city. The chief among these was that Dallington had been in a duel. It was shocking how few people knew, even now, that he was a detective. Most assumed that he had been drunk when he found his way into mischief.

Ten days, then eleven, then twelve, an aching inversion of time, since each day brought them not nearer to hope, even if it must inexorably mean they were closer to his waking, but farther from it. Lenox began to notice an alarming loss of weight in the young lord. His cheeks were thin, his shanks withering.

During this time, Lenox found that he took great comfort in the presence of his old friend Leigh. It had been his expectation that after Rowan was arrested, Leigh would breathe a sigh of relief and return to Paris. That return had been delayed by Dallington's misfortune—Leigh's own experience as a surgeon had been valuable, another voice—but in fact, even after a week, he seemed to have no interest in leaving London.

He quickly became a beloved and consoling presence at Hampden Lane. He had endless patience for Sophia's games; with Jane he would happily discuss books, people, ideas; and he and Charles barely needed to speak, though often they did, suppers lingering far past the warmth of the dishes that constituted them. It would be impossible to imagine a less intrusive guest, though he did keep odd hours, departing, sometimes, at midnight, and returning after dawn, sleeping very early one morning and very late the next.

"What are you occupying yourself with out in the city?" Lenox asked finally.

It was a late January day about a fortnight after Dallington's fall. Leigh was putting his scarf on in the front hallway, preparing to leave the house. "Eh? Oh—well, it's stuck in my head, you know. The Rowan business."

Lenox smiled wanly. "I can imagine, yes."

"Well, I'm having a whack at it, if you must know."

He would reveal no more than that.

Two weeks from the day after Dallington's accident, the patient suddenly took a turn for the worse.

That was the doctor's drab and unilluminating phrase, which Polly had repeated, but it didn't prepare Lenox for the reality when he visited him in the afternoon. McConnell was back, having been entreated by the Duchess of Marchmain to return and supervise. When he saw Lenox, he gave a slight shake of his head.

"What is it?" asked Lenox, when they finally had a moment alone together.

"The fever is back. I think there may be an infection internally."

"An infection."

"Yes." McConnell looked pale. "I must warn you that this kind of disease is wont to move very, very quickly at such a stage."

"What do you mean?" McConnell didn't reply. "Should he go to the hospital?"

"No. Not just now."

"Come now."

"Charles, you must listen. I think he will go."

Death took place at home, of course, a universal fact across all classes. You didn't go to the hospital unless you expected to get better. Certainly you didn't go there to die.

McConnell went back into the patient's sickroom, and Lenox went to wait.

He would never forget sitting alone in the duke's grand music room that afternoon. There had been a hundred evenings of amusement and celebration here. Now it was as desolate as an empty ocean, the light going iron gray as the sun faded, the carefully situated picture frames and sofas and silver bowls each reproached by their own frivolity. It was intensely sad. In Lenox's mind was the business of the next day. The terrible black-edged paper would have to be bought; the terrible black-edged envelopes; the terrible black wax, to seal the news in forever; the length of black velvet, fetched by a servant from some blessedly forgotten box below stairs, and affixed once more to the door knocker, to muffle its sound. All of the things that meant: A person is gone.

It was four o'clock when Polly came. Lenox, wishing to spare her the implications of McConnell's prognosis, tried to begin their conversation lightly. "Cold out?"

She flicked on a gas lamp, quite at home. "Yes, very."

"Where is Anixter?"

"Outside. He doesn't mind the cold, you know. But what about this—we have had news about Rowan, from Inspector Frost."

"Oh?"

"They have been trying to connect him to Middleton, and they have found a barman who remembers the two of them meeting at the

Collingwood more than once. He knew Rowan well, and happened to know Middleton's face because he had once worked at a different hotel closer to the chancery courts."

"Arrogant of Rowan to meet Middleton where he was known."

Polly tilted her head philosophically. "Perhaps. I doubt he thought it would end in murder."

"True."

"If only the Farthings would talk. But I think it would take a miracle."

Lenox hesitated, and then said, "Polly, when you told me that he had taken a turn for the worse—it's the very much worse."

"What? What do you mean?"

She had become so intimate a colleague of Lenox's that it was strange to see her, in that instant, for the pale, slender, beautiful young widow she was, making her way through life more or less alone. Her pragmatism, too, some-how diminished both her vulnerability and her femininity, in one's eyes—a necessity, in all probability. Lenox thought of when she had first come to their attention as Miss Strickland: her mischievous attempt to hire McConnell as a criminal investigator, her ingenious employment of a charcoal portraitist. A formidable person, Polly Buchanan.

Just at that moment McConnell came into the room.

Lenox knew instantly that something had changed. "What is it?" he asked.

"He is awake."

Polly half rose, her cheeks going red. "Awake! That is the most welcome news."

"Awake, but feverish. He is speaking almost exclusively about Mr. Labrenz."

They had confided that name in McConnell. "But this must be good news!" said Lenox.

McConnell nodded cautiously, but his face was flushed with color. "Yes. Yes, I think it is. It's possible that it was merely a fever he caught, in his weakened state, rather than an infection. He may be improving."

Polly looked at Lenox, realizing what he had been about to say. "May we see him?"

"At the moment—no. But I thought you would like to know."

They stayed long into the night. Lady Jane came over at eight o'clock, bringing them supper, then closeting herself with her old friend, the duchess, for a long, long time. There was no change in his condition; when at last they left, it was in an odd mood of optimistic anxiety. Their hopes had been relocated so many times they'd forgotten where they left them last.

The next morning was cool, steely, mundane, with a light sharp rain falling across the gray buildings. Lenox and Polly both had a tremendous amount of work to do in the office, and they had agreed that they would meet at Dallington's early to check on him before they went to Chancery Lane together.

She looked nervous. "It has been at least six or seven hours since I saw you," she said. Lenox noticed she was wearing a soft gray and pink frock coat over a dress, different than what she usually had on at the office. "How goes it?"

"I am ready for it to be springtime," said Lenox.

The person who came out to see them was the duchess herself. "There you are," she said. "Would you like to see John?"

"Is he well enough?" asked Lenox.

But the question had answered itself—his mother's face was a portrait of relief.

"He's in the finest fettle," she said. "I can barely believe it. So well that McConnell left at half two to get some rest—said that he wanted to catch up with the patient's, ha! The duke is asleep too, no less."

"I'm so very happy to hear it," said Lenox.

Polly didn't even speak; only nodded her fervent agreement. "He is very hoarse and very thirsty—not yet hungry," said the duchess. "Some head-ache, which as I understand it is to be expected. Weak. But alert, very alert. Indeed the first thing he insisted on doing was writing out an account of what happened."

"Did he?"

"Yes—after what seemed incredible labor. I have just given it to Mr. Barkley."

Suddenly Polly couldn't hold herself back anymore. "May we go in?" she said. "He is not asleep?"

"No! Go in—I have to send a wire. The nurse-maid is there, should he show any signs of disturbance. But the doctors are happy. For once."

Lenox barely knew what to expect. The room was unlit, the patient reclining upon the bed, his gaze turned toward the window, which was running with streaks of rain.

He turned his head and saw them enter. His face was ineffably different. Was it older? Was it more careworn? Or was this only a passing change?

"Hello," he croaked softly.

Polly, heedless of anything else, ran to the bed. "There you are," she said.

Dallington smiled, with a ghost of his old humor on his face. "Nowhere else."

She took his hand in hers and bent her head low toward his, by all appearances unconscious of Lenox's presence in the room. "You must marry me, you know. Will you?"

He looked at her for a long moment, with infinite exhaustion in his eyes, and then said, without any happiness, Lenox thought, and in a voice still hoarse, "Yes."

CHAPTER FORTY-ONE

T hroughout the entire spring of that year, Lenox drove himself very hard. He worked from morning to noon and noon to night, all Saturdays and most Sundays, over meals, after the house on Hampden Lane had gone to sleep— he gave himself to the business of the agency, compensating for Dallington's absence by redoubling his efforts.

A great deal of this involved the tedious but crucial work of reading through reports about various minor incidents at the businesses that kept Lenox, Dallington, and Strickland on retainer, to identify patterns that might foreshadow a larger crime, in particular a financial one. He found he had a gift for this kind of close, connecting work. Though that didn't mean he was fond of it.

Whenever he looked up, the agency had hired someone new—a medical specialist, a translator (so immediately useful that Polly was already thinking of adding a second), a new clerk or page. Suddenly, here was that elusive thing, success. They had never made more money.

And yet, as Lenox woke one late March Thursday, he discovered that he had no appetite for the day's work. He couldn't recall the last time he had investigated a case on his own, unless it was Leigh's.

This was a temporary state of affairs—they were looking for someone to do precisely his job, and indeed had offered Frost the position, though the inspector had declined—but it had worn on him.

And when he stepped outside to see what the weather was like, and saw the small, soft buds on the trees, saw the gentle yellow sun rising in the morning sky, and felt a mild warm breeze such as they hadn't experienced since the autumn before, he decided that he would take the day off. An hour later he was on his way to a place he hadn't been in a long time: Harrow School.

An interesting fact that Harrow illustrated was how much a distance of ten miles had changed in England in the last few centuries. The school's founder had left the overwhelming majority of his fortune to the maintenance of a highway that length, between London and the little village where he began the school. It seemed like nothing now, an hour's carriage ride, but in those early modern days it had been rather a long journey. His foresight had guaranteed that London's great families weren't sending their sons down a dank road, crossed with fallen trees and lined with thieves. As much as anything, this was the fact that had allowed Harrow to become so prestigious.

At about eleven o'clock, Lenox found himself passing up London Road, approaching the school grounds. Alongside the right hand of the carriage was an idyllic grove which Leigh, particularly, had loved, investigating the little tidepools and undergrowths between its close-ranged trees.

Lenox remembered a brilliant fall afternoon that the two of them had passed there, with huge banks of orange and pink clouds gliding through the sky, a smoky smell in the air. They'd gone out riding— Edmund, in one of his moments of decency, had let them have seconds on a pair of horses he and his friend St. Cross had hired for the weekend in order to ride into London, their rightful perquisite as monitors.

"Bring them back to the owner and you can have them for a few hours first," Edmund said. "He's just a quarter mile down from the school gate—Denham, the farmer there."

"Thanks, Ed," Charles had said.

"Oh, don't mention it. I shall be forced to murder you in your sleep if you lose them, incidentally. Probably by smothering you with a pillow. Understood?"

"Understood."

In truth Lenox probably would have selected Gray or Almondsley-West to go riding with him, except that there was a house cricket match that day, which he was missing because he had had a badly sprained wrist. He had therefore invited Leigh. He remembered it particularly well because Leigh had talked about his family, which he rarely did. They were very poor—shockingly so, by Harrow standards, and still more shocking that Leigh should admit it. Most of the boys of lesser fortune bluffed their way through conversations about money.

Leigh, though he didn't mention it much, told Lenox without any special ceremony that he and his mother now used their tea leaves three or four times. "We had a fearful row this summer about whether a fourth time was too much."

Lenox couldn't help but think about all the food he had consumed in Leigh's room, and vowed internally to repay him. He wondered how the mother spared that—but was too delicate to ask. Perhaps there was a kindly cousin or aunt involved. "I think I must be awfully spoiled," he said, by way of reply.

Leigh, sitting his horse awkwardly—he really was a squib—shrugged. "By any standard we all are," he said.

"Yes, I expect that's true."

"It would have been different if my father were still alive, of course. That's how it goes, though."

"Do you miss him dreadfully?"

They happened to be passing through a little clearing, and the bright sun had blinded both of them. Leigh lifted a hand. "I suppose I do," he had said. "We used to go to two hills along the seaside, about a half mile apart, and signal to each other."

"Signal?"

"Yes—a very rudimentary version of the telegraph. The kind the French still have. We each had nine little panels, and my father made us up two codebooks. Four white panels, one half white in the middle, and four blacks meant 'end transmission,' for instance, and there was an alphabet for spelling things out more laboriously. He was tremendous fun like that. Always had a plan. And I was his only son too—and so I think I always felt special. We would telegraph back and forth about specimens we found, and make plans for what time to meet and eat the sandwiches my mother had packed for us. In all honesty it would have been just as easy to go about together, but it was a thrill to have a secret code."

"He sounds a top."

"He was rather. My mother is much stricter. It's not half so fun. She's a good egg, but somehow it's less . . . less exciting, I suppose. We never have a proper conversation. She's always worrying at me about school, or my shirt being ripped, or writing a thank-you note to someone or other I don't care about."

They rode on in silence for a moment, and then Leigh spotted something and jumped down, leaving his horse, like a perfect fool, so that if Lenox hadn't been close by to grab the reins it might have run off. He had seen a plant. He plucked it carefully out in its clod of dirt and wrapped it in a bit of butcher's paper he had brought, which he then secured tenderly in his blazer pocket. He would plant it in his room—though that was strictly forbidden.

"If the MB *is* Townsend," Lenox had said cautiously, after they resumed their slow ride, "and you found that out for certain, what would you do?"

"Leave," said Leigh immediately.

"You want to leave anyway," Lenox pointed out.

"Sometimes I want to chase him down with a carriage of my own," Leigh said. "I daydream about that. In a way I would think worse of him if he were paying for my school. It would show that he has enough of a conscience to care—but not enough to pay for his crime. I would rather he were an unthinking toad than a thinking one."

"You mustn't kill him," said Lenox, alarmed.

"No. Only, why should he get to prance around?"

Lenox, who had in those days been rather literary from time to time in an insufferable sort of way, said, sonorously, " 'Why should a dog, a horse, a rat have life, and thou no breath at all?' "

"Yes, he is a rat," said Leigh.

Lenox felt that Leigh had missed the point, but nodded sagely. "I reckon it's your uncle anyway."

"Yes, maybe, sod him."

Passing by that grove now, Lenox felt many old Harrow memories crowding back toward him—

and not the ones he groped to recall, but the ones that arrived involuntarily, and were therefore sweeter, truer, deeper. He saw St. Mary's Church and could feel the worn bench under his bottom once more, as he sat bored through Sunday service, wishing he were outside. The way to the sporting grounds: He had walked this a thousand, a hundred thousand times with his particular chums, sometimes dreading the afternoon's activities, sometimes excited for them.

Here was the little stretch of fence where they had sat in a row during Shells, waiting to take turns with the rifle that one of the Latin masters let them shoot at a target. A darting little lane where all the boys had gone to buy sweets from Mrs. Carmichael, who boiled them herself. The steps of Druries, one of the school's houses, where he had once had a terrible falling-out with one of his closest friends, which had lasted almost six months, and made him unspeakably miserable at the time, though now he couldn't remember even its faintest lineaments.

At the distinguished brick schoolhouse near the school gate, Lenox stepped down. Inside it was very handsome, finer than in his own day—fresh white paint, portraits along the walls, prominent among them Harrow's two infinitely cherished Prime Ministers, Palmerston and Peel, among the most distinguished politicians of any age.

In the graceful entrance hall, with its black-and-white marble floor, he found a secretary taking notes. "Hello," he said. "My name is Charles Lenox. I was a student here once."

"How do you do, sir. Welcome back."

"I was wondering whether the headmaster might see me. I have a rather peculiar request, involving some old school records."

CHAPTER FORTY-TWO

The single stupidest person Lenox had ever met was Georgie Cholmondley, now Lord April, who had been at Harrow at the same time that he and Leigh had. He wasn't bad-natured— and a fine shot—but when you conversed with him it seemed a wonder he could stand upright, he was so dull-witted. And yet he had sixty thousand pounds a year, a hundred thousand acres, and probably eight seats in Parliament at his disposal.

When Lenox saw that the associate head-master he was taken to see—the headmaster himself being occupied in the classroom, at that moment—was named Alfred Cholmondley, he felt some trepidation.

"Are you any relation to Lord April?" Lenox said, entering a small, book-lined office and shaking the younger man's hand.

"George? Lord, yes. My cousin. From the much

richer and slower part of the family, however."

Lenox laughed. "He's an excellent sportsman."

Alfred Cholmondley—pronounced Chumley—smiled. "That's very true. He always sat a horse beautifully. I think he is the ideal lord, don't you? Not personally ambitious—scrupulously polite—dutiful—a wonderful husband and father—not likely to gamble away the title—content with his obligations and responsibilities, never shying from them. For my own part I cannot imagine anything less appealing."

"You've hit the nail on the head," said Lenox, sitting and accepting with a gesture the offer of a tot of whisky that Alfred made from the sideboard. "He's a brick, Georgie. You must be an Old Harrovian, too?"

"No, I was at Westminster. But after university I found that I was in want of a profession and a place to hang my hat, and there was an advertisement in the *Times* that the school wanted a professor of modern languages, with very generous pay. I had spent several years in Germany and France. And I must say that it is a comfortable place to work—a lovely place."

"Do the boys take to modern languages, I wonder? We only had the option of the classical ones, as I recall."

"Yes, it's new. Some rather like it. It's an option for Fifths and Sixths. I think they find it particularly useful if they mean to have a career

331

in the army or if they are planning to enter your own field—politics."

Lenox smiled. "My field! Yes—well spotted, I was once in Parliament."

"Oh, yes, we are very honored to have you back—many of the boys know the name, as belonging to two brothers from the school who have subsequently taken their place in the national dramas the newspapers deliver to us, as a consequence of their service in Parliament. I warn you that I am a conservative, myself."

"Like your cousin! Yes—that is me, or us," said Lenox, "though you are being too generous when you assign me a part in the national dramas to which you refer. My brother's career in Parliament has been more brilliant than mine. I am once again a private detective."

"And may I ask if it is work or personal inclination that brings you back here now?" asked the schoolmaster, in what Lenox thought was rather a neat way.

"Ah. Yes. The truth is that I am here on some business for a very old friend. A Harrow friend, to be precise."

"Who is that?"

Lenox had cultivated the storyteller's gift in the years he had been a detective. It was essential to have it, he felt—one of Polly's few weaknesses, for she was more inclined to directness. He started by telling Cholmondley about his schooldays with

332

Leigh, and then slowly built up to the events of the last year. He sketched these in vaguely, leaving room for interpretation.

The associate headmaster shook his head with good-natured consternation, hearing this story. "Dear me," he said. "A very interesting tale."

But anyone could see that he was undeceived. He was no fool, this fellow. Lenox decided to play his trump card, before asking his question. "I have a letter from Leigh here. It is—well, have a look."

The associate headmaster took it and read it quickly, frowning with concentration. He smiled when he reached the end, and then looked up. "An interesting letter. Its connection to your visit here is unclear to me, however."

Lenox smiled too, and took it back, glancing at it once more. Leigh had given it to him to allow Lenox to interview people from the Society on his own.

February 1877
With this letter, I, Gerald Leigh, the under-signed, grant to Charles Lenox authority to act on my behalf in any way he sees fit, legally, morally, etc, in all matters, though he cannot accept a knighthood for me. Please assist him.

Below this was a signature and an address, as well as the seal of the Royal Society, which was

Leigh's rightful appendage, now that he had finally consented to become a fellow.

Lenox had nearly invited Leigh to come along that morning; but his old friend had betrayed a certain diffidence, in their many conversations at the end of the winter, about the past. His whole mind was bent upon Rowan.

"It is this," said Lenox. "I would like to see his old school records. In particular, his billings."

"He does not have them?"

"No—he does not, and they may be of material use in the investigation I am conducting on his behalf."

"How so?"

"Ah—that is more difficult to answer."

"I see."

Cholmondley studied him. He was in an odd position, Lenox knew. Among the members of their class, there was a particular secrecy attached to all things private, but above all to matters of money. Lenox, sensing that the answer might be no, said, slowly, "I suppose I can tell you one thing: The person who paid his school bills may, unfortunately, be the same person who wishes him harm."

This blurred the line of the truth, but Cholmondley looked as if his interest was piqued. "Is that so? Rowan?"

"Not Rowan—one of Rowan's allies at the Royal Society."

"I see."

"You have my word that I have nothing but Leigh's interests at heart, Mr. Cholmondley. We may write him together, if you wish, and await his permission—or simply tell him that I have come here to do this. I will leave the letter in your possession. And honestly, what harm can there be in looking at a bill from thirty years ago?"

The associate headmaster sat motionless for several seconds, and then—whether it was Lenox's person, his name, the letter he bore, his story, for whatever reason—nodded slightly.

The school's record room was situated within the large basement of the same house, an impeccably clean space with long rows of shelves, lit by bright gas lamps. The archivist, Travers, was also the school's historian and comptroller, and his office was several floors up, but he had no trouble in taking Lenox down to the basement, where they retrieved Leigh's file.

"You are lucky in your choice of dates," Travers said as they walked back upstairs to his office. "Anything before 1830 and it's more likely than not that we wouldn't have it."

He took the file from its bound portfolio, after untying its crossed strings carefully, and then began to sift through the pages. There were ten or twelve of them.

Cholmondley's one injunction had been "nothing disciplinary." Lenox had assented to the condition readily. Now Travers was passing through pages of information, which Lenox guessed must have to do with Leigh's expulsion. A shame, these. Harrow had alienated one of its finest minds, which a tenderer overseer than Tennant might have nurtured in its infancy. Even Lenox had nearly noticed that Leigh was out of the ordinary.

Travers's face brightened when he reached one of the last pages. "What is it?" asked Lenox.

"Got it!" Travers said.

He read for a moment and then slid the sheet of paper across the smooth desk.

Record of remittance of fees
Student: Gerald R. Leigh
Term: Michaelmas 1846
House: Lyon's
Rate: 79 pounds sterling per annum; 19
    pounds boarding

REMITTED 8/8/46
Drawn on *Bank of Cornwall*,
account of P. Wilkins
£98.

At the bottom of the page were a stamp and then, in a scrawl dripping with loose ink, *"Fees partially refunded 11/12/46. Garnished at pro rata. Student departed Harrow School 11/14/46."*

"What about the same for the year before?" Lenox asked.

"The next sheet."

He took it from Travers and saw the same name: Wilkins.

After all this time, a name! Lenox, studying the paper, realized that he would need to go to Cornwall.

CHAPTER FORTY-THREE

L enox spent a pleasant few hours at Harrow, dining with the beaks at high table, then meeting the boys from his old house, enjoying their somehow simultaneously sly and ingenuous questions about being a detective. Late that afternoon he returned to London, back in time to have dinner with Lady Jane.

"Cornwall?"

"Yes, tomorrow, I think. It may mean staying overnight. But I could use the break. I'm sick half to death of the office."

She, who knew him better than anyone, said, "Why not ask Edmund to go with you?"

"That's an idea."

He went round to his brother's house after supper, and found him closeted with Lord Acton and James Hilary, discussing parliamentary matters over cigars and whisky. "Lenox," said Hilary after they had all exchanged hellos, "put your oar in. Do you think we should call the election this year or next?"

337

"This year," Lenox said confidently, sitting among them with his gloves in his hand—the old gamesmanship still in him.

It was up to the ruling party that would choose the new prime minister, an odd little wrinkle of Britain's constitution. "Your brother thinks next."

"He must be right, then."

Acton shook his head. "No, I am with you. We ought to take the wind while our sails are full."

The four men sat for some time, a little more than an hour, discussing the matter, a pleasant dip back into waters in which Lenox had once been immersed. When Acton and Hilary had gone, the two brothers remained in the firelit study, books and papers spilled across its surfaces, the remnants of a sandwich close at Edmund's elbow.

Lenox took it up and had a bite. "I have come to see if you wanted to take a day away from work. But it may be the wrong time."

"On the contrary—I haven't been less busy in some while. All of the questions Acton and Hilary came to discuss concern the longer term. But a day away to where?"

"Cornwall."

"Are you after King Arthur?"

"No—P. Wilkins."

"Who is he?"

Leigh and Lenox had sworn each other to secrecy, these many years ago, about the MB, but now Lenox broke his oath and told his brother a little bit about the problem. Edmund listened attentively, curious about Townsend. He knew the Earl of Ashe, Leigh's uncle. "But those candidates are now both disqualified. Which leaves it to discover who on earth Wilkins was, or is."

"Is he not a member of Leigh's family, then? A cousin, an uncle?"

Lenox shook his head. "I don't think so. All those years ago Leigh and I drew his family tree, looking for suspects—"

"How enterprising you were as a young detective!"

"Yes, I know! Without result, sadly. Anyhow, we studied it at length, and while I don't remember the names on the tree, I know they would come back to me if I saw them. The name Wilkins doesn't."

Edmund nodded thoughtfully. "Well, I'm curious," he said. "Is it tomorrow you intend to go?"

"Yes, if you can."

He took down his *Bradshaw's*. "What do you say to the eight thirty-three?"

"Capital! How about another splash of that whisky before I go?"

The brothers met on the platform at Waterloo the next morning at quarter past the hour. They were mirrors of each other, in their dark coats, each with an umbrella in the crook of his arm, each carrying an overnight bag.

The train ride west was beautiful, full of swooping hills and checkerboard fields, small farmhouses and outbuildings clustered away from the rails, the budding trees entangled with one another. Inside their compartment it was warm—there was a coal brazier at their feet—and they each had a flask of tea, which they sipped, comfortably, lazing back against the cushions, as the landscape sailed past. It had been quite a long time since they had so long to talk. Edmund spoke of his sons, who, after the death of their mother, had each committed to staying some while in England; his elder son, who had been venturing to make his own fortune in Kenya, had, with a maturity somewhat surprising in him, declared a desire to learn about the lands and estate that would one day be his own.

"That is something to make you feel old," said Edmund. "For my part I still think of it as Father's."

"No doubt he thought of it as Grandfather's."

"And he of the chaps before him. Therefore everyone goes through life feeling a charlatan. Is that what you propose?"

Lenox smiled. "I suspect that just around the time when you are about to die you'll begin to feel as if the whole concern is really yours once and for all."

"What a comfort you are, Charles."

Because their journey concerned Harrow they

spent some time discussing that; then Parliament again; then the downfall of a mutual acquaintance who had lost against the market, and was trying to rebound. The time slipped silkily away—though it was a four-hour ride, it felt as if it had lasted only twenty or thirty minutes, and they arrived in happy spirits, glad at having had the time together.

"Where do we go, then?" asked Edmund as they left the train. "I meant to ask you on the ride."

"Do you need lunch?"

"I can wait."

"Straight to the bank, in that case."

Charles had been to the Bank of Cornwall's branch in London the day before. In the distant days of their investigation, he and Leigh had discovered that Harrow accepted fees remitted only by banks in London. This meant that the ninety-eight pounds Harrow had received from P. Wilkins in 1846 must have been drawn on the London branch, and Lenox had thought that perhaps they would have information about him there.

In the event, however, it had only proved a tiny office, and they said it had always been this way: two men on staff, both clerks, without any clients in the metropolis, present there only to handle precisely the kind of business that needed to be cleared through London. They had advised Lenox that he had better make the trip out if he had any business to conduct with the local bank, and given him an address in Truro.

Lenox explained this to Edmund as they walked from the tiny platform down a series of stairs, ending at a cabstand where a local boy wearing a kerchief around his neck sat atop a cart, first in line, a donkey draped in a wool blanket patiently unmoving ahead of him.

They mounted this noble conveyance one by one. It was only a twelve-minute drive, the boy said; after that he spat continually, and if he was impressed to be carrying two gentlemen from the London train in expensive clothes through his hometown, he certainly kept it to himself, which Lenox rather approved.

The Bank of Cornwall was a low, handsome building in the style the Tudors had favored—possibly even original, Lenox thought, eyeing its black and white timbers. He and Edmund went inside, and found a cozy room dominated by a large round polished desk, with clerks sitting inside of it, facing outward, various pigeonholes and lockboxes at each of their stations.

A clerk greeted the brothers. "Good afternoon, sirs."

Lenox stepped forward. "I had a question about a customer here. I wonder whether I might speak to your manager?"

To the right of the young man, an older one, with white hair and a matching roundness in his spectacles and his belly, looked up. "I hold that position. Adams. How may I help you?"

"Ah! How do you do—I am Charles Lenox. This is my brother, Edmund."

They both passed their cards across the desk. Adams raised his eyes slightly at the second, and stood: a member of Her Majesty's government, after all. "What brings you to Truro, sir?"

"I am looking for a customer of yours by the name of P. Wilkins."

"Percival Wilkins?" said Adams.

The other clerks all glanced up, looks of recognition on their faces. "I believe so."

"He isn't a customer here," said Adams.

"No?"

"He banks with the Truro Limited. A sound establishment—none of the London quarrels here, business enough for all of us. And we occasionally come to Mr. Wilkins's assistance in his profes-sional line. Is it do with an inheritance? An estate?"

Lenox paused infinitesimally, and then said, "Yes."

"Well, there you are. Mr. Wilkins will be two streets down, three over, and one down again. Matching Lane. Where all the solicitors have their offices in Truro."

"Number six," said one of the young men.

Adams, looking intensely irritated, said, "That's what I said—Six Matching Lane."

The solicitors! Was this to be another dead end?

Edmund and Lenox followed the (very clear) directions of the bank manager, and arrived at a street that looked rather like Cheyne Walk in London, with small gardens in front of tidy squared-off white houses. Number 6 had—as all of them did—a brass nameplate.

P. Wilkins, Solicitor, 6
Mr. Percival Wilkins, private residence, 6 and ½

Lenox looked and saw that there were two symmetrical paths leading to two doors, one left, one right, the former, evidently, belonging to the professional life of Mr. P. Wilkins, the latter to the domestic.

They took the left path and knocked on the door. It flew open. A very young man stood there, with bright red cheeks and wild blond hair. "How do you do!" he said.

"We hoped to see Mr. Wilkins."

"He is with a client at the moment. Your business?"

"It involves an estate."

The young man nodded seriously. "In that case you may wait in the entrance hall."

Lenox smiled at Edmund after the clerk, who couldn't have been more than fifteen, turned his back and led them to a wall lined with several armchairs. There was a print of Queen Victoria on the wall, and another of the Battle of Blenheim. Deep England, they had found themselves in.

They chatted in low voices for some time, waiting—Edmund was getting hungry and wondering where they ought to eat—and then, at last, the young man reemerged, beckoning them back.

The office he led them into was neat as a pin, and overlooked a lovely garden, which, to Lenox's surprise, had a small stream behind it. And here was Percival Wilkins: just the right age, thank God, certainly nearing seventy. "Thank you, Percy," he said to the clerk firmly.

"Of course, Father," said the young man, and left, closing the door behind him.

The brothers once again presented their cards, and Wilkins inspected them. "I do not believe we have ever met."

"No!" said Lenox cheerfully. "No, we're here on behalf of a friend."

"Who is that?"

He had decided to be fairly honest. "Gerald Leigh," he said. "A local boy. Many years ago he was the recipient of a mysterious benefaction. His school fees were paid for him, when his family could not afford them. Now he wishes to know who did him that kindness, so that he might, having enjoyed success himself, repay the kindness."

Wilkins, to Lenox's surprise, let fall his

impassive legal countenance, and half smiled. "He *has* been a success, hasn't he? We worried once that he might not be."

"Who worried? You?"

"Well—I have been the family solicitor for some time, yes. Probably around fifty years now. I knew his father, bless his heart."

"Then you can tell us who paid the fees?"

"Gerald's fees for Harrow? Why! Who else? His mother!"

CHAPTER FORTY-FOUR

Several hours later, Edmund and Charles Lenox were ensconced in the Boscawen Arms, gazing out of its mullioned windows at the passing traffic. Each had a pint pot of bitter, and there was a carving board of bread and cheese between them, into which each made the occasional foray. A thoroughly contented hour of life's passage, Lenox thought. There was a 6:29 train back to London—the second-to-last of the evening—and they intended to catch it, in a little more than forty minutes.

"It only took you thirty years to solve your first case," said Edmund.

Lenox smiled. "Twenty-nine and a half."

"Better still! You should double your bonus for the year. That's fast work."

"You're very witty."

Edmund smiled. "No, no. I do think you did it well."

"And now the question. Shall I tell him?"

Wilkins had been very candid with the brothers, for the simple reason, he said, that Mrs. Leigh was dead now. She had insisted upon secrecy from her son while she was alive about the source of his school fees; but there was no need to prolong the secret now that she was gone, Wilkins thought.

"Why did she want it kept from Gerald to begin with?" Lenox had asked Wilkins, in his little office with its view over the back garden.

Wilkins had leaned back, thinking over the question. He was the picture of a small-town solicitor: reliable, comfortable, a friend as surely as a professional. "Because he wouldn't have wanted her to do what she did."

"What she did?"

Wilkins frowned. "I handled the estate of Gerald's father. Struck down in the prime of his life, now—just when he was setting out, certainly younger than both of you gentlemen, and therefore not having had a chance to accumulate much in the way of savings. There was no fortune there. He left them in a position that they might just squeak by—the cottage outright, and fifty or sixty pounds a year."

"Townsend never gave them money?"

"Townsend? No. No, no. What on earth gave

you that idea? The squire's wife, Mrs. Williston, gave Mrs. Leigh things here and there, when they could be disguised as other than charity—cloth for a dress, you know, or a pair of pullets from the farm. Not Townsend, however. No."

"And yet Leigh went to Harrow."

Wilkins nodded, his fingers steepled. "She was set upon it, Mrs. Regina Leigh. It was her obsession. She was in grief herself, I believe, though she was not a communicative person—not at all like her husband.

"But you see, she had loved him very, very much, and Harrow had been vital to his upbringing, to his sense of the world, and I believe she wanted to offer Gerald the same opportunity. I advised her against it, frankly. The fees were more than their entire remaining annual income."

"How did she pay them, then?" Lenox asked curiously. "Her family?"

Wilkins shook his head. "It is an impoverished earldom, you know, besides which there was a falling-out between the two branches. No, what she did was to invent this canard of an anonymous benefactor—with my reluctant consent—and then, while Gerald was away, she earned the money herself."

"How?"

Wilkins sighed. "Whatever her uncle was, she was the granddaughter of an earl, Mrs. Leigh, and very proud. But she had to have the money, and so she did two things. The first was to take in boarders."

"Leigh always said their house was small."

"Yes, two bedrooms. She let each of them during school term, and slept in the kitchen."

"Brought low indeed," Lenox murmured.

"And the second thing?" asked Edmund.

"She began to take in piecework, sewing at night, and during the day she began to teach lessons. Whatever came to hand—etiquette, piano, French, German, drawing, for of course she had all the accomplishments of her class, and she was happy to teach anything. The Ashe name means a great deal in these parts, and she priced herself reasonably, which meant that all the townswomen could send their daughters to her. A bragging right. That was how she scraped the money together for Harrow."

"And you transmitted the fees."

"I did. I would have helped, except—well, as a solicitor, once you begin to take pity on your clients, all of them need money, don't they? Or a great many. The best you can do is give it to the local societies, or the church, and help where help is needed direly. A public school—I respected her decision, and helped her arrange to send Gerald there. Not for long, as it happened."

"What about holidays?" asked Lenox, still stuck on Regina Leigh.

"The lodgers' terms always ended the day

before he came home, and she taught no lessons while he was in Cornwall."

"I see."

"It was only a period of two years, though they were brutally hard ones for her. After that, indeed, I believe he was able to send money back to her."

Lenox nodded. "That's true."

"She once referred to a bird trap, I think," said Wilkins, trying to remember. "I may have that wrong."

Lenox had felt a sudden stinging at the corners of his eyes then, quite unexpectedly. Why? Perhaps because Leigh had said, so often, how dull his mother was, how far less interesting than his father. Perhaps because she was gone. For his friend. For his own mother. Or perhaps it was universal: He looked over to his brother, who admittedly had had a very soft heart since Molly's death, and saw that his face was screwed up tightly and seriously, which had meant since he was five years old that he was determined not to betray his own emotions.

"Thank you for solving our puzzle," Lenox had said.

"Do you see Leigh?"

"Oh, yes."

"I hope he will return to these parts soon. He came for his mother's funeral, of course, and to settle her estate—but he still has many friends here, you know!"

Lenox nodded and said that he would give Leigh that message—conscious, however, that his friend was not likely to return to Cornwall, now that it had relinquished its one claim on him.

Charles and Edmund had taken their leave of Wilkins after this, thanking him again and complimenting his garden on their way, and wandered out into the street, a little aimless.

"What shall we do now?" Edmund had asked.

"We could have a look around Truro."

"Yes, that should be a thrilling eight minutes."

Lenox laughed. "Come along. Let's walk south and see what we may find."

As it happened Truro was a very pretty small city, with two rivers flowing through it, and many winding streets full of charm and character, teashops, a row of competing greengrocers, in the public square a half-indoor pantomime theater whose troupe was currently delighting a gang of small children. It was more like an English village overgrown than like a city—and they passed a diverting hour walking it, each of them picking up a few small souvenirs, Lenox, for Sophia and Jane, a pair of matching silver spoons with the city's name and motto engraved on the handles.

After some time they had found themselves—a little chilly, with the fall of the sun—seeking out the warm table by the fire at the Boscawen Arms where they now sat.

When Lenox ought to have known, he told

his brother, was when that mysterious Greek dictionary appeared after Leigh had lost it during half term. Who else but his mother could have known? A master, perhaps; a friend—but not Townsend, nor his uncle. Poor detective work.

"You must go easy on yourself," said Edmund. "You were inexperienced."

"Rum, isn't it, to be thinking back to clues from our days at school."

"Indeed."

Lenox felt a certain lonely dejection, as they walked slowly through the darkened evening toward the train station. He couldn't say exactly why. But the compartment they secured in the first-class carriage was cozy and warm, and each of them bought a cup of tea from the lady passing down the aisle, and soon they were warmly ensconced in the conversation they had been conducting for all these years, and which never, even in periods of remission, ceased, and Lenox felt better. Just past St. Austell, Edmund fell asleep, and Charles, taking advantage of the moment, began to sketch out with a nib of charcoal a long letter to Leigh. When this first draft was done he began to make a list of clients he ought to check in on the next morning, by wire or by letter; one thought led to another, and soon he was jotting down ideas for how they might improve, for example, the efficiency of their monthly check-ins at the soap factory in Birmingham.

CHAPTER FORTY-FIVE

By the first of April, Lord John Dallington was once more able to walk.

Not well, however. "Nor will he ever," said McConnell. He and Lenox were passing along Carlton Terrace, with its beautiful wisteria-lined alabaster houses, sunstruck on this mellow morning, on their way to have lunch at Lenox's club. "The left leg took too brutal a splintering."

"Will he be able to run again?"

"No."

That was a hindrance to a detective—and to a person, of course. "And yet he looks very well."

There were still ugly raised scars on Dallington's hands and arms, as well as one that ran up the back of his neck—and no doubt on his legs, too. But his face, always so alert and youthful, had mostly healed.

It was true on the other hand that it looked dimmer now, less full of light. His betrothal to Polly had been announced in the *Times*, a date set that summer for them to be wed at Marchmain House, and yet despite this good fortune, Dallington's manner seemed singularly joyless to Lenox these days. He had no interest in work, though he offered his dutiful thoughts on the cases

Lenox tried to interest him in, and smiled with inauthentic enthusiasm when one suggested that he would return soon.

McConnell, perhaps reading Lenox's thoughts, said, "There is always some period of despondency to be endured during such a recuperation."

"Is this the length you would expect?"

The doctor frowned, his long strides slowing slightly. "Perhaps. Perhaps it is slightly longer. I am not yet worried."

After they had eaten, Lenox asked McConnell if he wished to come and see Leigh. He had that morning returned from a week in Cambridge— of the two universities the more scientific in its strengths, whereas Oxford's lineage was in politics, letters, classics, history—where he had been meeting with colleagues. McConnell was very happy to say yes; and inquired, how did it go with Rowan?

Strangely, was the answer.

A city by all rights ought to spread rumors like fire, indiscriminately and evenly, without regard for whom they harmed or what they wrought. There was the famous story of the Dublin theater owner who bet a friend he could coin a new word: He wrote a random one on a few hundred pieces of paper and had his lads spread them all over town, waiting to see when the neologism would return to his ears. It had done so within a few hours—people thinking it was some kind of test, which was how the word, "quiz," had earned its meaning.

Rowan had shown that he had a bizarre immunity to that kind of circulation. It was a skill, perhaps; within the Royal Society, by all accounts, he was considered a wronged man, and in London at large there was some vague sense of injustice surrounding his case. He maintained his innocence steadfastly, and had many friends who did the same—and above all, Lenox suspected that some of the great fortune he held within his control, the one that extended so far and wide over the East End's racked tenements, was being used to defer unfavorable coverage in the newspapers and encourage favorable. He had attempted to find some explicit evidence of this, without luck. One of those conspiracies of omission, instead, which are so difficult to prove.

Nor had he and Frost been able to establish any definitive link between Rowan and Middleton. And both men had a great, great deal of other work to draw their attention away.

Thus Lenox and Leigh were in the bizarre position of knowing that a man who had held them at gunpoint might be restored without comment to his prominent life, and the esteem of civic opinion.

"He has not even been unnamed as president of the Society," Lenox told McConnell.

"Has he not?"

"Duties suspended temporarily. We could not wish for a better ally than Mr. Bartram—though perhaps a more prestigious one."

McConnell shook his head. "How mad it is."

The trial was to begin in a week. Lenox's hope was that the eye of the journalists must finally be drawn, the case too thrilling to ignore. But it was a slender reed.

They found Leigh at home in Hampden Lane. There was a small, dark room toward the west side of the ground floor, never of much use to anyone, which had gradually become his personal study in the last months. He popped his head out and greeted them cheerfully.

"Hullo!" he said. "Come in here a moment, would you?" The little room had a small yellow lamp lit, playing lazily over the book-covered wooden desk, and there was a comforting aroma of dry tobacco—a little ship's room, within the airy house. "Sit, if you would."

The months Leigh had been in London had been special ones. Friendship had always been very dear to Lenox; to have a friend so close at hand, and one who loved Jane and Sophia too, who was excellent company but never obtrusive. Occasionally he had asked if he was in the way, but had gracefully accepted their word that he was not, and soon become a thoroughgoing member of the little household.

As for he and Lenox, they had spent many

afternoons of the dawning spring in long walks together, prolonged lunch hours for the detective. Even in the densest block of the city, Leigh could spot a bird or a little shoot in the concrete, and name it, give its history—a naturalist to his bones. It reminded Lenox of their old walks at school. There was a fine joy in learning things like the ones Leigh taught him, which he never otherwise would have known.

All of this left Lenox's decision to investigate the MB a little uneasy in his mind—but only, he thought, defensively perhaps, because the result had been so personal. He remained unsure of how to disclose what he had learned to his friend.

In the study, Leigh handed Lenox and McConnell each a small pamphlet bound in plain brown paper. He had a stack of them. Lenox frowned. "What is that—have you taken to tracts? I am happy with the church I attend."

Leigh laughed. "No. A solution to a more earthbound problem."

Lenox opened the pamphlet and read through it, first with some confusion, and then with a growing sense of—of what? He was impressed; satisfied; and relieved. Also slightly overawed.

He and McConnell had apparently apprehended the document's meaning at the same time, because McConnell looked up just then. "Goodness me, Leigh," he said.

The scientist glanced at Lenox. "Charles?"

"We need to go and see Rowan."

"That's what I thought, too. But I wanted to wait until I spoke to you."

"Has anyone else seen this?"

"Only Bartram. He helped."

"I can't imagine the effort this must have taken."

Leigh shrugged. "I enjoy work."

"But what about the microbe?"

Leigh smiled. "The microbe has been taking care of itself for quite a while. Anyhow I find that my interest in it has waned, somehow, since this whole sordid business began."

McConnell looked alarmed. "I hope that isn't true. Your work is indispensable."

"The cemeteries are full of indispensable men, they say. In fact I find that I have a very great yen to return to Cornwall."

"Cornwall?" said Lenox.

"I've been daydreaming about the birds and plants of my youth. Birds especially. I remember them very vividly. I can't imagine there is much left to discover there—but then, I don't pine for that particular glory, and it would give me pleasure to conduct my own investigation. Count eggs, track mating patterns. Who knows what I might find. It has been quite a time since I was in England for long."

Lenox said, guardedly, "Have you heard from there recently? Cornwall?"

Leigh smiled, looking at him directly. "Yes, this morning. From an old family solicitor."

McConnell, unaware of the import of this last interchange, said, "Shall we go to Newgate and visit Mr. Rowan?"

"Yes," Leigh said immediately. "It is only fair to show him the pamphlet."

CHAPTER FORTY-SIX

L enox ate supper with Dallington that evening. They dined at a small private club without a name, in an unmarked house near Holland Park. There were only three rooms there, a library, a dining room, and a card room, only two servants and a cook, and fifty or so members—a place of profound superfluity, for it was the refuge of a group of gentlemen who felt that the great London clubs to which they belonged occasionally became oppressive in their social demands, and yet probably the favorite club of every one of its members. In the drawing room, filling out a racing form, sipping sherry, and being politely ignored, was the Prince of Wales.

Lenox had joined the year before and rarely wanted to dine anywhere else now, partly for its peaceable calm, partly because more than a quarter of the place's budget went to the cook, who had been stolen with bald wickedness from the Carlton Club, which had previously been reckoned to have the best food of any London clubhouse. He and Dallington began their supper with an exquisite leek and potato soup; it came in small silver tureens, immured within curves of crusty hot bread.

"My goodness, this is delicious," said Lenox after he had taken a spoonful.

There was a pleasant twilight in the windows. "Eh? Oh, yes—quite good, quite good," said Dallington.

Lenox eyed him critically. "I wish you wouldn't talk so casually. This might be the best soup I've ever eaten."

Dallington smiled—a real smile. "Short of writing a poem to the potatoes I'm not sure what I could do to satisfy you. This is why I never want to eat here."

"It's not the potatoes that make the difference, it's the celery root."

Dallington shook his head. "There is nothing I hate more on this earth than a connoisseur."

Lenox laughed. "Fair enough."

Dallington laughed too, but then, without any intermediate phase, the brief moment of sunniness passed. A shadow came over his friend's face. Lenox saw his hand go to his watch chain. He realized—not a detective for nothing—that in all probability that was where he kept a lock of Polly's hair, just as she would keep his in her necklace. The traditional exchange. By all the signifiers such as this one they were a happily engaged couple: Upon the fourth finger of her left hand was a ring, set with a diamond. In Lenox's day the women's engagement rings had been, without exception, of pearl and turquoise, but according to Dallington this was the new vogue, the diamond. Lenox thought it garish, though he kept the opinion to himself (and Lady Jane).

And even beyond these outward signs, the affinity between Polly and Dallington still seemed evident, every time the three of them were together.

Why, then, was his friend so sad, so low?

Lenox began a new plan of diversion. "We saw Rowan this afternoon. I have something to show you."

Interest flickered in Dallington's eyes. "Oh?"

Lenox took a copy of the pamphlet from the inner pocket of his jacket. "Have a look."

Dallington accepted the little typeset document, and soon his face had on it the same absorption that Lenox's own must have when Leigh showed it to him.

The book tracked Rowan's scientific career. It was a startlingly comprehensive piece of work. For the first time, reading it, Lenox had really grasped the tenacious forcefulness of Leigh's brain. His friend had gone back to the papers Rowan had submitted for consideration at Eton, back to the age of fourteen—obscure depths, indeed—and through to the most recent autumn bulletin of the Royal Society.

In nearly every one of these publications of Rowan, he had discovered some heretofore-unknown plagiarism. Case, after case, after case. Rowan's glittering reputation, founded upon a series of lies and thefts.

"Good heavens," said Dallington, when he was halfway through.

"Yes. Quite something, is it not? He consulted experts across every field. Many of Rowan's findings were taken from German sources, it seems. Leigh keyed in on them after he discovered that Rowan had spent a year at Göttingen."

"I am amazed," said Dallington, skimming now. "It has the scholar's art about it."

"Yes, indeed."

"And you showed this to Rowan?" said Dallington, looking up across his mostly full tureen. "How did he react?"

Lenox smiled faintly. "Ah."

When Napoléon had ordered the execution of the Duc d'Enghien, it was said, he had done worse than commit a crime—he had committed a blunder.

So it had been with Rowan, that afternoon. Lenox had never watched a man's identity disintegrate so wholly and completely before his eyes as Rowan's had, while Leigh stared impassively on from across the scratched, rickety table in his cell.

Rowan had looked up after some time with the pamphlet, bone pale. "You've murdered me."

Leigh had tilted his head, staring with a cool, scientific interest. He said nothing. Lenox replied instead. "Since it is just the three of us in this cell, Mr. Rowan—why did you murder Middleton?"

But Rowan's thoughts were no more on Middleton than they were on an insect he had mounted to a piece of board fifteen years before. He was still staring at Leigh. "Have you given this to anyone else?" Leigh didn't reply. "I have money. I'll admit to the crimes—just don't show this to anyone."

Still Leigh didn't answer, and Rowan, searching in his face, must have seen the truth. His eyes widened slightly and then he collapsed backward, his fine, handsome head buried in his hands.

"You might have had a perfectly happy life," said Lenox. "I cannot understand it, Rowan. In time you probably would have become the president of the Royal Society on your own merit!"

At last Rowan looked at the detective—but from a very great distance, as if he was not quite real. "My own merit," he had said.

"Yes! You have all the qualities of a man of science."

Rowan had stared at him, and Lenox had seen, in his face, some old fury for success, which had driven him into desperate action. Then his attention was gone, back on Leigh. He was still hoping to bargain with him.

But Leigh had stood up: And it seemed as if it was obvious to both of them, Lenox feeling strangely like an interloper, that Rowan had faced the only judge who actually mattered.

An account of this strange meeting took Lenox and Dallington through the arrival of a tender saddle of mutton, with crisped potatoes in a mountain over it. "What of the criminal charges, then?" asked Dallington, taking one or two.

"I'm not sure. Leigh has given the pamphlet you're holding to Lord Baird, at the Royal Society. I am hoping to convince him to give it to the courts reporter at the *Times*, too. A genuine 'scoop,' as they say in that line of work."

"It will strengthen your explanation for the crimes he committed against Leigh."

"Yes, I think so."

The conversation moved on to other subjects. After the mutton was cleared away came a plate of hard sweet biscuits. Lenox dipped them into his wine, a napkin in his left hand to catch any drops, as was the form, and savored their soft crunch. For his part, Dallington ignored them, as he had ignored most of the food. The succession of wine glasses too had come and gone from before him without his attention.

Lenox nearly said something—but his friend

seemed so fragile, in spirit and body, that he held himself back.

Afterward they were walking in the quiet spring evening, through the lovely verdure of St. James's Park. Dallington moved slowly along the stone pathways; he had a cane; his gait was one of studied evenness, as if he couldn't bear to reveal that he had a limp, though it meant walking far more slowly.

After a block or two, he stopped, leaning against a railing. He was out of breath, but feigned a pebble in his shoe, running a finger inside of it very deliberately to prove his word. Lenox looked away, keeping his face as close to neutral as he possibly could.

Then Dallington stumbled forward, unsteady on his feet. He righted himself quickly. But it had been one humiliation too many, and they walked on in a violent silence, Lenox's few conversational gambits met with barely disguised contempt.

They were near the gates of St. James's Park when suddenly Dallington stopped. "There's something I must tell someone, or I shall go mad."

Lenox looked at him curiously, careful to keep his voice temperate. "What is it?"

"The night of Labrenz—the night I discovered him."

"Yes?"

"I had been taking laudanum."

"Laudanum."

"Yes. It is an occasional vice of mine. I was feeling sorry for myself—and angry at you—angry at Polly—and I sat in my little alcove, the new one I chose that night, which is how Labrenz must have thought the coast was clear—and had several drops of the stuff, over a cube of sugar, dropped in a glass of wine."

"What does it do to you?"

Dallington looked for the words. "It makes the world seem nicer."

"Was it why you fell?"

"That's just what I don't know."

There was tremendous anguish in Dallington's face. Lenox, feeling that he had never wanted to choose his words more carefully, said, "You prevented a very serious crime—a crime against England. You ought to be proud."

"I remember falling. I remember being pushed, for that matter. But I don't know if it would have happened, had I been twenty percent sharper."

"John."

"And it is this I can't live with."

"Listen to me. It may feel that way, but I assure you—it means nothing. Nothing! You have suffered a serious injury, and you have suffered it protecting something important. As I say, you ought to be proud."

But the words were meaningless, and Dallington said, more to himself than to Lenox, "How can I marry Polly when she doesn't know the truth?"

Lenox hesitated, and then said, "Well, have you used laudanum again?"

"No. Nor will I ever. And yet—everything they have ever said of me, you know."

"Don't be absurd. It doesn't. And Polly will say so, too. Tell her."

Dallington shook his head. "No. I can't."

CHAPTER FORTY-SEVEN

E very day in that first two weeks of April, a different parcel—often several—would come to the house at Hampden Lane, addressed for Leigh. They contained ever more mysterious contents, nets, wooden cages, oscilloscopes and microscopes, weather gauges. All of them went into Leigh's ad hoc study, where they piled up as he sorted them with tender care into a pair of enormous trunks.

"A person would think you were setting out for the jungles of the Amazon," said Lady Jane critically one day, as Leigh opened a package containing several blank logbooks.

"I learned a long time ago that it is all the jungles of the Amazon, Lady Jane, looked at in the right light."

"What nonsense."

Leigh smiled. "Yes, probably."

He had another project upon which he was working, too. One day Lenox came into the house and Leigh was measuring the doorway. "What are you doing?" he asked his old friend.

"Nothing."

"Come now, you must answer that question in a man's own house."

Leigh smiled. "Well, it's a surprise."

Lenox frowned at him. "I don't want anything that you doubt might fit through this doorway."

"In fact it will be invisible."

"Eh?"

Leigh smiled, in his sphinxlike way, and walked off, humming.

As Rowan's trial approached, word seeped out into London that he was, in all likelihood, going to be convicted. It was hard to say what had prompted the change—the sudden escalation of the newspaper coverage, perhaps, or alternatively Rowan's eviction from the rolls of the Royal Society.

Frost and Lenox were often closeted together, going over their case notes in hopes that they might help the Queen's Counsel in his prosecution of the case. Lenox was set to testify. So was Leigh; the thing keeping him in London—except, except, Lady Jane kept saying, he certainly did seem fond of Matilda Duckworth's company.

"What bothers me," Frost said one morning in the coffee room at Scotland Yard, "is Middleton."

"What do you mean?"

"I like a tidy case. You and Leigh have survived. Middleton—we still don't know the circumstances of the meeting they had, the one that led to his death. Did Middleton object to something Rowan asked of him? Or did he simply know too much? Was it the Farthings who shot him, or Rowan? I would like to know."

Lenox looked troubled. "We may never."

"Yes, and that's why I say it bothers me."

In fact, the case held a few surprises still.

On the sixteenth of April, a day when the whole world seemed green, Lenox was working at the offices at Chancery Lane. Dallington was in his office, door closed, and Polly was out with Anixter, tracing a necklace that had been pawned by the impulsive daughter of a wealthy yeast merchant, who had used the money to elope to Spain.

These days Lenox had delegated some of the administrative work that had dominated his winter months, and he had the pleasure at that moment of reading a letter from one of his correspondents with the Liverpool constabulary, a bright young fellow named Thestreet who had read one of Lenox's essays on crime scenes and was asking for his assistance in the solution of a double murder near Anfield.

At a little after noon, Frost came in, his face flushed with excitement. "What is it?" asked Lenox immediately.

Dallington, having apparently heard Frost's entrance, limped into the room from next door. "Yes, I'd like to know, too," he said. "Is it about Rowan?"

Frost nodded. "One of them has turned. One of the Farthings."

"Which one?"

"Singh."

They had caught him the night before. He and Anderson had been separated a month or two before, and Singh had been charged, that week, with the murder of a rival gang member. He had been caught in the act—sheer good luck, Frost said—and now, facing the gallows, was willing to give away what information he could. All he wanted was to be shipped back to India.

"I can't imagine that even if we do, we've seen the last of him," said Frost. "He's thoroughly British now. But it will be worth it if he brings down the Farthings before he goes."

"He'll testify against Anderson?"

Frost smiled. "Everyone except Anderson."

"Loyalty among—well, 'thieves' is even too kind a word, I suppose," said Dallington.

Nearly everyone at the Yard had been jostling to get at Singh, once he had cut his deal. Frost had had to wait until midnight. But it had paid off.

"It was Rowan who killed Middleton," he said. "All that preceded it occurred exactly as we suspected. Rowan hired the Farthings, at a decent

370

rate of pay, mind you, which surprised me, and sent them after Leigh. But Middleton was his own business. After he had killed Middleton he apparently came to the Blue Peter in a panic, and had to be talked down."

"What were the circumstances of his killing Middleton?"

"As Rowan explained it to Anderson and Singh, Rowan went to the solicitor's office at his invitation. There, Middleton demanded more money of him."

"Gambling debts, perhaps," said Lenox. "That would also explain why they met when Beaumont was out of the office."

"Yes. According to Singh, Rowan grew confrontational, and it was then that Middleton pulled out his pistol, hoping, I suppose, to reassert control of the conversation. Instead Rowan panicked, he told the Farthings, wresting the gun away from Middleton and shooting him. He justified it by saying that Middleton's blackmail would never have ended. Then, in the same breath, he screamed at the gang's higher-ups, why wasn't Leigh gone, what on earth were they doing, that sort of thing. Singh said that most men who spoke like that to his bosses would have had their throats slit. But Rowan had certain protections."

"His social standing, his ownership of the buildings."

"Yes, exactly. After that he was a less honored

presence among the gang, however. According to Singh they still planned to murder Leigh, even after Rowan's arrest." Dallington and Lenox exchanged grim glances. "But the news that Rowan had been sending out threats, in the shape of those farthings in envelopes, pushed them away. They had a pigeon at the jail tell him it was all off."

"A sight too feudal, I suppose," said Dallington.

Frost, who had taken a seat and pulled out his pipe, tapped it happily against the arm of the chair. "He'll hang now. Thank heavens."

"Singh will testify?"

"Oh, yes. He'll do nothing but testify for about eighteen months. Fifty different cases. If nobody gets to him at Newgate, after that he'll receive new papers and a ticket to Calcutta. It's his lookout what happens from there."

It was good news. After Frost had gone, Dallington congratulated Lenox. "And yet, I always find it melancholy, a man's execution," said Lenox.

"Do you? So did Middleton, I am sure."

"The point must be that we are better than to replicate what we are punishing."

Dallington shook his head. "I cannot agree. A man like Rowan—given every advantage, every chance to be a civil member of society, he is the first who should know that killing a fellow human forfeits his own rights as one."

"That is the general run of thought," Lenox said. "As time passes I feel less and less sure it is mine."

"You have a soft heart."

He smiled. "So have you."

"I? No, I am a blight on the criminal class." Dallington smiled, too. "Just at the moment I'm hoping to put a fellow in Camden Town on the stanchion next to Rowan if I can."

"The fellow who drowned his wife?"

Dallington nodded soberly. They discussed the case for some time—the woman's family had hired the agency to chase down the finer shades of the truth, hoping that they would make the Crown's case irrefutable—and Dallington seemed absorbed and contented by the work. More moments like this; fewer like the other kind; that was the road back, perhaps, when someone had experienced what Dallington had. The restoration couldn't be expected all at once.

Lenox dined with Graham at Parliament, where they discussed in granular detail a new bill that was going to appear that evening. It was an extension of what Lenox considered his own gladdest moment as a politician, which was the Adulteration of Food, Drink, and Drugs Act, passed in 1872. The bill had outlawed a few dozen substances commonly found in food—chalk and alum in bread, for instance, which almost certainly made people sick, copper in pickles, for

373

color, even something as innocuous as arsenic, used in many foods to add tang, but which chemists, including McConnell, had persuaded Lenox might be mildly poisonous.

The Tories had cried bloody murder—government overreach!—but they had squeaked the bill through.

"We are hoping to add about fifteen substances to the list," Graham told him, as they sat back after eating, sipping a fine port. "Our goal is to allow every child to be able to drink water safely."

That was a lofty goal—nearly everyone, child and man, drank either beer or strong tea, which were both rightly considered safer, from first thing at breakfast to last thing before bed—but Lenox nodded. "Then I believe it will come to pass."

"The manufacturers are unhappy."

"When were they ever happy? And yet I observe that they prosper." Graham, looking out at the silvery flow of the Thames under the spring sun, smiled. "Last fall, the daughter of a manufacturer was presented at court for the first time. Even Lady Jane, who is a liberal soul, was unhappy about it. But I doubt there could be a clearer sign that the next age will belong to them. Restrict away. They won't stop turning coins into paper."

Lenox returned to the office from their lunch in a contemplative mood—still no mention of a betrothal, and he thought that it must be concluded Graham's gambit had been unsuccessful, which made him sorrowful—and was surprised to find that Frost was there again.

"Frost!" he said, hanging his hat. "Has something else happened?"

Frost, before so pleased, looked devastated. "It's Rowan. Gone."

"Gone? What do you mean, gone?"

"Just that—gone."

Lenox's heart lurched. "Where is Leigh?"

"I have no idea."

"No, you couldn't. I'm not thinking. Come—let's go find him—come with me, and you can tell me on the way."

Apparently Rowan had heard the news of Singh's apostasy that morning, and by some bribery had convinced his guards to let him go. There were nine of them on duty. Frost wanted all of them fired, or transferred, though it would only have taken one to slip him out, and Rowan could have offered each of the nine their salary ten times over without noticing the absence.

As they came to Hampden Lane, Lenox felt his heart pounding.

But Leigh was there—standing in the front hallway, with the strangest look on his face.

"What is it?" Lenox asked, though he was the one with news to deliver.

Leigh shook his head. "Have a look at this letter," he said.

"From Rowan?"

"Yes. In his bizarre way, I suppose there is nobody who loves science more. I have decided it will be exceedingly useful too, what he has sent— he is right in that."

> Leigh,
> If you are to live as you, and I cannot, I must know what the microbe is. I will be on the Continent by the time you read this, and likely never in England again; but I will look to the journals. This may help us meet there more often.
> Rowan

Enclosed was a check written to Leigh, drawn on the London bank Coutts, for twenty-five thousand pounds.

CHAPTER FORTY-EIGHT

On the June morning of Dallington's wedding to Polly, it rained steadily and torrentially, the light washed out of the sky, the people washed out of the streets.

"Fearful good luck," said Lenox.

Dallington, who looked sick, nodded. "Is it very full out there?"

"Tolerably full."

"I say, thank you again for standing up next to me."

"Well, I need the exercise."

Dallington managed a smile. They were standing in a tiny attending room at Marchmain House. Anything that was good of London society had found its way into the adjoining chamber, with its enormous windows. Lenox, peering into it a moment before, had seen Lady Jane, sitting with Toto and the duchess, the three of them speaking animatedly, Toto's hands upon her rounding stomach; McConnell and Edmund nearby, talking; and even Anixter, who for the first time in his adult life didn't seem to be wearing a peacoat; and who certainly wasn't speaking to anyone.

It was just passing six minutes before eleven o'clock now. Upstairs, Polly was no doubt busy with her final preparations. She was due to come before them in five and a half minutes, her first step down the stairwell, toward marriage. Lenox had no idea how he would make the time go.

And he felt sorry, sorry for his friend, who winced as they stood, the leg still painful, sorry for Polly, who had so few people here on her behalf—so few friends, Lenox had realized, and none of her first husband's family. A marriage day ought to be happier than this one was.

Still, a minute did pass, and then another minute. "Four minutes now," said Lenox.

Dallington, whose face was nine or so inches

from the enormous grandfather clock, said, "How very useful a notification."

"Well!"

Another minute—and then, suddenly, there was a loud murmur in the room. "What is it?" Dallington asked, alarmed.

Lenox cracked the door, and saw, to his astonishment, striding up the aisle, Polly. She looked lovely, her pale face made angular by the hair swept in a corona away from it, her simple rose-colored dress brightened by the bundle of yellow tulips she held.

She was headed for them.

At the very last moment Lenox stepped back from the door, making way for her to come in. The noise in the room outside was a clamor, now.

"Polly," said Dallington, more surprised than Lenox. "What—"

"Do you want to marry me?" she said.

"What?"

Her voice was steady, but there were tears in her eyes. "Do you want to marry me?"

"Of everything, it is what I want the most."

"Then *why?* Why have you treated me so coldly, John? I have made allowances, but I cannot marry you if—if—"

She was weeping. "Shall I leave?" Lenox asked.

He turned to the door and saw that the duchess was standing outside of it. He made a signal not to come in. Meanwhile, behind him, Dallington said, "I do not deserve to marry you."

"Deserve?"

"The night I fell, I had been taking laudanum, Polly. That is the truth."

More of Dallington's relatives had appeared at the door now—little so dangerous as people who wish you well—and Lenox, though desperate to leave, found that he had become the bulwark between his friends and their potential intruders.

"Listen," said Polly behind him. "Is that all? Is that really all that has been making you unhappy? Do you promise?"

"Yes. You deserve more than—more than a crippled, intoxicated liar."

And there, in the word "crippled," Lenox glimpsed the deepest truth of his friend's sorrows.

So had Polly. There was a sound which, though Lenox's eyes were turned studiously away, could never be mistaken for anything but a series of kisses upon a face. "You are the best person I know," Polly said, "and I love you better than anyone in the world, and you could be a million times more crippled and a million times more intoxicated and I would feel that way still."

"Would you?" said Dallington.

She kissed him again. "Charles," she said. Her face was shining with happiness when he turned to look. She was squeezing her betrothed's hand. "Would you mind clearing the way so that you and Dallington can go and stand by the priest? I'll walk from here—it's no matter—I would walk from a much less convenient place to marry you, John—go, go, we only have thirty seconds."

Dallington looked at Lenox, took a deep breath, and smiled. "Ready, then," he said, and started through the door.

It was many hours later when Lenox and Lady Jane returned home in their carriage. A good lunch was in them; and many happy memories, stored away now, of their friends' wedding.

Seated between them, curling her fingers through her doll's hair, was Sophia, who had stood near Polly with a basket of flowers, eaten too much soup, had a tantrum, and fallen asleep in her chair. Not one of her finest performances.

Lady Jane seemed sleepy, too. She had been awake late with the duchess, finalizing the layout of the room, the menu of the wedding luncheon. "I hope they are happy," she said.

"If he is as happy as I am he will have done well."

She smiled. "And she."

"Look," said Lenox. "Who is that on our front steps? With a hammer?"

It was a workman—but it was also Saturday, and they had hired no workman. Lenox's mind flew to the dangerous possibilities of this, immediately, but then Leigh came out of the house.

He was still wearing a black suit, having been a

guest at the wedding. He gave the workman a note, and waved him down the steps, then waved Lenox and Lady Jane and Sophia up the steps. He looked pleased with himself. "Hello! Hello, hello! How are you?"

"Who was that?" said Lady Jane.

"Aha. Come in, and you shall see. Kirk already knows—I think he might quit, however."

"You said you had to get back to Cornwall," Lenox said, as they came to the front door.

"And so I do. But I had a present to deliver to you first."

He led them very ceremonially down the front hall, and then stopped, with great pomp, just before the door to the study. Lenox looked around, but he saw nothing. "What is it?"

Leigh frowned. "Look, would you."

He pointed to the wall. There was a small black tab there, not more than half an inch long. It was new. "What is that?" said Lenox.

"I don't want that on my wall, Gerald!" said Lady Jane. "It looks very—very something."

"You couldn't even see it at first!" he said. "Anyhow, just give it a turn, would you? Or perhaps Sophia—perhaps you would like to do it. Yes, I think it ought to be you who turns it."

She looked up at her father for permission, and when he nodded walked over and pushed the little switch.

All at once, throughout the lower floor of the house, there was the most astonishing light—somehow brilliant and a soft yellow at once, flooding every corner of the hallway, casting itself evenly across every object, as if the sun had been divided into trillionth pieces and divvied out, this amount to their own house.

Sophia gasped softly. "What is it?" she said.

Lenox too had his mouth hanging open. Lady Jane half turned, speechless.

Leigh looked gratified. "My friend Swann has finally perfected his invention," he said. "One day you will be able to tell your grandchildren that yours was one of the first twenty private homes in London to use electric light."

"Electric light," Sophia repeated, wonderingly.

"Is it safe?" said Lady Jane, though Lenox could see that she was, already, enchanted.

"Safe? Pish posh, safe. That fellow you saw on the steps is installing it in Victoria Station—the Royal Albert Hall has it already—the *Times* has put it into their machine rooms. Even Buckingham Palace. But there are very, very few private homes, as yet. We had to run a wire from four streets over. Your brother helped with the permissions for that, Charles."

Lenox had read about the idea of electric light, but to see it in person was something else. It had already been, for him, a cathartic day; his dear friends married, and better still happy, happy. He felt something like a lump in his throat. "It's like magic, isn't it?"

Leigh smiled. "No, it's not magic, the future—it's science."

He was leaving that afternoon for Cornwall, and while Lenox and Lady Jane prevailed upon him to remain for another day, two days, a week, he insisted that he had to leave. ("I am overdue, and more importantly, when will I ever make a more spectacular exit?") Accustomed now to the idea of Rowan's money being his own, he had hired a carriage to transport him with his two trunks to Truro, where he had rented a cottage along the very same oceanfront cliffsides that he and his father had once explored. It would travel overnight. After a last cup of tea, he took his leave—promising Sophia, the most heartbroken of those he left behind, that he would be back soon.

And as his carriage pulled away, Leigh looked back up the steps toward the little family there and felt something funny and happy and a little sad. There they stood, father, mother, child, waving at him and smiling. It was how it ought to be—how it ought to have been for him when he was a boy. At least, he thought, as the carriage pulled beyond their good-byes, there was one truly happy family, here in this small corner of London. Already he looked forward to returning to see them again.

Center Point Large Print
600 Brooks Road / PO Box 1
Thorndike, ME 04986-0001 USA

(207) 568-3717

US & Canada:
1 800 929-9108
www.centerpointlargeprint.com